LUMARA

LUMARA

BY MELISSA LANDERS

HYPERION
LOS ANGELES   NEW YORK

First Edition, December 2022
10 9 8 7 6 5 4 3 2 1
FAC-004510-22294
Printed in the United States of America

This book is set in Bembo Book MT Pro/Monotype
Designed by Phil Buchanan

Library of Congress Cataloging-in-Publication Data
Names: Landers, Melissa, author.
Title: Lumara / by Melissa Landers.
Description: First edition. • Los Angeles : Hyperion, 2022. • Audience: Ages 14–18. •
Audience: Grades 10–12. • Summary: In a world where magical Mystics exist alongside
humans, sixteen-year-old Talia is thrust into the most powerful and secretive
Mystic family—and accused of trying to murder them.
Identifiers: LCCN 2021050317 • ISBN 9781368076562 (hardcover) •
ISBN 9781368076784 (ebook)
Subjects: CYAC: Magic—Fiction. • Secrets—Fiction. • LCGFT: Fantasy fiction.
Classification: LCC PZ7.L231717 Lu 2022 • DDC [Fic]—dc23
LC record available at https://lccn.loc.gov/2021050317

Reinforced binding
Visit www.HyperionTeens.com

For Kieran, whose creative spark
brought Lumara to life

CHAPTER
ONE

Maybe it was the jeweled autumn leaves swirling around me, or the oddly pleasant scents of car exhaust and woodsmoke on the breeze, or the cotton-candy sunrise I had watched from the train, but there was definitely magic in the air before I reached Mystic Con.

I tossed back my braid and looped a scarf around my neck as I left the train platform and headed north toward the convention center a few blocks away. The air chilled the skin between my pleated skirt and my boots, but I didn't mind. I grinned and lifted my chest, showing off the Saint Wesleyan Academy logo on my new sweatshirt. It was Saturday, which meant I could wear regular clothes if I wanted to, but why would I want to look regular when I had just scored a full scholarship to the classiest boarding school on the East Coast? Forget jeans and sweaters, I wore my uniform everywhere . . . except to bed. I wasn't a total nerd.

The convention center came into view a block ahead of me, where the sidewalk teemed with people. A sign floated above the crowd, proclaiming MYSTIC CON: THE WORLD'S BIGGEST AND BEST ENCHANTMENT EXPO, SHOWCASING YOUR FAVORITE CELEBRITY SPELL CASTERS. FOR ONE DAY ONLY . . . MAGIC IS IN THE AIR!

A miniature fireworks show had begun, multicolored bubbles that floated upward and popped into glittering rain. A few people reached up to catch the sparkles, even though the fireworks weren't real. They were only enchantments, and flimsy ones at that. The serious magic was inside, where we had to pay to see it.

A line of ticket holders had already formed at the main entrance, corralled into the sort of chrome partitions used at amusement parks. It looked like a thirty-minute wait to get in, maybe longer. Anxiety tightened my chest, urging me to hurry. I had already bought my ticket online, but something about a line full of people made me want to join it as fast as possible, and I doubled my pace automatically.

My heart put a stop to that nonsense.

I wheezed like I'd inhaled a cherry pit. Sweat broke out along my upper lip, my mouth already half-numb. The familiar spots dancing in my vision warned I would throw up if I pushed any harder, so I veered toward the nearest building. I tried to look chill while I caught my breath, hiding beneath my sweatshirt hood, pretending to check my phone. I had learned the hard way that strangers would call an ambulance whether I wanted one or not. They didn't know how much an ambulance cost, or how "normal" these symptoms were for me. And since a trip to the ER wouldn't do anything except stretch my dad's medical payments into the after-life, I avoided eye contact and waited for my pulse to slow.

By the time I made it to the convention center, the doors had opened, so the line was shorter than before. I took my place behind a group of old men who were probably there for the same reason as me. Modern medicine had limits. Take my Swiss-cheese heart, for example, full of leaky valves and weak, flimsy tissue that gave a surgeon nothing to work with. But a Mystic—a truly powerful healer—could manipulate the laws of science and make miracles. That was worth the price of admission.

Or so I hoped. It had cost me everything.

And judging by the phone blowing up in my pocket, my dad had finally noticed the withdrawal from our joint checking account . . . all the money I had saved for a car so I could drive home and visit on the weekends. We'd had it all planned out: I would find a Chevy Chevelle SS—late sixties or early seventies—something with a solid chassis and a working engine, not too much rust, and we would restore it together during school breaks. That was our thing, fixing up classic cars. Now I would have to start saving up again.

I cringed and peeked at my screen. Eleven texts and two missed calls.

call me right now

money missing from your account

a lot of money

holy shit talia

almost all of it gone

did you do this or

or was your card stolen

did you get hacked

should i call the bank

or the police

damn it call me talia

He wasn't using capitalization or punctuation. A bad sign. No way I would call him, but I could at least let him know I was okay.

Don't worry, I texted. *Wasn't hacked. Can't talk right now, but yes I used the money.*

For what? he asked, grammatically calmer. *Did you find an SS? I told you to call me before you pulled the trigger. I wanted to help inspect it, make sure it was a good deal.*

Not a car.

What then?

I didn't know what to tell him. It was bad enough that I'd spent my car money. When my dad found out how I had spent it, his head would explode. He didn't trust Mystics, and that was putting it mildly. He had low-key hated them ever since he'd bought my mom a healing spell from a "certified" Mystic website that turned out to be fake. Then, just to twist the knife even deeper, a famous Mysticgrammer jumped the line at my mom's favorite restaurant and stole the table she'd reserved for her and my dad's last anniversary together. Their *last one ever.* For my dad, it was personal. But my mother would have approved of me coming here. *These* Mystics were the real deal.

Tell you later, I said. *Can't talk now.*

Where are you? he asked. I didn't answer. But because I was an idiot and forgot to turn off my location services, he figured it out. *In the city??? The convention center???* From there, all it took was a Google search for him to put the pieces together, and he slipped into all-caps hysteria.

WHY ARE YOU AT MYSTIC CON???

NO YOU DIDN'T

SAY YOU DIDN'T

I TOLD YOU TO STAY AWAY FROM THOSE PEOPLE

LEAVE RIGHT NOW, TALIA

I MEAN IT, THEY ARE GREEDY AND THEY LIE

GO BACK TO YOUR DORM

I WILL GET YOU A REFUND

DO NOT . . .

I muted my phone and tucked it in my pocket. There was no point in trying to make him understand. He couldn't, because he had never seen a miracle. He would feel differently if he had met Amy Kwan, a sophomore at the academy. I'd seen yearbook pictures of how she used to look—a crutch under each arm, her legs encased in metal braces from a car wreck. Then last summer, her parents had paid a Mystic to come to their house in the Hamptons and heal her. Now Amy ran varsity track.

If it had worked for her, it could work for me. My dad would understand later, after I left the convention with a healthy heart. My ticket had cost me everything, but it was still cheaper than a transplant—and faster than waiting for a donor match that might never happen.

A bargain, really.

Just one thing bothered me.

What my dad had said about Mystic greed wasn't completely wrong. I had read a comic book once about a world where superheroes were managed by a giant corporation and contracted out like professional athletes. The superhero industry was a cash cow, fed by photo ops, movie deals, theme parks, product endorsements, you name it. Mystics did the same thing. They cashed in on their power instead of helping the people who needed it most, the ones who couldn't afford to pay.

But I tried not to think about that.

I made it to the front of the line, where an usher scanned my digital proof of purchase. "Talia Morris," he read from his tablet screen. "Photo ID, please."

I flashed my shiny new student ID from Saint Wesleyan Academy. The usher matched my name to my face and handed me a plastic lanyard on a string. My ticket had a special enchantment of a tiny beating heart in the upper-left-hand corner, to set me apart from general admission. I had paid extra for a private session with the "Legendary Madame Hector," the tour's master healer. I hadn't found much information about Madame Hector online—Mystics had a way of staying, well, *mystical*—but anyone who could charge nearly a thousand dollars a minute had to be at the top of her game.

"Don't lose this," the usher said, pointing at my ticket. "No replacements, no refunds, no exceptions. Got it?"

I nodded and looped the lanyard around my neck, tucking it into my bra for good measure. The usher waved me inside to the security checkpoint, two lines leading through a metal detector and an X-ray machine. The old man in front of me frowned as he emptied his pockets, grumbling to one of his friends, "Why do they need all this nonsense? They have magic, don't they?"

To me, the answer was obvious. No one was untouchable, not even Mystics. Normal people outnumbered Mystics ten thousand to one, and every once in a while, some psycho with a grudge managed to get past the concealment charms and protective wards into a Mystic community and make the news. Magic could only do so much against an ambush.

After making it though security, I picked up a map of the convention center. The main attractions all took place on the second floor, but that could wait. I couldn't risk losing my ticket or missing my session with Madame Hector. I found her station on the map—the third-floor ballroom—and took the elevator straight there.

I should have expected another line waiting for me. And since it wasn't moving very quickly, I sat down on the carpeted floor and surveyed the corridor. There were no more firework spells or floating signs, just the center's ordinary decor. I had hoped for more enchantments at a magical convention, but maybe the Mystics had saved their best work for the spells that mattered.

As time went on and my turn approached, a riot of anticipation fluttered in my stomach. It seemed surreal to think that in a few minutes, I would exit the other side of the ballroom a different person—stronger, faster, unstoppable. I wouldn't have to ride the elevator to the second-floor exhibition. I could take the stairs. I could speed-walk, or even jog, up and down the aisles of booths, without stopping to catch my breath. At the end of the day, I could run all the way back to the train station if I wanted to. And I *did* want to. The mental image excited me so much it hurt.

When my turn finally came, my hands trembled, and it took a few tries to show my ticket to the usher guarding the doors. I walked into the ballroom on shaky knees, vaguely noticing the stacks of empty tables and chairs lining the periphery. I only had eyes for Madame Hector.

I searched for her and found two people in the room, both of them men, one standing in front of the opposite doors with his arms tightly folded like a security guard, and the other sitting behind a long table draped in gold linens. The second man was brawny and bearded, dressed in a turtleneck beneath a black suit jacket. He seemed like the dramatic type, or maybe it was the candles floating in the air around him, casting shadows on his angular face. He clasped his hands atop the table and studied me as I approached, tilting his dark head, pinching his eyebrows together as if grading me for an exam I hadn't studied for.

I glanced from one man to the other. "I, uh, I'm Talia Morris. I came here to see Madame Hector. Is she—"

"*She* is me," the bearded man said with a grin that didn't reach his eyes. "It's a stage name—a nom de plume, if you will—forced upon me by the *vulgar* marketing department."

Definitely dramatic.

"They insist," he went on, "that eighty percent of the population prefer a female Mystic healer over a male." He waved a dismissive hand. "Antiquated notions of fairy-tale witchcraft, I suppose. Anyhow, I can transform myself into an elderly woman if you wish."

I shook my head. "That's okay."

"Then please," he said, indicating a chair that had just appeared at the opposite side of the table. "Make yourself comfortable."

I settled across from him and discreetly wiped my sweaty palms on my skirt. Both of us sat at the same height, but Madame, or rather *Monsieur* Hector's gaze had a way of making me feel small.

"So," he began, leaning forward and boring those dark eyes into me, "tell me why you're here, Talia Morris."

That part was easy. I had even brought a summary of my medical file, which I unfolded and slid to him across the table. "I have a congenital heart disease. Genetic, if it matters. My mother had it, too."

"Had?" he asked.

"She died two years ago."

"My condolences," he said. "Go on."

"Well, that's it, really." I pointed at the paper, which he hadn't touched. "I want you to fix my heart."

"Hmm. But that doesn't tell me why you're here."

"Doesn't it?"

"I want you to dig deeper," he said with a theatrical hand flourish. "Think beyond your physical symptoms and the clinical terms you use to define yourself, and tell me what it is you want. What does Talia Morris truly want?"

I didn't know why he cared, but I blew out a long breath and considered his question. "A future, I guess."

"You already have one."

"A longer future, then. Longer than the one my mother had."

"That's fair. What else?"

"Strength," I said. "And stamina."

"But why?"

"So I can walk to class without wheezing like a grandma."

"But *why*?" he pressed.

I shook my head, unsure of what he was looking for.

"Think, girl. Think!"

Frustrated, I threw my hands in the air. "Because I don't want to be a spectator anymore. I'm tired of sitting on the bleachers and watching other people play. *I* want to play. I want to run." *And dance*, I thought to myself. Especially dance. With homecoming a week away—my first big event at Saint Wesleyan—the only thing I had to look forward to was wearing a dress that showed off my legs. "I want to have fun. I want to be normal."

Hector raised an eyebrow. "Normalcy is a terrible thing to wish for, my dear."

"That's not what I meant," I told him. "I just want to act my age, do what my friends are doing. Right now, my roommate's at a corn maze—something I can't handle. Tonight she's going out with her boyfriend." And probably hooking up, something else I couldn't handle.

"You can date," Hector said. "Nothing is stopping you."

"Maybe," I agreed. Except the only boy I wanted to date was Nathaniel Wood, and he made my heart do sprints and cartwheels and all sorts of acrobatics. Just thinking about him set my cheeks aflame.

A slow smile curved Hector's lips. "Ah, there's a boy."

I blushed harder.

"Tell me about your boy."

"He's not mine," I admitted. Not yet. But unless I had misread a hundred signals, it seemed like he wanted to be.

"Is he special?"

That made me laugh. Only the president of the junior class, homecoming prince, first-string quarterback, and former child actor. Oh, and crazy rich, too. Nathaniel came from old money, the kind of family that had a wing of the academic building named after them. But none of that mattered to me. The best part about Nate was everything we had in common. We both liked pineapple on our pizza. We watched the same true-crime dramas. We listened to classic rock. We had grown up with a love of American cars, and—get this—had both helped our dads restore vintage Impalas when we were kids. It was eerie how well we matched. Nathaniel couldn't be more perfect for me if I had made him in a computer.

"Sure," I said. "I guess he's pretty special."

Hector nodded. "Well, now that you've manifested your desires to the universe, all you have to do is take what you want. The only thing holding you back is you, Talia Morris."

"And my heart," I reminded him.

"There's nothing wrong with your heart."

I probed my chest with my fingertips. Had he healed me while we were talking? I didn't feel any different, but sitting down, it was hard to tell. "Did you fix me already? Is that what you mean?"

"No, I mean there's nothing wrong with you."

I blinked, waiting for the punch line that didn't come. "Excuse me?"

"Your heart is healthy."

"No, it's not." I pointed again at the printout he hadn't bothered to read. "I almost threw up walking here from the train."

"Bad food, perhaps?" he offered.

I glanced at the security guard for some sort of explanation, but he stared blankly ahead with his arms folded.

"I'm confused. Are you saying . . ." I swallowed a lump that had risen in my throat. "Are you saying you can't fix me?"

"I'm saying I can't fix what isn't broken."

"But . . . you haven't even touched me. How could you possibly know anything?"

"I don't need to lay hands on my clients to diagnose them."

"You didn't chant a spell."

"My gift doesn't work that way."

"Your *gift* didn't work at all," I said, my voice rising. I pulled in a calming breath. "I want you to try again. Please."

"Very well." He peered at me for the span of two blinks and said, "My diagnosis hasn't changed."

Panic rose up inside me. None of this made sense.

Except it did.

My dad had warned me, but I had wanted so desperately for him to be wrong that I hadn't listened. Now I could see the flaw in my logic. I had known there were powerful Mystics in the world.

What hadn't occurred to me was that the "Legendary Madame Hector" might not be one of them. Hector could obviously cast enchantments—levitate candles, summon a chair—but he didn't have the power to heal me. And he would never admit it, because that would mean no more sold-out tours, no more lines of idiot ticket holders willing to empty their bank accounts for a chance at a miracle.

Idiots like me.

And still, I wanted to believe Hector. Hope was such an easy thing to cling to, and I had come here with mountains of it, built during weeks of picturing a new life for myself. I couldn't let go of that dream. I had to try again.

"My heart—"

"Is healthy," he interrupted.

"No, it's not."

"Your symptoms aren't real. You're in denial, my dear."

That did it. My control snapped.

"Liar!" I yelled, bolting to my feet. "Tell it to my cardiologist! Tell it to the blood thinners I take every day, or the lab techs who know me by name! Tell it to my dad, who works a second job to pay for my insurance, or my mom, who's in the ground!"

Hector swallowed visibly, darting a glance at his security guard. He held a palm toward me. "Now, now, my dear, I can see you're upset—"

"I am not your dear," I ground out. And hell yes, I was upset. "Don't try to mansplain to me what's going on inside my own body. It's *my* body! My life! I was there for all sixteen years of it. You weren't."

"That's not what I'm trying to do."

"I know exactly what you're trying to do," I spat. "There's even a name for it. You're gaslighting me." I had learned about it in psychology class. It was a mind trick used by abusers to cover up their lies by fooling people into thinking their suspicions were all in their heads. "It won't work on me. I know what's real and what's not."

"Perhaps I can offer you a different service," Hector said, changing tactics. "I could clarify your skin or . . . add gloss to your hair? Or perhaps you'd like to eat as much as you want without gaining weight."

"I didn't come here for party tricks." I gripped both hips and planted my feet. "I came here for a new heart. So make that happen, or give me my money back."

"There are no refunds," he reminded me, glancing again at his guard. "I don't make the rules. You agreed to the terms and conditions when you bought your ticket."

I stood firm and faked a confidence I didn't feel. Hector couldn't do this, could he? Lie to me and take my money? It was starting to look that way, but how could I stop him? I couldn't talk to his manager or file a complaint. Mystics didn't operate like that. They had all the power, and they knew it.

"No" was all I could say. I gripped the back of my chair and repeated, "No. I won't leave until you make this right. I want my money back."

Hector snapped his fingers, and the chair vanished from my grasp.

"Fine." I sat cross-legged on the floor. I knew how desperate I looked, but I couldn't stop myself. I couldn't let him win. "I'm not going anywh—"

My voice cut off as my lips froze in puckered formation. I couldn't speak. Or move, I realized, except to breathe and dart my eyes from side to side. Out of the corner of my eye, I saw the security guard staring at me and chanting under his breath. I couldn't hear his spell, but I fought against it, pushing back with my mind, holding my breath and straining until my face felt like an overinflated balloon.

I exhaled hard. Nothing worked. His magic was too strong.

Hector hooked a thumb toward the exit. "Take her out the back. Use the service elevator. Make sure no one sees you, and disable the cameras. I don't want video of this leaking to the media."

The guard nodded. He murmured another incantation, and the next thing I knew, my body was standing up from the floor. The act felt dreamlike, similar to how I sometimes walked in my sleep, but with more awareness. I had no control over my movements or my voice. I glared at Hector, or tried to, but the gesture was ruined by a tear spilling down my cheek. I hated—absolutely *hated*—how helpless he had made me feel.

He gave me a pitying look that boiled my blood. "Oh my dear," he said, one hand pressed dramatically to his chest. "I am sorry to have disappointed you, and for the unique predicament that brought you here. I do hope you'll take my advice and shape the future you want for yourself. No one can make you a spectator in life without your consent."

Consent? I couldn't even lift my hand to wipe the rage tears off my face, and he was lecturing me about consent? My father was right. Mystics were nothing more than gold-digging, lying, power-hungry, hypocritical assholes.

The guard didn't ask for my consent to puppet me out of the room. He put my feet in motion and walked behind me to the service elevator, down two floors, and along a maze of empty corridors leading to the staff exit. He set a slow pace for our walk, pausing twice when I started to wheeze. Not that I would thank him.

He pushed open an exterior door and guided me into an alley lined with dumpsters. When we were just out of view of the sidewalk, he lifted my lanyard and said, "Your barcode is flagged, so don't bother trying to get back in. As for my spell, it expires with distance. You have to go a little farther before you get your body back. I'll start you off going south. You should have control by the time you make it to the street."

I *should* have control? What if I walked into a car?

He looped a swag bag in the crook of my elbow. "Here, take this. There's some cool stuff in the bags this year. At least you won't go home empty-handed."

He forced my feet to obey him, calling, "Bye, kid," before he left me all alone under his spell. With the scent of garbage in my nose, I ambled like a zombie onto the crowded sidewalk in front of the convention center, bumping shoulders with strangers, fumbling along as a passenger in my own body. A spectator, as usual, in my own life.

I would never—*never*—trust a Mystic again.

CHAPTER
TWO

ONE YEAR LATER

#*BoycottMysticCon and starve the beast! Be part of the solution, not the problem!*

Mystic Con had returned, and magic hung like sparkling dust motes in the air. Sadly, Lysol didn't make a spray for that, but I had the next best thing: a popular social media account dedicated to exposing Mystics for the scammers they were. And at the moment, my hashtag was trending.

I hit *send* and read the post out loud for the benefit of my roommate, Farah, who was digging under her bed for a sweater to wear to the convention center. Traitor. "Part of the problem," I repeated. "That's what you became when you bought a ticket."

She flipped me a clumsy bird with her free hand.

"You know I'm right," I said, sitting cross-legged on my bed. "They'll never stop touring as long as people like you give them money."

Farah found her sweater and held it up in triumph. "Good, I

don't want them to stop. I live for this con. You know who's going to be there this year?"

I groaned.

"Joshua Hartwell." She fluttered her lashes, clutching her sweater to her chest. "He's on tour promoting the sequel to *High School Magical*. I don't care how much it costs, I'm bringing home one of those enchanted posters of him . . . you know, the sexy dancing one, where he's peeling off his shirt and rolling his abs. I'm going to hang it right there"—pointing at the ceiling—"so I can fall asleep every night watching him."

"Oh god. Please don't."

She sighed dreamily. "Could you imagine if he went to school here? If any Mystics could go here? That would be awesome."

"For them, maybe," I said. "They could cheat their way to the top. That's what they do best." Personally, I was glad Mystics couldn't enroll at Saint Wesleyan. It wouldn't be fair to the rest of us, especially scholarship students like me. We had to keep up our grades to qualify. "I worked too hard to let anyone *abracadabra* me out of valedictorian."

"You're seriously racist against Mystics, you know."

"That's not a thing," I said.

"All right, then, you're Mystiphobic."

"That's not a thing, either."

"Sure it is. It's about hate. You hate Mystics." Farah zipped up her boots. "I dare you to tell me I'm wrong."

I opened my mouth to argue with her, but I couldn't. She was right. I did hate Mystics. I hated everything they stood for and their entire way of life. And I especially hated the way people like Farah worshipped them just for being different. "They're liars and manipulators, and they get way more attention than they deserve."

"Special people always get attention."

"Special?" I asked. "What's so special about winning the genetic lottery? They don't earn their magic. They're born with it. That's privilege, not achievement, and it doesn't entitle them to my respect."

"In case you haven't noticed," Farah said, pulling the sweater over her head, "life's not fair. Some people are luckier than the rest of us." She delivered me a burning look. "Like the senior with the highest GPA—who's also the homecoming queen *and* Nathaniel Wood's girlfriend."

I beamed. "Next week is our one-year anniversary."

She pretended to gag herself. "Of course it is. He's probably taking you to Paris to celebrate."

"Manhattan," I said, ignoring the jab. "He wants me to come home with him for fall break and meet his family."

If only I could convince my dad to agree . . .

"Ugh, you're unbearable, and I have to go." Farah grabbed her phone and made for the door. Smiling sweetly, she added before she left, "I'll tell Joshua you said hi."

I cringed, seriously hoping she didn't bring home one of those posters.

But now that she had left, I could retrieve last year's Mystic Con bag from its hiding place at the bottom of my closet. As it turned out, Hector's guard had been right about the cool swag. But my roommate didn't need to know that. She would never let me hear the end of it if she caught me using a magical gadget.

My favorite contraption was a prototype called Blaze Connect. I had originally thought it was a flash drive, but then I'd discovered that if I plugged it into my phone, the person on the other end would appear in front of me, life-size and so realistic that I'd tried to hug my dad and passed right through him into the wall. Now I used it all the time to talk to him, and mostly to my cousin Katja, who doubled as my best friend.

I nestled against my pillow and called her. She answered before the first ring had finished, making me flinch when her image suddenly appeared, cross-legged and leaning toward me from the foot of my bed.

I would never get used to that.

"So what do we think about him?" she asked, holding up her tablet to show me a picture of a random guy. All of our phone calls began that way, straight to the point, no greetings. "He's in a band, if that sways you."

I glanced at the image. Shaggy but cute. "What does he play?"

"Drums."

"Oh, come on. Instant veto."

"Ugh," she groaned, throwing back her dark hair. "I know, I know. Never date the drummer."

"Then why did you ask?"

"Because I *waaaaaant tooooooo*."

Kat definitely had a type. I could blindfold her in a room with a hundred guys, and in less than a minute, she'd sniff out the wildest, most emotionally stunted butt-scratcher in the pack. "It's your heart to break," I told her, "but I say keep looking. The world is full of guys. You know, plenty of fish and all that."

"Not in the Dead Sea." She pointed her tablet at me. "This town's so small the zip code is a fraction. You forgot the struggle, city girl. Not all of us are scholarship geniuses living in gold-plated dorm rooms with our trust-fund billionaire boyfriends."

I glanced around my room: two twin beds and two desks pushed against the wall. "Don't forget the private chef who cooks unicorn bacon for breakfast."

She jutted out her lower lip. "I miss you, that's all. You took all the fun when you left, packed it up in your little suitcase. Now there's none left for me."

I smiled. I missed her, too. And I missed her house—the plush lavender carpet in her bedroom, the lawn-scented breeze through her open window, the creaky wooden floors that led to the kitchen, where my auntie was usually stress-baking fresh sourdough. For as long as I could remember, I had spent more time at Kat's house than my own. Especially after my mom died.

Thinking about my mom made me wonder how my dad was doing, and if he was lonely without me at home. He didn't like talking about his feelings, but he had mentioned that growing up in foster care had given him an appreciation for family that the rest of us couldn't understand. I hated the idea of him rattling around the house all by himself.

"Hey," I said. "Have you seen my dad lately?"

"Not since church last week. Why?"

I touched the pendant at my neck, an oval locket containing a single dark coil of my mother's hair. I never took it off, not even to shower. That way she was always with me. "Her birthday's coming up. You know how he gets."

"Oh." Kat slouched and made the sign of the cross. "Yeah, my mom, too. I learned a long time ago to stay away from her when she gets dark. Nothing I say or do helps. She says I can't understand the pain of losing a sister, because I don't have one"—tipping up her hands—"like it's my fault I'm an only child. But she forgot about you. You're better than a sister. You're my person."

"Aww." I covered my heart. "I love you."

"I love you more," she said. "So I can imagine how she feels, because a giant hole opens up in my chest when I think about losing you." Her gaze went soft and sad, like a cloud had passed over her. "That can't happen. I'll do anything to stop it."

"Hey, don't worry. I take my pills. I get plenty of rest. I drink those nasty medical shakes that taste like concrete." I didn't mention that I had to stop to catch my breath in between sips. "I'm hanging on."

She stared at her lap for a few silent beats, then asked, "What about Nathaniel Wood?"

Her question caught me off guard. Kat didn't like talking about Nathaniel. She rarely brought him up, and she would get salty if I talked about him for too long. I didn't think she had a problem with him as a person. She seemed to resent the time he spent with me. In a way, it had to feel like he had taken her place.

"What about him?"

"How's"—she twirled a hand—"all that going?"

"Right now he's at an away game, but he's taking me to dinner tonight. He says he has something important to tell me. I think it's about fall break. He wants me to come home with him and meet the family." Which would mean missing fall break with my own family. I waited for Kat to realize that and complain, but instead, her face brightened.

"That's great!" she said.

I blinked at her. She was in a weird mood today.

"So he hasn't introduced you at all?" she asked. "No video calls, like when I met him?"

I shook my head. Nate didn't talk to—or about—his parents very often. I assumed they weren't close. But he'd told me all about his sister, Olive. She was seventeen years older than him, with some kind of health condition that forced her to live at home. Nate and Olive had different dads—Olive's father had abandoned the family when she was young, and her mom's next husband adopted her. But I had never heard Nate call Olive his half sister. He idolized her, probably because she'd spent so much time taking care of him when he was little. I had tried looking her up, but she didn't have social media. None of the Woods did, except for Nate.

"Huh," Kat said.

"So you're okay if I go?"

"Yeah, but only because he's loaded, and I want to know how the one percent lives."

Now for the hard part: convincing my dad. He only saw me during school breaks, so our time together was considered untouchable. He even took off work when I came home, to pack each day with activities. He would probably want to plan another family trip to the pumpkin patch. I smiled, remembering last year, when my aunt had seen a garter snake and stumbled backward so fast she'd landed on the prize pumpkin, breaking it in half. We'd had to pay for it, and it hadn't even tasted good in the pie we'd baked later.

"Hey," I said. "Tell your mom to watch out for snakes this year."

Kat wrinkled her brow. "What?"

"The pumpkin patch," I reminded her.

She shook her head.

"You know, when your mom almost stepped on a snake?"

"Oh, right," Kat said, slowly nodding. "Yeah, that was scary."

Scary? We had laughed about it for hours, even my aunt. Weird that Kat didn't remember.

My phone beeped. I glanced at the screen: *Dad calling.*

"Hold on," I told Kat. "My dad's on the other line. We'll do a three-way."

She wrinkled her nose. "That sounds so wrong."

I tapped *accept*, and my dad's image appeared by the door, where he stood holding a bottle of his favorite cream soda. He'd cut his hair in the usual style, short on the sides and *way* too long on top, a failed effort to hide the silvery wisps that receded a little farther every year. My dad had gone full gray during his senior year in high school, and he'd had no luck with his hair ever since. I kept telling him to shave his head. He had the right kind of face for it: strong brow, straight nose, high cheekbones, and a bold, angular jaw. Maybe one day he'd take my advice.

"Hey, Button," he said to me, then tipped his bottle at Katja. "Kitty Kat. How are my two favorite girls today?"

Kat spoke up before I had a chance. "Talia was just saying we might not see her for fall break. Nathaniel wants her to meet his family."

I tensed my shoulders and waited for my dad to explode. Instead, he made a *hmm* noise and took a drink of soda. His nostrils didn't flare. His face didn't turn red. He patted his chest to release a quiet burp and said, "Well, a boy from that kind of family doesn't bring home just anyone. Sounds like he's serious about you."

"I . . . I guess so," I told him, dazed by his reaction.

"I hate to miss out on our time together," he said. "But that's all right. We can make it up over the holidays. Tell the Woods you can stay with them."

"Really?" I asked.

"Sure, I can share you for a week."

Since when? I thought. Not that I was complaining, but I had expected major pushback—from both my dad and from Kat. Convincing them had felt too easy. I couldn't help wondering if they were hiding something, if there was a reason they didn't want me to come home.

I looked back and forth at them, studying their faces. "Is everything okay?"

They nodded and said yes, their expressions normal.

"Nothing's wrong at home?" I asked.

Dad chuckled, and Kat told me I was paranoid. Maybe she was right. Maybe not. I knew a weird mood when I saw one, but I let go of my suspicions and thanked my dad before he had a chance to change his mind.

He had given me what I wanted. No need to question my luck.

That night, I made my way across the campus to the boys' dorm to meet Nathaniel for our date. I knocked on his door and floofed my hair while I waited for him to answer. When he yelled for me to come in, I opened the door and immediately stopped short.

My boyfriend was nowhere in sight. The room was dim, illuminated by a single candle on the floor, where Nate had spread out a blanket and arranged a private picnic for us. I recognized the Chinese takeout cartons from my favorite restaurant, Third Wok from the Sun.

"Surprise," he said, his voice coming from a dark corner of the room. "I wanted to stay in tonight. I hope that's okay."

I stepped inside and shut the door behind me. This was more than okay. Nathaniel didn't have a roommate—one of the perks of being a zillionaire—so it would just be the two of us, all alone in the candlelight, surrounded by spicy goodness and the promise of a whole evening to do whatever we wanted.

"Kung Pao chicken?" I asked.

"With extra peppers."

"You really do know the way to my heart."

A flame sparked as he lit a second candle that illuminated his smile. "Same."

"It's perfect," I told him, gesturing at the picnic. I didn't say, *Just like you*, but I was thinking it.

We sat on the blanket, our knees touching as we ate. Now that my eyes had adjusted, I watched Nate over my fork, and my chest turned warm in a way that had nothing to do with Kung Pao chicken. I could never believe how breathtaking he was: eyes as dark as a secret, set in an angel's face, framed by glossy black curls that were made for my fingers. And that mouth. Full, soft lips that

turned down a tiny bit at the edges, just enough to give him a soulful pout.

A masterpiece.

I was so wrapped up in admiring him that I finished my whole
plate before I noticed he'd barely taken a bite. He should be on his
third helping by now, not pushing around a half-eaten egg roll.

"What's wrong?" I asked. "I never clean my plate before you."

He bit his lip and scratched a spot he'd missed shaving. "You
know that thing I wanted to talk to you about?"

"Yeah."

"It's sort of a good-news-bad-news deal."

"Then start with the good news," I said. That always made the
bad news seem like less of a downer.

"My cousin Lucy is getting married."

"That's awesome."

"Yeah," he agreed in a tone that didn't sound convincing. "My
mom and dad are her godparents, so they're hosting the wedding
at their place. My sister said Lucy went totally overboard, and now
it's the wedding of the century or something." He took my hand.
"Anyway, I get to bring a date."

I tapped my chin. "Hmm, I don't know. A romantic night with
my boyfriend, all dressed up at Manhattan's wedding of the century? Sounds like torture, but I guess I can take one for the team
and go with you."

He didn't smile.

"Hey," I said, nudging him. "I was kidding about the torture
part."

"Yeah, sorry." He shook his head as if to clear it.

"What's the bad news?"

"The wedding is Saturday."

"As in . . . a week from today?"

He nodded. "We'll have to leave on Friday to get there for the rehearsal dinner. Then after the wedding, we can stay for fall break. My dad already cleared it for both of us with the headmaster. We can make up the work from Friday. It won't hurt your ranking."

"But . . ." Next week was the homecoming dance.

Nate cringed. "I know. I'm sorry. We'll have to miss the dance."

"But . . ." I repeated. We had won the vote for king and queen. I had never dreamed I could be the queen of anything—the center of attention, the popular girl standing onstage in a twinkling crown and a sash, admired by all. For once, I was going to be the star instead of the spectator.

Nate groaned. "You're disappointed."

I didn't bother trying to hide it. There was no use. I had absolutely no poker face, worst liar ever. "I really wanted that tiara."

He kissed my hand. "I'll buy you ten of them. Twenty."

"One will do," I told him with a sigh. "But what should I wear to the wedding? If it's formal, my homecoming dress might not work."

His fingers went cold in my hand. I noticed he wasn't looking at me.

"What's wrong?" I asked.

"There's more."

"More bad news?"

"Kind of." He swallowed hard, peeking at me and away again.

"But before I tell you, I need you to promise you'll listen to everything I have to say."

"I always listen to you."

"This is different. Promise you won't get mad and leave before I can explain."

I froze, instantly thinking of the one thing that would make me walk out on Nathaniel and never look back. "Did you cheat on me?"

"No! God, no. Nothing like that."

I gently shoved his chest. "Then stop scaring me and spit it out."

"Promise," he insisted.

"Fine, I promise I'll sit here and listen until you're done."

"All right." He took a deep breath and blew it out slowly. "The wedding's not in Manhattan, because that's not where my parents live. My whole family lives on a private island called Lumara. It's about two hours off the coast in international waters. My mom and dad pretend to live in the US so I can go to school here."

"Okaaay," I said, drawing out the word while I processed the absurd amount of money it would cost to live on a private island. How rich *were* these people? Then I began to understand the issue of residing in international waters. "They're not citizens, are they?"

"Not exactly."

"And you?"

"Not me either."

That complicated matters, but I still didn't see the problem. I could keep Nate's secret. And even if the academy found out, his family had the kind of wealth that made those problems go away. Money fixed issues like missing documents and passport paperwork.

"What's your citizenship?" I asked.

He inhaled another deep breath as if strengthening himself. It took him three tries to finally say, "I belong to the IFC."

"The IFC?" I asked. The International Federation of Conjurers, the Mystic government that negotiated treaties with different countries so Mystics could live in weird sheltered communities and observe their own laws.

"That's what I'm trying to tell you," Nate said, his fingers positively freezing in my grasp. "That's the reason I have to lie to go to school here. And why I made you promise to let me explain, because I know how you're going to react when this sets in."

I stopped breathing. The moment felt surreal, like the time Hector's guard had enspelled me and stolen control of my body. I had resisted the truth then, and I fought like hell against it now. I wanted to protect my own version of the truth, the story I had written in my heart—a year-long collection of realities that Nathaniel could shatter if he kept talking. I silently begged him to take it back, to say he was joking. But he didn't.

Instead, he crushed my denial with four little words.

"Talia," he said. "I'm a Mystic."

CHAPTER
THREE

"Say something."

I heard the words, distant and fuzzy, as if spoken underwater.

"Talia?"

Cool hands squeezed my fingers.

"Tals, talk to me. Please? You're starting to scare me."

My alertness returned with a blink, and I demanded, "Prove it."

Nathaniel sat back. "Prove . . . that I'm a Mystic?"

"Seeing is believing," I told him. And my heart wanted evidence. "Show me. Do some magic." I indicated the cartons of takeout next to us on the blanket. "Turn the egg rolls into butterflies, or levitate the crab fried rice or something."

"I can't," he said. "I'm a Core. That means—"

I cut him off with a lifted hand. I knew what it meant. Core Mystics drew their energy from a place—for him, probably his island—and their magic weakened away from it. There were two other groups: Bloods, who drew their power from their ancestors, and Auras, who were fueled by chaotic life energy. Most of the jerks at Mystic Con were Auras. They settled in major metropolitan areas and joined the convention circuit. If I thought about it for too long, it creeped me out to imagine them feeding off my energy.

"I can't give you proof here," Nathaniel said. "Only on Lumara. I can't do magic away from the island."

I went quiet again. I didn't know what to say or even to think. My mind reeled with disjointed thoughts, making it impossible to process this new reality, or more important, what it meant. Because this changed everything. Nathaniel was one of *them*. He belonged to the same league of con artists who preyed on people like me. Even if he didn't steal money or sell fake spells, he had lied to me since the day we'd met. Now our whole history was a question mark. Which moments were real? Which were fake? And the unfairness of it hurt, too. I had never lied to Nathaniel, not one time. He knew me, inside and out.

What did I really know about him?

Suddenly, it clicked—Nate's popularity, his looks, his money, his athletic skills—too good to be true. Not to mention the instant spark between us, the parallel of our lives, the eerie perfection of how much we had in common . . . as if I'd made him in a computer.

I gasped as a horrible thought occurred to me. "Did you use magic to make me love you?" But then I wondered why he would do that. I wasn't important. No one at the academy had even noticed me until Nate and I started dating.

"Talia, listen to me." He took my face between his hands and spoke to me like a parent to a child. "I can't. Do magic. Away from the island."

Oh. Right. He had already said that.

"You're not thinking straight," he said. "I would never use a spell on you."

"How do I know?"

"Have I ever lied to you before?" He quickly added, "I mean, except for—"

"Except for your identity?" I snapped. My heart pounded, and I drew a deep breath to slow my pulse. "Who you are? Where you're from? Everything about you? All you've done is lie."

Hurt flashed in his eyes. "That's not fair."

"Isn't it?"

"No," he said. "Because if I was just some ordinary guy from China or whatever, you wouldn't care that I lied to go to school here. It's not about the lie. You're mad because I'm a Mystic."

I folded my arms. I couldn't deny his point. "You know what they did to me. You know how I feel about them."

"I do," he said, pulling one of my hands free. "That's why I was afraid to tell you. Put yourself in my shoes. I had just met this incredible girl. We had fun together and liked all the same things. She was cute and smart, honest and kind." He grinned. "And a *really* good kisser. I was excited—and scared, too, because I knew she was special. I didn't want to mess it up. So imagine how I felt when I took her to the homecoming dance, and she spent half the night telling me how much she hates Mystics."

I dropped my gaze, my cheeks warm.

"I totally get why you felt that way, but what was I supposed to do?" he asked. "We had just started dating. You didn't love me. You had no reason to give me a chance. So I told myself I would come clean in another month or two, after we got to know each other. But then I fell for you, and it was even harder to tell you the truth, because I had more to lose every day." He tipped up my chin, pleading with his eyes. "I'm sorry for keeping a secret from you. I should've had the balls to tell you sooner. If it makes you feel better, I've hated myself this whole time."

That didn't make me feel better. The boy I loved had spent the last year thinking I wouldn't accept him for who he was. Guilt washed over me when I imagined how unsafe I had made him feel. I couldn't blame him for hiding the truth. How could I expect him to be honest with me when I had created a whole social media account to trash his people?

But how could I trust him now? I didn't know what to think.

"I hate that I made you feel that way," I said.

"You didn't do anything wrong. If a Mystic ripped me off, I would be pissed, too, and I *am* one. Guys like Hector and thirsty Mystigrammers give us a bad name. Now I can show you we're not all like that. Lumara is different. No one cares about power or fame there. No one does magic for hire or posts videos of spells. They don't post anything at all. They want to be invisible. That's why the whole island is cloaked. It's not even on the charts."

What he was telling me didn't make sense. Mystics who didn't want attention? Who didn't take advantage of their power?

"All they want on Lumara is to be left alone," he said. "And to live naturally, the way they were meant to. The magic is incredible, Talia. It's beyond anything I can describe. Sometimes I think the island is actually alive."

"Then why are you here?" I asked. "Why would you go through so much trouble to leave a place that sounds like paradise?"

"Because even paradise has downsides. Lumara is small. Seriously small. As in claustrophobic."

I could relate, coming from a tiny town. "As in everyone knowing each other's business?"

"And good luck finding someone to date who's not related to you. That's not what I want for myself. I want something bigger, and that means living in the real world and blending in and going to school so I can have a career."

"Your parents are loaded," I reminded him.

"I can't mooch off them forever. Besides, doing nothing gets boring after a while. Money doesn't change that." He peered at me. "So, will you come with me?"

"Oh," I said, almost forgetting the plans we had made. The wedding. Fall break. Meeting his family. I had pictured Manhattan as our destination, not a cloaked, magical, potentially living island that didn't exist on navigational charts. Now we had a new problem. Because even if I decided to go, my dad would never agree to it.

"I know it's a leap of faith," Nate added.

He didn't know the half of it. I would have to lie to my father, and my inability to deceive was practically a reverse superpower.

"Maybe this will help convince you," Nate said, unfastening the leather band around his wrist. It was a simple bracelet, just a wide brown strap with an adjustable brass buckle, but I had never seen him take it off. "It's the only magical thing I own."

"What does it do?"

He tried to put it on me, and I instinctively jerked away. "It's all right," he promised. "The magic can't hurt you. It's basically a lie detector."

"You think I'm lying to you?"

"No, not at all. The bracelet only works for whoever's wearing it. It vibrates when someone's not telling you the truth."

I extended my hand, and he buckled the bracelet around my wrist, the brass still warm from his skin.

I thought back to last week's math class. "It didn't tell you when I gave you the wrong answer in Calc."

"That's because intent matters," he said. "Lying is different from being wrong."

I nodded. "Right." One was on purpose. The other wasn't.

Nathaniel smoothed a thumb over my wrist. "Your honesty is my favorite thing about you. I could never tell you before, but"— tapping the buckle—"this is how I know you're the only person who's always been real with me. I hate liars. And I hate that I had to lie to you, because I know how it feels to be on the other end of it. People have been trying to use me since I can remember. Mostly for money, but it happens on Lumara, too. My mom's a big deal there, so I never know if someone is only being nice to me to get to her." He cupped my cheek. "But not you. You're genuine. That's why I love you, and why I want you to come home and learn about the real me. I promise to be totally honest, and this bracelet will prove it."

I chewed my inner cheek and wondered what to do. I believed Nathaniel. I didn't need a bracelet to trust him. Ironically, the main reason I was hesitant to go to Lumara was the same reason he loved me. I didn't want to lie to my dad. And then there was a part of me that still couldn't believe the Mystics on Lumara were as wonderful as Nathaniel claimed.

"Please come with me," he said, his beautiful, dark eyes brimming with emotion. The candlelight had dimmed, but not enough to hide his fear when he asked, "You *do* love me, don't you?"

The question was so easy it answered itself. "Of course I do," I told him. But going home with him . . . I didn't feel as sure about that. "I just need some time to think."

"How much time?"

I knew I couldn't keep him in limbo forever. That wouldn't be fair. "Give me until morning," I told him. "I'll make up my mind by then."

When I returned to my room that night, my worries started to solidify, mostly about my dad. I didn't know how I could spend a whole week on Lumara without him finding out. If lying wouldn't work, maybe I could try avoiding him. But he would expect me to check in during fall break. It would look suspicious if I didn't call.

I needed to talk to Kat. She would know what to do. She had always been the sneaky one. Since my roommate would be at Mystic Con for at least another hour, I dialed Kat on my Blaze Connect.

"Psh, that's easy," Kat said, completely unfazed by everything I had told her. Her reaction didn't surprise me. Kat had always admired Mystics the same way she admired sharks at the aquarium—with fascination but enough common sense to keep her hand out of the tank. "It's your voice that gives you away when you lie. So just make up a reason why you have to text your dad instead of calling him. Tell him the signal is bad."

"In Manhattan?"

Kat shrugged. "Towers go out. It happens. A bad storm can knock out a phone network and still leave people with power for Wi-Fi."

"You're good at this. It's almost disturbing."

"I'll take that as a compliment."

"So you're not scared for me, not even a little bit?" I asked. "To go to Lumara?"

"No way," she said. "The opposite. This could be a huge win for you."

"What do you mean?"

"Core Mystics are supposed to be the strongest. I heard it's some kind of trade-off for being stuck in one magical place. I don't know, whatever. Anyway, you said Nathaniel's mom is a big deal on the island. That has to mean she's more powerful than everyone else—way stronger than the guy who scammed you at Mystic Con. Maybe she can fix you."

I covered my heart. I hadn't even considered that. "But Nate said his sister is sick, too. Why wouldn't they heal her, if they're so powerful?"

"I don't know. Maybe Mystics are harder to fix?" She tipped up her hands. "But you have to try. Let me worry about your dad. Call me when you get to the island, and we'll figure it out."

I chewed the inside of my cheek. Was it decided, then? Was I going to Lumara?

"You're still on the fence," Kat said.

"A little."

"What's holding you back?"

"Trust," I said. I believed Nathaniel would never hurt me, but what did I know about the rest of his island? The only decent Mystic I had ever met was Nate. Those weren't great odds. "Think of it like this," I told Kat. "What do we know about drummers?"

A dreamy smile crossed her face. "They're fun and wild . . . and hot."

"*And* they break your heart."

"Well . . ."

"Every single time," I reminded her. "One hundred percent of the drummers you've dated have let you down. So imagine you were invited to spend a week on an island full of them."

"Oh hell yes!"

"Seriously?"

"I would trade my left boob for that."

"You're hopeless."

"Hey, sometimes the disappointment is worth the ride," she said. "Let me ask you a question. What's the worst thing that can happen if you go to Lumara?"

"I could get murdered."

"The worst thing that's *likely* to happen."

I took a moment to think about it. "I could find out all the Mystics on Lumara are liars and scammers, just like the rest of them."

"And you and Nathaniel would probably break up."

I nodded. "That too."

"Okay. Breakups suck. But now tell me the *best* thing that could happen."

Strangely, that outcome was easier to imagine. "I could have a great time, and fall in love with Nate's family, and come home with a healthy heart."

Kat grinned, tipping up both hands. "That's worth the risk, don't you think?"

When she put it that way, I couldn't say no.

"So it's decided: You're going," she said. "Now, the first problem is getting them to accept you."

I tried not to roll my eyes. More like getting *me* to accept *them*.

"They'll see you as an outsider," she went on. "You have to make an extra-good impression by bringing a present for the wedding."

"Of course I'll bring a pr—"

"No, wait," she interrupted. "This is the wedding of the century. There'll be a hundred presents. Yours won't stand out." She snapped her fingers. "The rehearsal dinner, that's when you give them yours. Make sure it's special, some personal token that'll make the bride go mushy. She'll be so touched that she'll talk you up to the rest of the family, and then *bam!* You're in with Nate's mom."

"I thought I was already *in*. They're letting me in on their secret island. That has to mean they trust me, right?"

"Don't be so sure. You're overlooking a few things." Kat began ticking items on her fingers. "First, Nate's parents are rich. Rich people always think their kids fart rainbows. Second, he's the only son *and* the baby of the family. He's probably never heard the word *no*. And third, you're not one of them. Just because Nate loves you doesn't mean his parents will. Especially his mom. Moms can be a tough nut to crack."

A pit formed in my stomach. I didn't want to have to win over Nate's family any more than I wanted to be the only powerless person on an island populated by magicians.

"Hey, don't stress," Kat said, scanning my face. "Stress will give you pimples."

"You're not helping."

"You got this."

"Sure, all I have to do is find the perfect gift for two people who can buy or conjure anything they want. All with a twenty-dollar budget and six days to go. No pressure."

"I'll pitch in," Kat promised. She dug under her mattress and pulled out a wad of bills. "I have enough to . . . double your budget." She cringed. "Money's not everything. It's the thought that counts."

"Then we'd better think harder."

It would help if I had ever been to a wedding before. I touched my pendant, wishing my mom were there to tell me what to do. I couldn't go to her for advice, but maybe my aunt could step in. "Ask your mom if we have any wedding traditions in the family," I said. "Maybe that will jog an idea."

"On it!" said Kat.

And she signed off before I could say anything else.

My aunt did end up saving the day, though, with a suggestion for a homemade gift that would melt any bride's heart. Even better, all of the supplies and equipment I needed were right there at the academy, including a staff of teachers to help make it perfect.

I pulled out a pad and pencil and sketched a preliminary draft of my idea. Excitement kept me awake for seven more drafts, until I knew I had a winner. I couldn't wait to begin the next step, to bring my inspiration to life in physical form. The knot in my stomach loosened as my confidence crept back in. Because I remembered that magic wasn't everything. I had power, too—creativity and heart— and my project was a chance to prove it. I wanted my gift to do more than stand out. I wanted to make myself unforgettable.

I'm in, I texted Nathaniel that night. *Just tell me what to pack.* ☺

CHAPTER
FOUR

One week later, fall break started off with a bang when I woke up on the floor and opened my eyes to the shirtless image of Joshua Hartwell gyrating on the ceiling. I groaned and sat up, fully dressed in my academy uniform, except for my feet, which were bare and covered in dirt, a dried leaf peeking out from between my toes.

"Great," I grumbled, pulling the leaf free. It looked like I'd gone wandering in my sleep again. That shouldn't have surprised me, considering my stress level, but it had been six months since the last episode, and I thought I had grown out of it.

Apparently not.

Farah was watching me, propped up on one elbow in her bed. "You're an entertaining roommate. I'll give you that."

"Glad I amuse you."

"I don't suppose you remember anything from last night," she asked, grinning in a way that told me she remembered enough for both of us.

My mind was blank. "How bad was it?"

"Well, on a scale from nutty to bananas, you were raw fruitcake batter."

I dragged a hand over my face, torn between wanting to know and wanting to stay oblivious. Sometimes amnesia was a gift.

"I didn't hear you leave," she said. "I was dead asleep, or I would've stopped you, or at least followed you around so you wouldn't walk off a cliff or something. But you forgot to take your key, so I definitely noticed when you came back. You pounded on the door and gave me a heart attack."

I winced. "Sorry."

"No worries," she said, flapping a hand. "It was worth it to watch you breeze in here like some kind of drunk Christmas elf, all loaded up with ribbons and wrapping paper and a little box for the present you made."

I glanced around the room, seeing none of what she'd described.

"Oh, you cleaned up after yourself," Farah added, with a dry chuckle. "Even in your sleep, you're a nerd." She pointed behind me, where a beautifully wrapped gift rested on my bed. "It took you half an hour to do that—bent over the box, all slow and meticulous, like you were defusing a bomb. And here's the best part. When I asked what you were doing, you said *the Lord's work*."

I couldn't help laughing. "Are you serious?"

"I swear," she said, holding up a hand. "You should sleepwalk more often."

The buckle on my wrist didn't vibrate, so Farah's story was

true. At least I had been productive in my sleep. Now I didn't have to worry about wrapping the wedding gift before Nathaniel came to pick me up. I did, however, need to wash off last night's dirt and finish packing, so I put the episode behind me and got to work.

When I returned from the showers, Farah had left for class. I dug my Blaze Connect out from beneath my mattress and tucked it carefully between two T-shirts in my suitcase. Kat had made me promise to bring the gadget to Lumara so she could experience the island for herself. I added the wedding gift and an extra pair of sandals to the bag, and then I was ready to go.

Nathaniel arrived at my door with a powdered sugar doughnut and an even sweeter smile.

"All set?" he asked. A second question lingered in his gaze. He searched my face, holding his breath as if afraid I might change my mind.

Secretly, I had changed my mind a time or two, but he didn't need to know that. I reassured him with a kiss and sealed the deal by locking my door behind me.

"I can't wait," I told him, surprised to discover a thrill of excitement rising above the nervous flutters in my belly. Nate always had that effect on me. Apparently, it even overcame my dread of all things Mystic-related. I threaded my arm through his and said, "Lead the way."

He carried my bag outside to a limousine parked at the curb. I had never ridden in a limo before, so I couldn't stop myself from gawking at the assortment of snacks and candy, even a tiny refrigerator stocked with drinks. The backseat was plush and warm—not to mention private enough for a bonus make-out session—and the ride to the marina didn't last nearly long enough. But the limousine, with all its luxury, didn't prepare me for the hundred-foot yacht waiting for us at the end of the dock.

Gleaming from bow to stern, its teak decks polished to a reflective shine, the *Seas the Day* offered a full outdoor lounge and a two-story interior cabin, all while maintaining the sleek, sporty lines of a craft built for speed. I knew nothing about boats, but even I could tell the *Seas* was made for living fast and going faster. I also knew that the autumn wind would force us inside as soon as we started moving, so I insisted on a full tour before we set off.

Nathaniel showed me the pilothouse and introduced me to our captain, a middle-aged man of very few words. He greeted me with a nod and then called for our butler, an equally quiet balding man, who led us to the entertainment room and recited the ship's lunch menu. I ordered a bacon cheeseburger and fries, nothing fancy, but as the butler backed out of the room, I thought I caught him glaring at me.

"Is it just my imagination?" I asked Nathaniel when we were alone. "Or did he give me the stink eye?"

Nate pulled me down beside him on the leather sofa. "It's not you. It's me. I dated his daughter when I was fourteen and broke it off when I moved to the academy. He's still bitter about it."

"So he's from Lumara?"

"The captain, too," Nate said, wrapping an arm around my shoulder. "I should tell you not everyone is happy that I moved away. The last person who left Lumara didn't come back, and people try to use that as a reason to get in my business. They see it as a betrayal for me to live on the outside, like I'm turning my back on my roots or whatever."

Now I understood the butler's dirty look—and what my cousin had meant about the islanders not accepting me. "And here I am, the outsider you're bringing home . . . the weed killer to your roots."

He kissed the top of my head. "Don't think of it like that. Most people on the island are chill. And, honestly, if it weren't for my mom, no one would care what I do."

"You never told me why she's important."

He drew a long breath, as if gathering his thoughts. "The easy answer is she's the boss, but it's more complicated than that. Her official title is Grand Lumara. Every generation has one. It's the person who's most connected to the island. She's responsible for the homeostasis on Lumara, making sure no one's throwing off the balance by using too much magic or pushing too hard against the flow."

"The flow?"

"It's kind of like fate," Nate said. "The way it's told in Greek mythology, where a mystical being is pulling strings and setting events in motion. The flow is basically the will of the island, or maybe it's the will of the magic *inside* the island, like a spirit inside a body. I don't know. No one does. But every once in a while, the island tries to make things happen, and if we fight it, the ecosystem breaks down."

I looked up at him, my mouth hanging open.

"It's not as weird as it sounds," he promised.

I held up my lie detector bracelet. "I think this thing is broken. It should be vibrating like crazy."

"Really, I didn't describe it right," he said. "I swear everything will make sense once we get there and you can see for yourself."

"I guess you weren't exaggerating when you said Lumara feels alive."

"Yes, but I also meant what I said about the magic," he told me. "It's more beautiful than anything you can imagine. So don't get too bogged down by the freaky parts."

That was easier said than done, but I tried my best to push aside my doubts. We cuddled on the sofa until lunch was ready, and then Nathaniel told me stories about the island while we ate. Mostly he tried to help me understand "the flow" by giving me examples of how Lumara made its wishes known. He said one of his earliest memories involved going for a walk in the meadow behind his house. He was looking for berries when the grass in front of him parted and formed a path, which he followed until he reached an injured bird hiding in the underbrush. He took the bird home to his sister, who taught him his first healing spell.

"Right after we released the bird," he said, "we found out it was the last female left on the island."

"So Lumara used you to save an endangered species?"

"Pretty much."

When he put it that way, the flow didn't sound so creepy. I could also see why resisting the island could cause a breakdown in the ecosystem. "Why would anyone fight it?"

"Bad timing," he said. "If you're in a hurry, or in the middle of doing something important. The promptings don't always make sense, either. It can get annoying after a while, like having an invisible parent who gives you confusing chores."

He went on to describe the ways the island communicated through nature. A branch might brush against someone to draw their attention elsewhere, but they might not know the reason. Blossoms might open to guide a path, or lightning bugs might fly in unison like a personal airstrip. The more Nate told me, the more I wondered why he would ever want to leave such a place, even if the community felt tiny.

Then our frosty-eyed butler returned and reminded me of the downside to small-town living. He handed each of us a patch, the kind that people wore for seasickness, and informed us that we were approaching Lumara's protective wards.

"Put these on," he told us.

I looked at my patch, imagining all the ways the butler could have jinxed it. I knew I was being paranoid, but I couldn't help myself. The man clearly hated me.

"It's safe," Nate promised. I trusted him, but I waited for the butler to tell me in his own words so I could see if my bracelet vibrated.

"Completely safe," the man agreed.

No vibrations. *Now* I believed him.

Nate applied a patch to the side of his neck before helping me with mine. "These stickers are enchanted," he explained. "To let us pass through the first layer of wards."

I touched the smooth patch. It felt like a Band-Aid. "What happens if we're not wearing them?"

"We'd start getting mixed up, sort of scared and dopey. The spells make people feel disoriented so they'll want to turn around if they get too close."

"What about the next round of spells?"

"The second ward kills navigation. Electrical equipment dies, compasses stop working. There's total cloud cover to block the sun, and fog so thick you can't see your hand in front of your face. And if *that* fails," he added, "the island kicks up its currents. Then the party's really over."

"Sounds like vampire lore," I said. "You can't come in without an invitation."

"You're not wrong."

"What about a Trojan horse maneuver?" I asked. "Has anyone ever—" I cut off with a gasp of pain, my temple throbbing. "Ow!"

"You okay?"

"Headache," I whispered.

But it was more than that.

As I cradled my head, a flashback appeared behind my eyelids. The images were brief and teasing, and unfamiliar enough that I couldn't tell if the memory was real. I saw my mother lying in bed, her cheekbones sharp and her face pale, the way she looked in the days before she died. My father sat on the edge of her mattress while I watched from the corner of the room. My mother looked at me and told my father, *You have to find a way to stop it before it gets this bad.* While he cried and muttered promises to her, I said, *I want to help. You have to let me try.* I felt an urgency to do something, but I couldn't remember what. The answer was so close. I knew that if I reached a little further into the memory, I would understand it, but the missing link was just beyond my grasp, like a dream beginning to fade.

The pain ended as abruptly as it had begun, and I opened my

eyes to find Nathaniel watching me in a panic. I realized he was gripping my shoulders. Odd that I hadn't felt his touch until now. I must've really been out of it.

"Where did you go?" he asked. "Tals, that was scary. Is that a new heart thing you didn't tell me about? Side effects from your meds?"

"What do you mean? It was a headache. It lasted for a second."

"Talia, you were out—we're talking eyes rolled back, staring at the ceiling like your spirit left your body." He pointed at our butler, who had reappeared in the doorway. "Long enough for me to call for help."

I touched behind my ear and noticed my patch had peeled partially off. I smoothed it back down. "It must have been the wards. You were right; those spells are no joke."

Nathaniel traded a look with the butler. No words passed between them, but I understood the universal body language of raised eyebrows.

"What?" I asked.

"The wards don't work like that," Nate said. "They cause confusion, not"—gesturing at me—"whatever that was."

I tried not to panic, but I wondered if the island was rejecting me. What if Lumara could sense that I hated Mystics, and it didn't want me here? "Does the island treat non-magical visitors differently?"

"No," Nate said. "Well, I mean, technically, yes, but not like that. We don't let a lot of non-Mystics through the wards, and we erase their memories as soon as they leave. But the island doesn't mess with them out of spite."

My heart thunked with a sudden, unwelcome suspicion. "Will my memory be erased? You never mentioned that."

Nate shook his head. "You're an exception."

"Good," I told him. "Maybe someone turned up your magical security settings."

"Maybe," Nate said, but in a tone that implied the opposite. "I'll ask my mom about it later. We're in the second layer now."

I turned around and peeked out the window, where the dense white fog resembled a blizzard. "How much longer?"

"A few more minutes and we'll be out of the wards. Then we can go up top for a better view."

I bit my lip. I didn't know if I wanted to go to the upper deck. I couldn't help envisioning the pissed-off spirit of Lumara shoving me overboard.

"But first, I'm putting you in a life vest," Nate added as if reading my mind. "Just in case you zone out again."

True to his word, he found me an enchanted life vest that would supposedly catch me before I hit the water and return me to the deck like a human boomerang. A slightly disturbing mental image, but it made me feel better anyway.

After buckling me up, he cupped my elbow and supported me as we climbed the interior stairwell to the top deck. I had to stop a couple of times to rest, but the effort was worth it when we opened the door and stepped outside.

I braced myself for the autumn chill, but to my surprise, tropical warmth blew back my hair and caressed my cheeks. I noticed right away the air had a special quality to it, crisp and clean, with none of the usual humidity that left a sticky film on my skin.

The *Seas the Day* had slowed to half throttle, allowing us to walk forward while gripping the handrail. The fog was thinning now, enough that I could see the dark water churning below us. We had nearly made it to the seating area at the bow of the ship when Lumara came into view, and my steps halted, along with my breath.

The boundary was impossible to miss—the murky Atlantic morphing into a turquoise sea as clear as bathwater. The gentle waves seemed to radiate brightness, as though a second sun had risen at the bottom of the ocean. Their swells rolled toward an island of rich green dotted with red blossoms, colors so vibrant I had to blink twice to believe my eyes.

Nestled farther back from the coastline, I could make out a lagoon, its placid waters surrounded on all sides by curved stretches of sandy white beach. Behind it all stood a single mountain, its peak disappearing into a mist of thin, feathery clouds. Something about the mountain gave me chills. Even from a distance, it gave off a charge that was practically electric, and I knew without asking that if Lumara was alive, the mountain was its beating heart.

"Wow" was all I could say.

Nate held me close. "Just wait. Here comes the best part."

The boat slowed and cut its engines, drifting to a stop as it crossed into the turquoise waters. In the silence, I could hear bird-calls and the distant roar of the surf. And then, as if Poseidon himself had cupped us in his hand, a wave arose from the depths and cradled our ship high in the air. I gasped in delight, clinging to the hand-rail while the sea rolled us toward the coast, closer and closer, until we reached a docking harbor, and the wave lowered us back to our rightful place.

I laughed as the boat gently bobbed up and down. Maybe Lumara didn't hate me after all. I was about to tell Nathaniel he was right—that *was* the best part—when I felt the sensation of being watched. I glanced over my shoulder and found a tall boy standing a few yards behind us on the deck.

The boy must have been swimming and used magic to come aboard, because his entire body was soaking wet. He wore a pair of red plaid swim trunks, and he peered at me with a curious expression, not hostile, but not warm, either. I figured he was a friend of Nate's. They seemed close in age, though the boy was an inch or two taller and noticeably wider in the shoulders. I didn't usually describe guys as beautiful, but for him, the word fit—high cheekbones; wide eyes fringed by impossibly thick lashes; and dark, wavy locks of hair dripping water down his chest. And not that I was trying to notice or anything, but the guy had muscles for days.

I cleared my throat to get Nathaniel's attention, then hooked a thumb behind us. "Friend of yours?"

Nate turned around and glanced the stern. "Who?"

"Him," I said, nodding at the boy, who was still watching me . . . and only me.

Nate tipped up a palm.

"That guy." I pointed directly at him. "Right in front of us."

Instead of acknowledging the boy, Nate shielded his eyes from the sun and peered out over the water. "Where?"

"Oh my god," I huffed.

I stomped toward the dripping boy with the intention of taking him by the wrist and leading him back to my farsighted boyfriend. But the stranger took a step away from me, and before I could reach him, he climbed over the railing and jumped. I rushed to the hand-rail and leaned down, searching for him in the crystal water. I could see all the way to the sandy bottom, but there was no sign of the boy. He'd disappeared.

"Careful," Nathaniel said, gripping my arm as if afraid I might fall.

"*Me* be careful?" I pointed below. "What about the guy who just jumped?"

Nate looked at me like I'd grown a third eye.

"You really didn't see him?" I asked. "The tall guy, about our age, long hair, likes to work out . . ."

Nate shook his head.

And then it hit me that I had probably been pranked. If one of Nate's buddies was salty enough about his friend moving away from home, he might want a sneak peek at the new girlfriend, to scope out the enemy, or maybe even scare her into turning around and leaving. Not very original—more like an episode of *Scooby-Doo*—but Mystics were petty like that.

"Can you make yourself invisible?" I asked.

"Sure."

"But invisible to everyone except one person, like me?"

"I never tried it, but I don't see why not. We can't teleport or fly or time-travel. But aside from that, the possibilities are open. You just have to figure out the right spell to connect to the magic. That's the hard part. Spells are like family recipes. It can take generations to get them right, so you don't give them away for free."

"What about invisibility?" I asked. "Is that an easy one?"

Nate flashed a grin and whispered something under his breath.

His body started to fade around the edges, continuing inward until he vanished completely.

"Effortless," he told me, his voice at my ear.

I squeezed his arm to test his solidity. He was definitely all there, but I could see through his physical form to the deck. I heard him whispering again, and his body reappeared.

"Then that explains it," I said. "I think I just met one of your friends. For the record, he's kind of an asshole, and you can tell him I said so."

Nate chuckled. "I can think of a few guys who might fit the profile. Sorry about that. As soon as I figure out who he is, I guarantee it won't happen again."

I nodded, peering out at the water. Only one thing didn't make sense. Two things, actually. Because now that I thought about it, I wasn't sure I heard a splash when the boy jumped overboard. And glancing at the spot where he had stood, I noticed the teak decking was dry and polished to a flawless shine. No traces of pooling, or wet footprints, or even dried water spots to indicate anyone had been there.

I guessed the boy could have planned ahead and used extra spells to cover his tracks, but that seemed like a lot of work for a prank.

Petty, I reminded myself, and ignored the heaviness in my stomach.

CHAPTER
FIVE

The harbor bustled with activity as wedding supplies changed hands—floral arrangements, linens, decor, wine crates, chairs and tables—not to mention new guests arriving by the minute. I had learned the bride and groom, Lucy Vila and Leo Green, both belonged to powerful Mystic families. Nate's cousin Lucy, the local, was the niece and goddaughter of the Grand Lumara, while Leo had grown up outside Los Angeles in a big Aura community founded by his grandfather. So for the Mystic elite, an invitation to the wedding was a golden ticket that no one had refused. According to Nate, more people would occupy Lumara during the next two days than the island had ever accommodated before. And because Lumara wasn't a tourist destination, no hotels had ever been built.

"Which means they're all crashing in houses, including mine," Nate said as he loaded our bags into a retro black car parked at the end of the dock. "Let's just say things are about to get . . . cozy."

"I guess not even magic can stop wedding chaos, huh?"

"Everything has limits." Nate closed the trunk and then used his shirt hem to buff a tiny smudge near the latch. He swept a hand toward the car, reminding me of an old-school game-show hostess. "Anyway, what do you think?"

"About the car?"

"Of course about the car."

"It's nice."

He cocked his head. "Nice? That's all you have to say about a flawless, factory-restored time capsule from the glory days of American auto-body design?"

"Um. *Very* nice?"

Shoulders sagging, he jutted out his lower lip in an adorable pout that hurt my heart. I hadn't meant to disappoint him. "I thought you'd be more impressed," he said. "Since you and your dad restored one like this."

"We did?" I asked. I was pretty confident I had never restored a car. I didn't know the first thing about the process. I massaged my forehead against the building pressure. "Are you sure?"

"That's what you told me." Nate pointed at my bracelet. "And I know you weren't lying. You said your dad bought a rusted-out Impala, and you guys spent a year working on it."

"Oh!" Suddenly I remembered the entire project from start to finish, every moment in a rush. I had no idea what had happened to me. It felt like a mental hiccup. "I can't believe I forgot about that."

"Neither can I," Nate said, giving me the same worried look as before. "When you spend a whole year on something, it tends to make an impact. Do you think . . ."

His words faded away as I watched another flashback unfold

behind my eyes. This time, I recognized part of the memory. My mother had just given me her locket, a cherished family heirloom that she had worn religiously. I would never forget the impact of that moment. It was the first time her diagnosis had felt real, and I ached with a loss so sharp it nearly doubled me over. What I didn't remember was opening the oval pendant to insert a lock of her hair, and then recoiling when I found bits of bone and dried blood inside it. *Don't be afraid,* my mother whispered. *And don't ever forget me.*

As if I could.

The instant my headache passed, I ignored everything around me—the sun, my senses, Nathaniel's voice—and tugged my locket out from beneath my shirt. I had to see what was inside it. My fingers trembled, but I managed to wedge the pendant open. I held my breath while I inspected its contents. There, resting in the center of the golden oval, was a tight black coil of my mother's hair. No dried blood. No bone splinters. Nothing out of the ordinary.

I exhaled in relief.

But what did the flashback mean?

"I think your island is screwing with me," I said to Nate, who had crouched in front of me. I had somehow ended up on the ground with my back against a tire. "What did I do to trigger Lumara?"

"Maybe it read your tweets," he joked, helping me to stand. "But seriously, your tour of the island can wait. I'm taking you home to see my mom."

I didn't argue with him, even though I felt fine. So far, the episodes had snuck up on me at random times, so I knew better than to trust a normal moment.

We climbed into his Impala—which was equally show-worthy

on the inside, restored with wood-inlaid detailing and sport leather seats—and drove along a narrow road leading toward the mountain. The road began to zigzag as it steepened. I admired the way the Impala handled, with very little play in the wheel and more than enough power in its rumbling, throaty engine to scale the mountain with ease. While we drove, I asked Nate to tell me about the engine rebuild. I already knew he'd used updated modern fuel injection, but I wanted to show extra interest, to make up for my brain blip at the harbor. I chewed on my thumbnail and tried not to overthink what had happened, but it scared me that I had forgotten a lifetime of knowledge in an instant. All of my memories had returned, but what if next time they didn't? What chunk of my life would vanish next, and for how long? What if the last part of my flashback was real, and my mother had asked me not to forget her because she knew it might happen?

The possibility turned my stomach. I had to stop thinking about it.

I gazed out the window and focused my attention on the jungle greenery until we reached a fork in the road. A stone sign marked WOOD ESTATE pointed toward a private drive that disappeared into the trees. We followed the lane for another mile or so, and then I caught my first glimpse of Nathaniel's home.

I had seen pictures of earth-sheltered homes, little hobbit burrows carved into hillsides, but nothing as grand or as seamlessly blended with nature as the multistory mansion ahead of me. Built into a mountain cliff, the foundation was supported by natural stone columns that seemed to have pushed up from the ground of their own volition. The island trees had joined their branches to create a wraparound porch leading to an observatory that stretched beyond the cliff face. Wooden walls and a thatched roof provided enough camouflage that I might not even notice the home . . . if it weren't for the blacktop driveway that formed a circle at the entrance before continuing to a six-car garage.

Nate parked at the front door and wasted no time leading me into the foyer, its marble floors so shiny I could almost see up my own skirt. I barely had a chance to notice the soaring ceilings and the majestic dual curving staircases before he ushered me into an adjoining living room, where a woman in her early thirties sat alone on a sofa, a hardcover book hiding the lower half of her face. Her hair was blacker than a raven feather and pulled into a high ponytail. She'd draped a blanket over her lap, despite the warm temperature, and even with the yarn's added bulk, I could see her legs were painfully thin. This must be Olive. She struck me as fragile, as though a breath of wind could come through the open window and shatter her like a porcelain teacup. She lowered her book and glanced at Nathaniel, and her whole face transformed in a smile bright enough to blind the sun.

I liked her at once.

"Where's Mom?" Nate asked her.

She scoffed. "Well, hello to you, too."

"Sorry." Nate waved a hand between us. "Talia, Olive. Olive, Talia." He gently pushed me toward the sofa and told his sister, "I've got to find Mom."

He jogged out of the room without another word.

Olive shook her head, laughing. "Are all brothers this rude?"

"I'm an only child," I answered. "I wouldn't know."

"Ah, well, I'd say you're lucky, but that would be a lie." She patted the spot next to her on the sofa. "He's the best . . . most of the time."

I left a few cushions between us when I sat down, a comfortable amount of space that I hoped didn't make me seem standoffish. Briefly, I glanced around the room, taking in an assortment of expensive-looking artwork and decor. The room was lovely, but something was missing. I realized there were no personal touches, no framed mementos or family portraits . . . or any pictures at all. That seemed odd, or at least cold, but I tried not to read too much into it. Maybe the family photographs were displayed somewhere else in the house.

I pointed at Olive's book. "What are you reading?"

"A history of contemporary critical law," she said.

"Are you a lawyer?"

She nodded. "I got a health waiver and took all of my classes online. I handled my cases remotely, too. I don't practice anymore, but it's still a passion of mine."

"Were your clients Mystics? Or ordinary people?"

"I'm licensed to represent both, but most of my cases were non-magical. There isn't much of a demand for attorneys in the Mystic culture."

"Culture?" I asked. "What does that have to do with the law?"

She chuckled softly. "You must not know about the Federation legal system."

I shook my head.

"Their idea of justice is . . ." She paused, looking for the right word. "Archaic. So most Mystic communities handle disputes and criminal issues internally. It's not in anyone's best interest to get the government involved."

"My history teacher would say it never is."

"I'm surprised Nate didn't mention any of this."

"I didn't even know he was a Mystic until last week. But he told me more about you than anyone else. I even heard the story about the bird you saved together."

Olive placed a hand over her heart. "He's always had the sweetest spirit. That's why I want to thank you."

"For what?" I asked.

"For coming here," she said. "I know it couldn't have been easy, but you did it anyway, for him. That tells me a lot about you. I love Nate more than anyone on this earth, and I can't be happy unless he's happy." She pointed her book at me. "You make him happy. So thank you for that, too."

My cheeks blushed, and I studied my lap.

"Oh no, I embarrassed you," she said, hugging the book to her chest. "You're a sweetheart, Talia. I can see why Nate fell for you. He didn't stand a chance."

Her words triggered the briefest flicker of a flashback. I didn't know when or why, but I had said something similar to my cousin about Nate. *He won't stand a chance.*

Nate came skidding into the room, pointing at me. "Look!" he called to someone in the foyer. "She's doing it again!"

"I'm not," I assured him. But to be sure, I asked Olive, "Did I zone out?"

"You closed your eyes," she said. "I assumed you were tired."

Three other people joined Nate, one man and two women, all

of them in their sixties, or so I guessed, judging by their gray hair and lined skin, and the slow, careful way they moved. If I didn't already know Nate had been a late-life surprise baby, I would've assumed the man standing beside him was his grandfather. But those familiar dark, soulful eyes, now peering at me curiously, belonged to his dad. I glanced between the two women and couldn't tell them apart. Both were petite and slim, dressed in tailored pantsuits, their silvery hair pinned in similar French twists. They stood with the same regal posture, hands at their sides, chins lifted, looking down their noses at me. I noticed a slight difference in the shape and tilt of their eyes, and the sentiment behind them. One woman studied me like a math equation to solve, the other like a wad of gum she'd found on the bottom of her shoe.

As if reading my mind, the first woman told me, "We're twins."

"Fraternal," added the other.

"Yes, it runs in the family," said the first woman. "And because my son has so rudely neglected to introduce us"—cutting her eyes at Nathaniel—"I am Lillian Wood." She indicated Nate's father. "This is my husband, Adrian. And my sister, Camilla."

"Welcome, Talia," Adrian said in a deep voice so much like his son's. "Nate hasn't stopped talking about you all year. It's a pleasure to finally meet you."

"You too," I told him with a small wave. "I'm excited for the wedding." I asked Camilla, "Are you the mother of the bride?"

"Yes," she said. "I'm delighted that you could join us."

Something buzzed against my skin, and I peeked down to find my bracelet buckle vibrating. I muffled the sound, glancing at Nate to see if he'd heard. He seemed oblivious, as did everyone else, except for his mother, who looked at my wrist and back to me before avoiding my gaze completely. It shouldn't have surprised me that she'd noticed the alarm. As the most powerful Mystic on the island, she had probably enchanted the bracelet herself.

Still, Camilla's lie shook my confidence, and I didn't know how to act. I wished I could tell her that I didn't really like her, either.

"Yes, yes," Nate said, flapping a hand. "Now that we're all introduced, can we get back to the important part? Talia's been having weird episodes ever since we crossed the wards."

"Episodes?" Lillian asked.

"Like seizures," he said.

"No, not seizures," I objected, giving him a look that told him not to correct me. There were already enough people who didn't want me here—first the butler, then Nate's disappearing friend, and now his aunt Camilla. None of them needed another reason to be suspicious of the outsider. "More like migraines. I get them sometimes when I don't drink enough water."

Nate clenched his jaw, staying silent but not happy about it. I thanked him with a nod. I knew he would understand when I explained my reasoning to him later.

Lillian strode forward and delicately lowered onto the sofa cushion between me and Olive. Though there was plenty of room without making physical contact, Olive scooted an inch away from her mother. *Interesting.*

"Let's see what the island has to say," Lillian told me.

I sat up straight. I didn't want the island talking about me. "No, that's okay. You don't have to do that."

"It's no bother," she said while reaching toward the open

window. A vine appeared, slithering on the breeze until it encircled her hand and interlaced with her fingers. I held my breath as she closed her eyes, parting her lips in silence, motionless except for a shimmer of energy rippling around her. A moment later, the vine unwound itself from her hand and snaked back out the window. I chewed my lower lip, afraid to move, staring at Lillian for some hint of what Lumara had told her.

Lillian opened her eyes. "The island wants to help you."

I exhaled in relief.

"Why?" Camilla blurted before she caught herself and cleared her throat. "Lumara has never acknowledged a non-magical guest before."

"I want to know, too," I told her.

Lillian shook her head. "That remains to be seen."

So Lumara was messing with my head . . . but with good intentions? I couldn't imagine why the island cared, but I was glad it didn't tell Lillian I was a Mystiphobe.

A tall, suited gentleman entered the room and addressed the Grand Lumara. "Excuse me, ma'am. We've hit a minor snag and need to discuss some changes to the rehearsal dinner."

Camilla's brows shot up. "What snag?"

"And," the man added with an apologetic cringe, "the groom's parents would prefer accommodations in a west-facing room."

"Oh gracious," Lillian whispered. "Duty calls." She patted me on the knee and suggested to Nathaniel that he give me a tour of the island, starting with the lagoon. "Just be back in time to receive guests for dinner," she told him, and strode away with her sister and husband.

It didn't escape my notice that Lillian and Adrian, and even Camilla, had left without exchanging a single word with Olive or acknowledging her in any way. But if Olive felt slighted, she didn't let it show. She tucked her blanket in place, inviting Nate to use her old scooter to take me to a place called Jumping Rock Waterfall. Then with a smile and a nod goodbye, she reopened her book and went back to reading.

CHAPTER
SIX

I followed Nathaniel to a shed, where he dug out Olive's scooter and dusted off the seat. He told me the engine had been enchanted to run on ocean water instead of gas, and with the tank full, we were ready for our adventure. While fastening my helmet, I noticed an outbuilding set farther back on the property where the lawn began to surrender to the wild underbrush. The building reminded me of a studio or a small guesthouse, its rounded hexagonal walls painted white in stark contrast to the jungle.

"What's that?" I asked, pointing.

"Ah," he said. "Fun fact. That cottage is the only place on the island where your lie detector bracelet won't work."

"Interesting. Why not?"

"Because every inch of it's been warded to block magic. Spells won't cast in there, no matter how good they are. And any enchantments that already exist—like the one on your bracelet—go dead as soon as you walk through the door. It's basically a power vacuum."

"For all magic?" I asked. "Or just the kind that comes from the island?"

"All of it."

I could think of only one reason for Mystics to build a structure that stripped them of their power. "It's a jail cell, isn't it?"

"Good guess," Nate said. "We don't call it that, but, yeah, pretty much. It's a place to stow people until we figure out if they're guilty."

"What if they are?" I asked. Olive had mentioned the reason Mystics handled their own justice, but she didn't share any details. "Like, does the death penalty exist here?"

Nate shook his head. "The worst punishment is exile. But for a Core Mystic, that's severe, because we can't—"

"Do magic away from the island," I finished. I shielded my eyes and squinted at the cottage windows, checking for signs of life. "What's to stop someone from picking the lock or breaking out through the window?"

"Nothing. But they wouldn't get past the perimeter wards."

"Is anyone in there now?"

"No," he said, and winked at me. "But I'll bet you five bucks someone gets drunk enough at the wedding to win a one-night stay at the Inn of Shame. Probably after midnight."

"*Before* midnight," I countered. "It's a bet."

We shook on it, and I settled behind Nathaniel on the scooter as he fired up the engine. With my arms around his waist, we set off toward the main road. In the open air, I noticed a blend of fragrances I had missed from inside the car—sweet, tantalizing scents that seemed to be coming from a stretch of black-and-white-striped lilies growing wild along the road. I inhaled and felt a tingle of euphoria spread over my body. The sensation passed quickly but left me smiling . . . and wishing I had a magical dopamine garden at home. The jungle greenery was an arm's length away now, and if I looked closely, I could see the vines pulsing and the leaves expanding and contracting, as if the ivy was breathing in the fragrance, too.

Smart ivy. I couldn't blame it.

I found myself relaxing a little more as we traveled away from Nate's family, and I was finally able to appreciate the island's magic. We took the fork opposite his estate and climbed another mile or two up the mountain, until we reached a well-worn dirt path that veered off the pavement. The ride was bumpy but worth it when we came to a stop at the end of the trail. Ahead of us, a spring-fed waterfall flowed directly out of a cleft in the mountainside and into a crystalline pool at least twenty-five meters below.

Nate pointed at a hiking trail leading to a stone slab above the spring, the perfect leaping-off platform for someone with a death wish. Definitely not for me, even if my heart could survive it. I would never understand the appeal of cliff diving. If I wanted to meet my ancestors, I would hire a psychic.

"There it is," Nate said. "Jumping Rock Waterfall."

"Have you ever done it?" I asked.

"No way. I'm not a fan of heights. But my sister has."

"What?" His sister, Olive, who looked like she could snap in half with a sneeze?

"I know," Nate said. "I can't picture it, either. That was a long time ago, when I was just a baby. Supposedly, she was wild as a teenager. I've heard all the stories. But that was before she got sick."

I was glad he'd brought up her illness. I had been waiting for a chance to ask about Olive's condition without coming across as nosy. "What happened to her? It must be serious if your mom can't fix it."

"It is," he told me, his voice softening. "Just like there are regular diseases, there are magical ones, too. We don't know why or how they happen. They're super rare. Olive is the only person on Lumara who's ever gotten sick like this. She grows tumors in her organs, and no matter how many times my mom removes them, they keep coming back. Olive will get better for a week or two, just long enough to put on a few pounds, before it all starts over again. It doesn't help that she's stubborn. She always waits until she's half-dead before she lets my mom heal her."

I caressed Nate's shoulder. That sounded terrible. I had never heard of diseases exclusive to Mystics, and now I wondered what else I didn't know about them.

"Anyway, this is her favorite spot," he said. "She still comes here sometimes, when she feels up to it. She likes to watch the jumpers. I think they remind her of happier days."

I wanted to bring Olive back with us to the falls, maybe pack a picnic and stay for an afternoon. It was none of my business, but I couldn't stop myself from suggesting to Nate that he give his sister and his mother a gentle shove and convince them to remove Olive's tumors before the wedding. Selfishly, I wanted to spend time with Olive before fall break ended, and that couldn't happen if she was hiding behind a book.

Nate agreed with my idea, and with that settled, we turned around and motored back the way we'd come. As we descended the mountain toward the lagoon, I held on to Nate with one hand and used the other to text my father.

I'm here, I told him. And this time, I had actually remembered to remove him from my friends list so he couldn't use location settings to find me. *Too busy to talk, but all is good. Love you!*

I waited for his response, hoping he didn't insist on a phone call.

Love you too, Button, he replied. *Behave yourself.* ☺

Always, I told him, and added an angel emoji.

I tucked my phone in my pocket and relaxed. I hated lying, but so far, Kat's strategy had worked. Now to avoid talking to my dad for the rest of the week . . .

Nathaniel and I reached a different path veering off the main road, this one noticeably sandier, which slowed down the scooter. Before long, we had no choice but to park off to the side, take off our shoes, and walk the rest of the way. Though the sand was deep and shifted beneath my feet, it didn't stick to me or chafe my skin—a very clever enchantment. I also appreciated the absence of mosquitoes and sand fleas, and especially the sticker burs that often grow near sand dunes.

I had to admit Mystics had perfected island living.

The lagoon was even more striking up close, with water so placid and so vividly blue I could stare at it for hours and never get my fill. A glittering school of rainbow fish zigzagged below the surface, darting away from a glowing barracuda in pursuit of his lunch. In the distance, a pod of dolphins performed acrobatics that looked almost choreographed, their leaps and flips perfectly timed with one another. No aquarium could compete with this show.

I had been waiting to call Kat until I found the right spot. This was it.

Nate and I sat down on the sand, just near enough to the water to wet our bare toes. I plugged in my Blaze Connect and dialed Kat, who answered on the first ring and appeared sitting cross-legged beside me, diving into the conversation with her usual lack of chill.

"No way!" She sat up straighter and gawked at the view before uttering a chain of swears that made Nathaniel snort. "It's not fair. I should be there with you. If you loved me, you would've packed me in your suitcase."

"Next time," I said. "Go work on your contortionist skills."

"But for real, this is nuts." She swept a hand from the lagoon to the flat stretches of white sand and beyond, to the jungle greenery. "I'll bet it's even better in person."

"It is," I told her. "Watch this." I scooped up a handful of sand and released it, then showed her my palm. "It doesn't stick to your skin."

"Or clothes," Nate added while dumping sand on my head. I cringed, but the grains didn't touch me as they fell to the ground. "It's the only way to live at the beach."

"You two are killing me." Kat slumped over, pouting. "But I'll consider forgiving you if you promise me an invite."

"I'll see what I can do," Nate said.

Someone shouted his name, and we turned to see a blond guy about our age waving to us from the path where we'd parked our scooter. Nate stood up and shouted, "Hey, loser!"

Kat and I rolled our eyes at each other. "Boys," she said.

"Do you mind?" Nate asked me while thumbing at his friend.

"Go ahead," I told him.

"It'll give us a chance to talk about you," Kat added with a smile.

Nate jogged off to join the boy. They ventured out of sight, and Kat turned to face me. "So tell me how it's really going."

"About how you'd expect," I said. "Some people like me, some don't. Especially the mother of the bride, Camilla. She hates my face."

Kat scowled. "That bitch. How dare she not see how awesome you are?"

"I know. I'm too sensitive for this."

"But you've got the wedding present, right?"

"Yep. I'm bringing it to the rehearsal dinner."

"That'll change the game. You'll see."

I noticed movement in my periphery, and I glanced at the lagoon just in time to see a dark-haired boy surface from beneath the water. One look at his chiseled face and his impossibly long lashes, and I recognized him as the boy from the boat. He locked eyes with me, standing chest-high in the lagoon, and then strode forward in slow, methodical steps, as if entranced. The skin on the back of my neck prickled, but I held his gaze and refused to show fear. I didn't want to give him the satisfaction of knowing how much he bothered me.

"What are you looking at?" Kat asked.

"Someone you can't see," I said, watching him move closer.

"Uh . . ." Kat peered across the lagoon. "That's because there's no one there."

"Trust me, he's there." He was waist-deep now. I could see the top of his red plaid swim trunks. "It's a friend of Nate's, I think. He's using some kind of invisibility spell to freak me out. He's coming toward us right now."

"Well, it's a good spell," Kat said. "Because the water's not moving."

I realized she was right. The boy's forward steps caused no disruption in the placid lagoon, not even the slightest ripple. Water dripped from his upper body and from the tips of his long hair, falling to the surface without making contact.

The boy wasn't simply invisible. He had made himself intangible.

"You okay?" Kat asked.

I nodded. The boy would probably be gone soon. And without a body, he couldn't hurt me . . . I hoped.

Ankle-deep, he took two more steps and then reached the sand, leaving no footprints behind as he closed the distance between us. The boy's intense stare made my pulse rush, but I held still and resisted the urge to back away. He continued until an arm's length separated us, and he dropped to his knees, swallowing as if preparing to speak.

"I'm not," I began, and cleared my throat. "I'm not afraid of you."

But he quickly made me a liar when he opened his mouth and water poured out in a gush. I gasped, scrambling backward like a four-legged crab while Kat jumped to her feet and asked what was wrong. I couldn't answer her. Or think. Or exhale. All I could do was watch the water flow from the boy's lips. He reached for me and pleaded with his hands. Raw emotion filled his eyes, the frustration of trying and failing to communicate. He seemed to know talking wouldn't work, because he abruptly closed his mouth, scrambled to his feet, and strode back toward the lagoon. At the water's edge, he beckoned for me to join him.

I shook my head. No way.

Nothing on earth would get me into that water with him. Not now, not ever. I sat on the sand, shaking, and watched him wade into the lagoon. He turned away from me and didn't look back, venturing deeper and deeper, until he finally dipped below the surface and vanished.

I blew out a shuddered breath.

"He's gone," I told Kat. My voice trembled. My hands, too. Even though my instincts told me the boy meant no harm, the experience had left me shaken.

"What the hell *was* that?" she demanded.

I had no idea. But whatever it was, it didn't feel like a prank. I glanced around for Nathaniel, still not seeing him. I had assumed the disappearing boy was a friend of Nate's, but now another possibility came to mind. I peeked at my cousin and worked up the nerve to ask a borderline stupid question. "What about ghosts?"

"What about them?"

"Do you think they're real?"

She shrugged and sat back down beside me. "I've never seen one. But magic is real, so it's not that big a stretch to believe in ghosts."

"It's either that, or I'm hallucinating," I told her. Then I chuck-led, because both scenarios might be true. I explained to Kat how the island had been messing with my head, and the theory that Lumara wanted to help me. When I told her about the blood and bone fragments I'd seen in my vision, Kat went stone still. Her gaze darted to my locket. "There's no blood in there," I said, and opened it to show her.

"You didn't take it off, did you?" she asked.

What a weird question. "No, I never do. You know that."

"Okay, yeah," she said, nodding and fidgeting with her fingers. "Listen, I have to go. Call me tonight after the rehearsal dinner. Promise you won't forget."

"I prom—" But before I could finish, she disconnected.

Just like that, her image was gone.

CHAPTER
SEVEN

I couldn't stop thinking about the disappearing boy.

At the rehearsal dinner, I shook hands and smiled, pretending to listen to introductions and anecdotes while mentally replaying the events at the lagoon. When I took my designated place at the table, I kept examining the details of the day, over and over, so distracted that I barely tasted my food.

But in the end, my questions only multiplied.

Who was the boy? Was he a ghost of a real person, or maybe a simulation the island had created to try to communicate with me? What did he want to tell me? Why had he wanted me to follow him into the lagoon? And most intriguing of all, what was his connection to the water? Because there had to be one. I had wondered if he might be a merman or some similar creature. Nathaniel had told me nothing of the kind existed, but I knew the boy was tied to the sea. I just didn't know how.

"Right, Talia?"

I blinked at the sound of my name. Nate was looking at me from his seat across the table, his eyebrows raised, waiting for an answer to a question I hadn't heard.

"Mm-hmm," I told him. "Totally."

I needed to pay attention. I tucked away thoughts of the boy and focused on the dinner party, which was beginning to wind down.

We sat at the end of a long table that took up the entire width of the Woods' cliffside observatory. In the darkness below, fireflies swirled and danced, occasionally coming together to form a tight spiral like an electric tornado. Above us, floating lanterns cast a romantic glow over a tablecloth made exclusively of white rose petals, its surface festooned with bejeweled candles and silver platters full of leftover cuisine. Best of all, each place setting offered a faceted crystal goblet paired with a wine carafe that refilled itself after every pour.

And there had been *many* pours.

None of them ours, as Nate and I had agreed to behave ourselves. But it was still fun to watch the bottomless wine lighten moods and heighten laughter, and in some cases, strip away all traces of maturity. Several seats down, a pair of groomsmen were engaged in a magical shootout, finger-gunning each other with crouton pellets. Beyond them, two bridesmaids pressed their cheeks together to take a selfie, then got distracted and ended up kissing. Not to be outdone, the bride and groom kissed so often they wore out the staying power of her enchanted lipstick.

It made me smile. For Mystics, they seemed like good people.

Drink flowed at the opposite end of the table as well, where both sets of parents were having a spirited discussion about Lucy

and Leo's choice to combine their last names into something new.
Nate's parents listened along, as did Olive, who had been healed by
her mother that afternoon and now glowed with vitality.

I placed a hand on the gift resting on my lap. A glance at Lucy
and Leo found them locked in an intense discussion with the maid
of honor. I'd been waiting for a chance to give the couple my gift
ever since the toasts and speeches had ended, but it wasn't easy competing with twenty other guests for their attention. So I watched,
poised and ready, and when the maid of honor stood up to use the
restroom, I took her vacant chair.

I congratulated Lucy and Leo and handed my wrapped package
across the table. "I know it's early," I said to Lucy. "But we have a
tradition in my family to give the bride and groom a homemade
present before the wedding day. I hope you like it."

Lucy's mouth popped open. She held up the box. "You made
this?"

"For you."

She melted at once, turning to Leo with a squeaky, barely coher-
ent, "Oh my god isn't that the sweetest thing you've ever heard. I
can't believe she took the time to make this for us. Baby, can you
believe it?"

Leo smiled at me. "Especially since we just met. You're very
thoughtful, Talia."

I blushed at the attention. The table had gone silent, everyone
watching us.

Lucy tore off the wrapping paper, revealing the small cardboard
gift box my art teacher had given me. I'd painted the box white,
stenciled with glittery wedding bells. Lucy gushed about that, too.

She lifted the lid, set it aside, and parted the tissue paper encasing her gift. On opposite ends of the box rested two brushed-copper puzzle pieces that formed a heart, one half darkly engraved *Lucy* and the other *Leo*. Though hidden, a second engraving existed below their names, thinly etched and concealed by my shop teacher's expert brushwork. With his help, I had machined and wired the two pieces and powered one half with a tiny watch battery.

I pointed and explained, "Each side is special on its own, but they shine brightest when they're together. Just like you two."

Lucy connected the puzzle pieces. They clicked into place, completing a circuit and illuminating *Lucy and Leo Vilagreen*, their new last name at the core of the heart.

"Copper is a natural conduit," I explained. "And it symbolizes unity, so I thought . . ."

But Lucy wasn't listening. She had broken into a surprisingly beautiful ugly-cry, both her nose and mascara running, her lips contorted in a wet sob. Twice, she used magic to fix her makeup before destroying it all over again. When she could finally speak, she told me, "Talia, this is the most priceless gift anyone has ever given me. I'll treasure it. Thank you."

She passed the heart to Leo, who turned it over and admired the handiwork before handing it to the best man, who gave me a thumbs-up and passed it down the line. One by one, the puzzle made its way through the wedding party until it reached Lucy's mother, Camilla, who left my gift sitting on the table, untouched.

I couldn't win them all.

But I had won the hearts that mattered to me, so I rewarded myself by snagging a few extra macaroons on my way back to my seat. I handed one to Nathaniel. He beamed at me and shoved the whole cookie in his mouth.

"I'm proud of you," he said, one cheek full.

"You already told me that," I reminded him. I had shown him the puzzle the instant I'd finished it. Anything important to me, I shared with Nate first.

"I'm telling you again. It's my job to make you feel special." He leaned forward, delivering a smoldering look that turned my insides to jelly. "I have lots of ideas on how to do that. Want to get out of here so I can show you?"

"Yes," I said, cookies forgotten. "Hard yes."

Sticking with our good behavior, we couldn't leave without saying goodbye. So we made the rounds, smiling and waving until we reached the end of the table, where Nate's parents were sipping wine with Olive and Camilla.

"We're going to head out," Nate said to his mother.

"What? No." She indicated a pair of empty chairs. "Stay a little longer."

"We can't. We're on our way to—"

"Whatever it is can wait," she interrupted. "I only see you on school holidays, and we've barely traded ten words since you got here. Is it so wrong to want to spend a few minutes with my son?" She swept a hand toward me. "And his lovely girlfriend?"

Nate and I traded a look of defeat. We dragged two chairs over and joined the group. Olive grinned at us, lifting her wineglass in a toast. I could tell from the impish gleam in her eyes that she knew exactly why we had wanted to leave.

"Did you get to see Jumping Rock Waterfall?" Olive asked me.

"Oh, I saw it. And I can't believe you actually jumped . . . on purpose."

She laughed. "That was another lifetime."

"The lagoon is more my speed."

Nate squeezed my knee and raised his eyebrows at me, a signal to tell the group what I had seen in the water. I gave him a tiny shake of my head. I wanted to keep the disappearing boy a secret, especially from Camilla. But I couldn't resist asking a question.

"There's so much magic here," I said. "And it seems like the island has a mind of its own. Are there . . . Could there be . . . ghosts on Lumara?"

I waited for the group to laugh. They didn't.

"No," Camilla answered, simply and without malice. She should drink more often.

"Not at all?" I asked.

Nate's mom shook her head. "Not at all."

My bracelet didn't vibrate. But her answer eliminated my strongest theory about the boy.

"How do you know?" I asked.

"Because when you consider what a ghost is," Lillian explained, "it's essentially a prisoner, a spirit trapped in the mortal realm, confused and tormented because it doesn't belong there anymore. My connection with Lumara has taught me that when a life ends on the island, it passes on in peace. I can't say with any degree of certainty what happens to spirits in the outside world, but Lumara doesn't bind the dead."

Something niggled at the back of my mind, a thread of aware-ness trying to work its way to the surface. Without thinking, I blurted, "What about a curse?"

That raised some eyebrows, specifically Camilla's. Nate and his father both cocked their heads to the side, while Lillian's eyes wid-ened in perfect sync with Olive's.

"Could a curse do that?" I asked. "Bind a spirit to the island?"

Lillian took a long sip of wine before she answered. "In theory, I suppose, but I've never heard of anything like that happening. Even for the most skilled Mystic, the level of spell work it would take to reach into the afterlife—the amount of power they would need—is unimaginable. I don't know anyone capable of it."

Olive slid her mother an icy look. "I can think of one."

"Olive!" her father chided.

"What?" she asked. "Someone had to say it."

Camilla drew a breath to speak, but Lillian cut her off with a lifted hand.

Lillian maintained her graceful posture, her face giving nothing away, but she couldn't hide the vein throbbing at her temple. She faced her daughter and paused to pick a bit of lint off her blouse. When she spoke, it was in a tone that a CEO might use to address a mail clerk. "It's true that the power of the Grand Lumara is unimag-inable to most. But anyone entrusted with that magic would know better than to use it for harm. The island doesn't make mistakes in the leader it chooses."

Olive exhaled bitterly and mumbled into her glass, "All hail the island."

The air turned thick with tension. I sat still, unsure of what to do or even where to look while the two women glared at each other. My bracelet didn't vibrate. Whatever cold war was brewing between Olive and her mother, each of them believed she had told the truth.

"Yes, my duty is to serve Lumara," Lillian said to her daughter. "It's also my privilege. This is what I was born to do."

Olive's eyes narrowed to slits. She leaned closer to her mother, her face flushing red, and hissed, "Don't I know it!"

"Whoa, whoa," Adrian said, standing up and taking away both women's wineglasses. He chuckled awkwardly and remarked that they'd had enough, as though alcohol was the problem.

"We should go," Nate suggested, and this time, no one stopped us.

On our way back to the house, I asked him, "What's going on with your mom and your sister?"

"I honestly don't know." He splayed his hands. "They've never been close. None of us have. We're just not that kind of family. But, god, we don't hate each other."

"It almost sounds like Olive is jealous of the island."

"That's what I don't get," he said. "Olive has always complained about my mom's priorities. She has it in her head that our family doesn't matter. But I don't see what she sees. I never have. Our mom has a demanding job, yeah, but she'll stop in her tracks and make time for us when we need it. Like today, she skipped a council meeting to stay home and fix Olive's tumors. Isn't that what prioritizing your family looks like?"

"Pretty much," I agreed. "Maybe something happened while you were away."

"I guess. But I don't want to talk about them anymore." He waggled his brows as he opened the back door. "I want to take advantage of this empty house."

"And me," I suggested, though he couldn't take advantage of the willing.

He leaned down to kiss me but then paused and cupped my face. "Are you sure you're okay, though? Your heart? It's been a long day; I don't want to push you too hard."

"I'm fine," I told him. But I realized he was right. I had done a week's worth of living in one day. I should have collapsed in bed hours ago. Instead, I felt stronger now than when I had woken up that morning. It made no sense, though I wasn't complaining. I tapped my wrist and said, "Time's wasting . . ."

He flashed a devilish grin. The next thing I knew, he hauled me over his shoulder and carried me, firefighter style, into the house.

CHAPTER
EIGHT

*M*y heart pounded. I held my breath and tiptoed across the attic floor,
picking my way through a maze of cardboard boxes and plastic bins,
discarded furniture and rolled-up rugs. Tension locked my shoulders. I had to
be silent, had to hurry before someone caught me rifling around where I didn't
belong. I scanned the room, looking for a file cabinet or an office safe, anything
that might contain important papers with my mom's name on them. I didn't
know what I expected to find, but a cold urgency told me my life depended
on it.

I dragged an office box to the window. By the light of a single moonbeam,
I leafed through receipts and bank statements, deeds and death certificates.

I slammed the papers down.

No mention of my mother.

Next, I opened a cedar chest and dug through an assortment of family
keepsakes: baby clothes, loose photographs, stacks of letters bundled together
with twine.

No hint of her there, either.

Panic set in. My pulse rushed, making it hard to breathe.

Soon, the sun would rise. I had to go, before anyone caught me. But I couldn't leave without finding a record of my mother on Lumara. That was the only thing that mattered, the whole reason I had turned my life upside down to come here.

I needed more time.

In my mother's voice, the house spoke to me.

Be ready, it said. There will be time. Be ready for it.

I felt the sensation of falling and gasped awake on the same wooden floor as my dream. The early morning sun cut through the window, highlighting a flurry of dust motes that tickled my nose and watered my eyes. I pushed to sitting and recognized the stacks of boxes, the unused furniture and rolled-up carpets. Then I noticed a scattering of paper documents all around me, and I froze.

Oh god.

It wasn't just a dream. I had actually gone through their things.

What was *wrong* with me?

Fear set me in motion. I sprang onto all fours, scooping up papers and shoving them into the nearest box. I had to put every-thing away—fast—and get back to my room, or who knew what these Mystics would do to me. Maybe Nathaniel would understand. He knew about my sleepwalking. But Camilla and anyone else who saw me as an outsider would probably demand to have my memory erased before they ejected me from the island.

I didn't know where the office box belonged, so I hid it behind an old armoire and then tiptoed out of the attic, brushing the dust from my pajama shorts and my tank top. I closed the attic door and crept down the stairs to the second-floor hallway, relieved to find it empty. All of the noises of activity seemed to be coming from the kitchen below. If anyone left their room and found me wandering the hallway, I could just ask for directions to the bathroom.

But no sooner had I reached my bedroom door than Nate opened it from the other side and scared me out of my skin.

I squeaked as my hand flew to my chest.

"Sorry," he said, gripping my upper arm. "I knocked and you didn't answer, so I came in to check on you." He glanced up and down the hall. "Where were you?"

I refused to lie to Nate. Even if I could get away with it, I wouldn't want to. "I was sleepwalking," I whispered. "But I'm really embarrassed, and I want to forget it ever happened. So please don't ask me about it, okay?"

"Of course." He wrapped me in a hug, surrounding me in his warmth and the spicy-sweet scent of his cologne, and just like that, my worries melted away. "I got you."

"How do you always know the right thing to say?"

I felt him smile against the top of my head. "Because I'm a magic man. You know, like the old song."

"Makes sense," I said, playing along. "It was probably written about you."

"Definitely, before I was even born. That's how magical I am."

I peeked up at him. "Maybe my magical boyfriend can fix me a cup of coffee while I take a shower?"

"I'll make you a protein shake."

I groaned.

"You're not supposed to have caffeine," he reminded me.

"I know," I said. And normally, I wouldn't ask for it. But

yesterday's adrenaline boost had vanished—at least that's what I was calling it—and now that the shock of waking up in the attic had worn off, I felt more sluggish than usual. I probably had enough energy for the wedding that afternoon, but if I wanted to make it to the reception, I would need help. "It won't hurt this one time," I pressed.

But there was no swaying him. Nate left me with a kiss and a promise to return with a heart-healthy drink. I accepted defeat and consoled myself with a long shower. After I returned to my room and put on a sundress, I texted Kat an apology for not calling her after the rehearsal dinner.

Sorry I flaked, I said. *Stayed up too late doing dirty things.* ;)

Eww, she answered. *Did they like the present?*

THEY LOVED IT!

Good! I knew they would.

Gotta go, I told her.

No worries. Call if you need me. I'll have my phone all day, so I'll be ready for it.

"Be ready for it," I whispered, remembering the echo of my mother's voice in my dream and how desperate I had felt to find traces of her in the Woods' attic. I wished I understood what all of it meant—the dream, the sleepwalking, the flashbacks and visions, and mostly the boy in the water. Deep inside, I sensed they were related, but I couldn't imagine in what way.

A knock sounded on the bedroom door. Nate came in, bearing a pink smoothie in one hand and a gift box in the other. Olive was with him, her movements a little slower than the night before, the color in her cheeks muted.

"You look how I feel," she told me.

Her abruptness made me laugh. "I know, right? What happened to us?"

"I can only speak for myself," she said. "Every time my mother heals me, the tumors grow back twice as fast as before. That's why I don't ask her to do it very often."

Nate's brows jumped. "I didn't know that."

"Well, now you do," she said, and then shamelessly changed the subject by lifting her own smoothie toward me. "He made me one, too."

Olive and I took a long pull from our straws. The sweetness of berries crossed my tongue, blended with a rich, creamy flavor—Greek yogurt, maybe—that added a hint of vanilla and balanced out the tartness. Nate was right. He made a mean smoothie.

"It's perfect," I told him.

"Yes," Olive added. "Thanks, baby brother."

"My pleasure. I gotta take care of my girls. Speaking of which . . ." Nate turned to me and opened the gift box, revealing an elegant silver tiara, set with hundreds of faceted crystals that caught the light and sprayed prisms across the room. "For my homecoming queen."

For a long moment, I didn't know what to say. I stared at the dazzling tiara, entranced by its beauty, until my eyes welled up and turned everything into a rainbow-colored blur. I couldn't believe Nate had done this for me. Just when I thought I couldn't love him any harder, he forced me to completely redefine the emotion. "You actually did it. You bought me a crown."

"I promised you ten," he said.

"Twenty," I corrected.

"But who's counting?"

"I thought you were joking," I told him.

He brushed back my hair and settled the tiara on top of my head, then gently pressed down the combs to hold it in place. "There," he said, caressing my cheek with his thumb. "Now my queen is properly adorned."

"*Your* queen?" Olive cut in. "Remind me to have a talk with you about misogyny later on."

"I didn't mean it like that," he promised.

"What about your crown?" I asked him.

"I don't need one," he said. "I already feel like a king when I'm with you."

"Oh, we're definitely having that talk," Olive told him. "But it can wait. You guys go ahead and . . . carry on. I'll see you at the wedding."

We shut the door behind her, and then we "carried on" for quite a while, until my choppy breathing turned into a full-on wheeze, and Nate made us stop.

"The day is all yours," he said, checking his watch. "We have six hours until the wedding. Tell me what you want to do and I'll make it happen."

"Nothing near the water," I told him. "Not today, at least. I'm not in the mood for a ghost encounter."

He pretended to take notes. "No haunted-cemetery tours. What else?"

"And I'm also kind of tired, so—"

"Say no more." He scribbled on his imaginary notepad. "How about we go to the theater room and watch movies in the hot tub?"

My body relaxed just thinking about it. "You have a hot tub . . . in your theater room?"

"With extra jets."

"I feel so *seen* right now."

"I know my queen," Nate said. "Even better than she knows herself."

I smiled at him. He was probably right.

If magic was rationed on the island, then Lucy and Leo's wedding venue must have taken up half the budget. At the lagoon, a hundred white chairs, each adorned with a translucent bow, faced the horizon in straight and tidy rows on the water—not *near* the water, but quite literally on top of it. Feeling slightly nervous in my seat, I couldn't stop peering at the fish while I tapped my shoe against the lagoon's hard, invisible surface. The experience reminded me of a glass-bottom-boat tour, but without the security of a boat.

Dividing the chairs into two groups, an aisle that seemed to be made from mother of pearl stretched from the beach all the way to a covered pavilion in the heart of the cove, where the ceremony would take place. Leo was already there, trading jokes with his best man, and beside them stood a tall, elderly cleric in a white robe, his hands loosely clasped in front of him as he watched the last guests take their seats.

"That's Father Tim, my great-uncle," Nate whispered to me. "He married my parents at this beach."

I thought that was sweet. I tried to imagine how Lillian and Adrian had looked back then, young and vibrant and in love, before they had become the stoic couple seated at the end of our row, staring at the horizon without talking or touching. Camilla, however, looked happier than I had seen her, smiling as brightly as her yellow chiffon gown. She patted Olive's knee and whispered something to her, probably *Don't worry, you'll find a husband*, because Olive rolled her eyes hard enough to see her own brain.

I threaded my arm through Nate's and admired him in his tuxedo and bow tie, his black curls slicked back and secured at the nape of his neck. The moment he had finished changing and stepped out of his bedroom, I had told him, "James Bond *wishes* he could be as hot as my boyfriend." And I'd meant it. But Nate had been too distracted by my strapless dress to notice anything except my curves. Since then, he hadn't kept his hands, or his eyes, off me.

I could get used to that.

Music filled the air, a soothing instrumental that seemed to originate from above, though there was no orchestra in sight. Along with the other guests, I turned around in my seat to face the beach, where the wedding party had assembled.

Bridesmaids and groomsmen lined up, two by two, and then Pachelbel's Canon in D played, and each pair began a slow, steady march toward the pavilion. When the maid of honor finished her procession, the music paused, and everyone stood up, craning their necks for a glimpse of the bride.

A thick curtain of fog had appeared on the beach. It held there, blocking our view, heightening the anticipation with each passing second, until all of our hearts seemed to beat faster in unison. Then the fog parted, and Lucy appeared, standing at the end of the pearlescent aisle.

There was a collective intake of breath.

Lucy was a vision. Her hair spilled in glossy waves over her shoulders, her face radiating such pure joy that I had to blink back tears, even though I barely knew her. She'd chosen a simple dress, a white satin chemise that hugged her to the waist before flowing freely to the ground. But as the music resumed and she began to stride forward, I saw that her dress wasn't simple at all. Behind her, a train of glittering white satin ribbons hovered above the aisle, dozens of them, each catching the light and sparkling as they moved in the hypnotic, tranquil sway of jellyfish tentacles. The sight was so mesmerizing that I couldn't look away, not until she reached her groom and took his outstretched hand, and the ribbons drifted, as if in slumber, to the floor.

"Wow," I whispered to Nate.

He gave me a proud look, as if saying, *See? I told you magic can be beautiful . . . and that not all Mystics misuse it.*

I was starting to agree.

Father Tim gave the signal to sit down, and I linked hands with Nathaniel as we took our seats. I had never been to a wedding before, but I'd seen plenty of them in movies. The ceremony began the way I had expected, with a welcome message, followed by an inspirational talk about the meaning of love and the value of partnership, and how to protect that love and make it last a lifetime.

"Despite what you might think," Father Tim said. "Love doesn't come from romance. Real love—and real trust—is like a house built from a thousand bricks. The bricks don't represent expensive gifts or candlelight dinners, or your wedding ceremony or even the birth of your children. Instead, the bricks represent the accumulation of each small, everyday choice you make to protect your partner's heart." He paused, letting his message sink in. Then he smiled and added, "It's that simple . . . and that challenging."

I had never thought of love that way, but he'd made an interesting point. I was still thinking about it when a sudden movement from beneath the water caught my eye, and I glanced down to find a face staring back at me. By some miracle, I didn't flinch. My hand tightened around Nate's, but he must have mistaken the squeeze for affection, because he gave me one in return and stayed focused on the ceremony.

It was the beautiful disappearing boy, of course. He floated, belly-up, on the other side of the invisible barrier, like a swimmer trapped beneath ice. The effect was chilling, even though I knew he wasn't really there.

I wondered what would happen if I ignored him. Would he go away, or would he keep escalating things until he showed up in front of me with water spewing from his mouth? I decided not to risk it. I looked at him and made a face that said, *WHAT???*

He mouthed a word to me and then another.

But I wasn't ready, so I missed it. I tilted my head, inviting him to try again. His lips moved in a slow, exaggerated way, and this time I had no trouble reading them. I recognized the words from watching Nate use them so often with me.

I . . . love . . . said the boy.

I waited for him to finish the sentence and tell me who he loved.

I . . . love . . . he repeated.

Who? I mouthed.

I . . . love . . .

Before I could ask him again, someone in the wedding party cried out, and I jerked my gaze to the pavilion just in time to see Lucy lose consciousness and crumple to the floor. Leo barely had a chance to call her name before he passed out, too. Then the best man and the maid of honor collapsed, followed by the bridesmaids and the groomsmen, one by one, until the only person left standing was Father Tim, whose mouth hung open in shock.

Nate and I shared a blank look. What just happened?

Part of me wondered if it was a joke, maybe the start of some weird flash mob dance. But nobody got up. In fact, two more people passed out. The groom's parents were now slumped over in their chairs. The guests in the front row rushed to the pavilion. I glanced down, and the boy in the water was gone. When I looked back up again, Lillian was pushing her way toward the fallen bodies.

Lillian reached Lucy and knelt down to examine her. It only took a moment before the Grand Lumara stood up, her face visibly pale, and announced, "This is a curse."

I gripped Nate's arm while gasps and murmurs of "dark magic" filled the crowd. Guests stood up and wrung their hands, scanning the lagoon as if they might be the next to fall. A man from two rows behind me paced the aisle and then turned to leave. I was about to ask Nate if we should go, too, when Lillian flashed her palm and raised a wall of water to block the exit.

"Do not panic," she ordered. "Stay in your seats. We need to keep the aisle clear so we can transport the victims to a safe location."

Reluctantly, the guests made their way back to their chairs.

Lillian raised her hands to the heavens. The sky rumbled, and out of nowhere, a transparent dome appeared around the island, rising like a bubble to contain us.

"No one is leaving," Lillian said. "Not until we find the person responsible. Until then, Lumara is officially locked down."

CHAPTER
NINE

A total of fourteen victims—ten members of the wedding party, the bride and groom, and the groom's parents—were levitated to the Woods' estate, where the basement had been magically converted into a quarantine medical facility, accessible only to Lillian and her most trusted colleagues.

While all of that took place, the rest of us were stuck in our seats, left to wonder how and why the attack had happened, not to mention whether we were in danger, or how long we would have to stay in lockdown.

"I knew Lumara sounded too good to be true," I whispered to Nate as my heartbeat ticked to a new rhythm. "You said the Mystics here were different. You told me we were safe!"

"Try to breathe," he said, which was better than telling me to calm down, but not by a lot. "We *are* safe."

"We're trapped in lockdown with a criminal," I reminded him. "On an island that you described as claustrophobically small.

And we have no idea how long we'll be here. Are we talking days? Weeks? Months?"

"It won't be months."

"How do you know?" I asked. What if the person wasn't caught before the end of fall break? What would I tell my dad if I didn't make it back to the academy? My father thought I was in Manhattan. He would lose his mind if he discovered the truth . . . and for good reason. I obviously shouldn't have come here.

Instead of answering my question, Nate shook his head, his eyes glassy and focused on nothing in particular. "Why would anyone do this?" he murmured. "Who would want to hurt Lucy, of all people? She's like the human equivalent of sunshine."

I stroked his hand to comfort him. I'd forgotten Lucy was his favorite cousin. But more than that, he seemed shaken, maybe even betrayed, as though such an ugly act shouldn't have happened on Lumara, and now he had to question everything he thought was true.

"Maybe Lucy wasn't the target," I said.

"She was. They all were. Curses don't hit at random like stray bullets." His gaze slid to the other side of the aisle. "It had to be one of Leo's people," he whispered.

"Why?"

"Because magic leaves a signature, even dark magic, and my mom can trace it. Every Grand Lumara can do it—it's one of the secret spells they pass down to each other. And the whole island knows that."

I understood his logic. "So a Lumaran would never cast a hex here, unless they're an idiot."

"Either that, or they want to get caught. Which would make them an idiot anyway, because they'd end up in the cottage with their magic stripped. So it has to be someone who didn't grow up here, someone who doesn't know my mom can trace the hex."

I felt a stirring of hope. "So you're sure your mom will catch the person?"

"All it takes is one spell to trace the source of the curse—it might be something the wedding party ate or drank or touched—and another spell to track down the person who cast it." He furrowed his brow. "I just don't know why anyone would hex a wedding. It doesn't make sense. What do they stand to gain?"

Other guests were speculating, too, some of them in low murmurs, others in voices loud enough for us to overhear. One person, the same man who had tried to escape, had a theory that the real target of the attack was Leo's grandfather in California, the leader of a powerful Aura community.

"It's all about ransom," the man said. "You watch. Whoever did this will come forward with a message, something like: *If you want the hex lifted, you have until tomorrow morning at dawn to give me*"—flapping a hand—"I don't know . . . whatever it is he wants."

"Eh," disagreed another man. "I think it's more personal than that." Then he went on to explain that emotion, not greed, was the motivating factor behind most premeditated crimes. "If you want to find the culprit, find out who didn't want the wedding to happen."

Camilla snorted in disdain but didn't look up from her phone, except to cast occasional glares at me. I wouldn't be surprised if she thought I had somehow turned magical and hexed the wedding party myself.

A woman raised an index finger. "What about the best man, what's-his-name?"

"Kavanaugh," someone supplied.

"Yeah, Kavanaugh," the woman said. "Didn't he have a crush on Lucy in college? Maybe he never got over her, and he couldn't stand to see her with his best friend."

"But why would he hex himself, too?" the second man asked.

"To avoid suspicion?" the woman guessed. "It's kind of brilliant when you think about it. What better alibi than to hide among the victims?"

"I think it was someone else," Camilla said. Her eyes hardened and locked on me. "Someone who hates Mystics so much she posted about us under her own name." She read from her phone, *"Mystics are nothing without our money. Starve the beast and take back the power! Mystics want us under their boots—it's time to rise up! Are you awake yet, because Mystics want to own you!"*

My cheeks heated under the weight of a hundred gazes. I couldn't bear to make eye contact with anyone, so I stared straight ahead and confessed. "Yes, I posted that. A fake healer stole my whole savings at Mystic Con, and I wanted to do something to fight back. But I would never hurt Lucy, or anyone else." I raised my bracelet. "This proves I'm telling the truth."

"Plus, she doesn't have magic," Nate said.

"So what?" Camilla argued. "She could be working with someone who does. Or maybe she's part of one of those anti-Mystic terrorist groups. They could have contracted out a black-market curse and sent her to infiltrate our island and destroy us from within."

"Oh, come on," Olive said. "That's such a stretch, I'm surprised you didn't pull a hamstring."

A voice from behind said, "This is no ordinary curse."

It was Lillian. The Grand Lumara had returned. She stood in the aisle, holding a paper-wrapped bundle. "My friends, I know you've been waiting for an update, and I thank you for your patience. I wish I had better news to share, but I've been unable to wake our victims. They seem to be suspended in time. Their hearts have stopped beating, their organs have paused, but their bodies haven't shut down . . ." *Yet.* The unspoken word hung in the air.

Camilla wilted in her seat, glancing at Lucy's fallen bouquet. "You'll keep trying, won't you?"

"Until my last breath, sister," Lillian assured her. "But we have to work quickly. I traced the source of the magic to a single cursed object. When I stripped away its magic, a message revealed itself." She waved a hand over the paper-wrapped bundle, and out of nowhere, a man's deep voice boomed, *"Your sleepers will die in seven days, unless the Lumaran responsible for cursing my family comes forward and removes their spell."*

"Cursing his family?" Nate asked. "Whose family? Whose voice is that?"

The island must have been messing with my head again, because the man's voice reminded me of my father's. I kept that thought to myself, though. It would make me sound even guiltier than the posts.

"The speaker didn't give a name," Lillian said. "Whoever the perpetrator is, they seem to believe they've been hexed by someone on the island."

Olive blinked owlishly. "And he's willing to let fourteen people die because of it?"

"What if it didn't happen at all?" Camilla asked, her skin pale. "What if he's wrong, and no one confesses?"

"We have to find out who the family is," Nate said. "They must have left a signature behind."

"They did." Lillian indicated her bundle, the mysterious object that had cursed the wedding party. Peeling away the paper, she revealed a gleam of copper . . . and then lifted my puzzle for everyone to see.

I stopped breathing.

Gasps and mutterings broke out, all eyes on me.

"No," I said, shaking my head. "I had nothing to do with this."

I turned to Nate, clutching his arm, silently pleading for him to believe me. Deep down in my heart, no one else mattered as long as he believed me.

The look in his eyes told me there was never a doubt.

That, alone, allowed me to exhale.

"The puzzle is benign, now that I've stripped it," Lillian said, showing off the front and back sides. "But for those who touched it, the damage is done. I want to be transparent and warn you I've never seen magic of this kind. It's the work of a true master." Her gaze passed over me, as though she knew I couldn't possibly fit the description. "An *insidious* true master."

A chill snaked down my spine.

"Now it makes sense," Camilla said. "Lucy was the first to touch the puzzle at the rehearsal dinner. She gave it to Leo, and Leo gave it to the best man and the maid of honor, and then they passed it to the others."

"And they fell in that exact order," said the man who'd predicted a ransom note. "That can't be a coincidence."

"It's not," Lillian told them. "The spell was designed with a time delay. The victims fell twelve hours after contact."

Camilla jabbed a finger at me. "I knew something was wrong with your puzzle. My instincts warned me not to touch it."

"I swear I didn't do this," I told her.

"Were you trying to 'rise up' and put us in our place?" she demanded.

My fear turned to anger, heating me up inside. I hadn't done anything wrong, and I refused to sit there and let Camilla throw me under the bus. I stood up and thrust a finger right back at her. "I'm not a Mystic! You read my posts—I can't stand Mystics! So what makes you think I can do a spell—*any* spell—let alone the work of a true master?"

She didn't have an answer for that.

But I did. "It's obvious someone's setting me up."

"Who would do that?" she asked.

"I don't know, maybe someone who doesn't want me here," I guessed. "It's a long list, and you're at the top of it."

"Lucy is my daughter!" she snapped. "I would never endanger her life for *you*. If I wanted you gone, I could accomplish that in my sleep."

Nate stood up beside me and clasped my hand. "Any one of us could have cursed the puzzle. We all had access to it. The box was sitting right there on the table for at least an hour before Talia gave it to Lucy."

"Even before the rehearsal dinner," I said. "There were tons of people who had access to the puzzle in my luggage."

"That's right," Nate confirmed.

Camilla had gone quiet. Too quiet, almost placid in the way she relaxed her stance, folded both hands in front of her, and delivered a knowing look to her twin sister.

Lillian nodded and addressed the group. "There's one more tracing spell for me to cast. My power doesn't extend beyond Lumara's borders, so I can only identify the person who cursed the puzzle if they're on the island. But regardless, this should give us a clue. If the spell-caster is outside our borders, it could indicate the cursed object was brought here—"

"To invade us," Camilla interrupted. "Like a Trojan horse."

I shivered. Just yesterday, I had asked Nate if anyone had ever outsmarted Lumara's protective wards by using a Trojan horse maneuver. Camilla couldn't possibly know I had said that, could she?

Lillian motioned for us to be silent as she drew a deep breath. With her eyes closed and her palms outstretched, she chanted an incantation in another language, uttering the words softly at first, and then increasing in volume until I had to resist the urge to cover my ears. An electric charge thickened the air. It congealed into something visible at Lillian's fingertips, like a static cloud. She commanded the mass, "Seek out the dark spell-caster among us. Reveal them to me."

The static cloud did not hesitate to obey.

I blinked, and it had already surrounded me, hot and heavy

and suffocating, its energy drowning me, crushing me, pushing me down until my knees collapsed beneath the magic's weight. I splayed both hands against the floor and cried out, desperate to make the pressure stop. Then suddenly the cloud lifted, and my body was a hundred pounds lighter.

But the relief didn't last long, because a new gravity settled over me. I didn't have to look up from the floor to know what had happened or what it meant for me.

I had been framed.

And as the only non-Mystic on the island, I was powerless to stop it.

CHAPTER
TEN

Voices clamored all around me, but I absorbed none of their words. I sat on the floor and felt my skin go numb, one inch at a time, until I no longer sensed the contact between my body and the glassy surface of the lagoon.

Nate's voice broke through the haze. I heard him shout to someone that I wasn't a liar. "And I know it," he yelled, "because the bracelet she's wearing is enchanted to detect lies. I wore it every day for the last year, and I can tell you she's the most honest person I've ever met!"

In defending me, Nate stirred another hidden memory.

I was in my house, standing in my parents' bedroom.

You're too honest, my father had said to me. He sat beside my mother and smoothed a hand over her pillowcase. He wanted to touch her cheek—I could tell—but her skin had become too sensitive to tolerate the barest amount of friction. She seemed to be getting worse at an exponential rate now, deteriorating so quickly I was afraid to blink and miss her last breath. *You're a terrible liar,* my father added. *One look at your face, and they'll figure it out.*

I can do better, I told him. *I can learn how to lie. It's basically acting. Just sign me up for an acting class.*

He shook his head. *It's not in your nature, Button. A fish can't learn to be a snake.*

But, my mother had rasped through thin, parched lips, *in the right hands, a fish can be transformed into anything . . .*

The flashback was like all the others: more frustrating than useful, giving me a distorted snapshot of the past without letting me understand what it meant. I wished the island would stop scrambling my brain. It wasn't fair to turn my memories into nonsense.

Nate's voice brought me back to the present. He was kneeling beside me, one arm wrapped around my shoulders while he pointed at his mother and argued, "You said it yourself: Lumara wants to help her."

"And the island doesn't make mistakes," Olive added. "You said that, too."

Lillian held both palms forward to shush her family and the wedding guests. "Listen, please. I understand your confusion. I share it myself. It's clear we're missing critical information. That's why we need to take our time to gather the facts before we jump to conclusions. And while we investigate, the safest place for Talia is in the cottage on my estate."

Jail, I thought. *I'm going to magical jail on a magical island.*

My heart began to pound. I shouldn't have come here. Why had I thought Nate's family would be any different from the rest?

"The cottage is warded," Lillian continued. "No magic can exist within its walls, so—"

"So," Camilla interrupted, "it's safest for *all* of us to keep her there."

I fired a glare at her and pushed up from the floor. "You people are the threat, not me! I have no magic, no power, and whoever is setting me up knows it!" I looked to Nate. "Tell them!"

"She's right," he said. "Think about it: Even if Talia *could* cast a spell—even if she wanted to hurt us—she's smart enough to do it without getting caught. She wouldn't curse her own puzzle. It points right to her!"

"I agree," Olive said. "The evidence is too convenient. It looks like a setup."

"These are all valid points that we can discuss at the cottage," Lillian said.

I looked Nate in the eyes. "I'm not going there. I want to go home."

"I know," he told me. "I'm sorry. I can't—"

"Now," Lillian said.

Nate looked at his feet. That was when I knew the matter was decided, so I lifted my chin and tried to scrape together some pride. If the locals wanted to lock me up in their mystical power-vacuum guesthouse, I would rather get it over with than sit around and wait for Camilla to throw more stones at me.

"Will you go with me?" I asked Nate.

His grip on me tightened. "I dare anyone to try and stop me."

He walked me down the aisle to the beach, and together with Lillian and Olive, we drove back to the estate in the Impala. During the ride, Nate tried to convince his mother to change her mind and let me stay in the main house.

"Come on, you can't put her in the shack," he said. "This is Talia. I know her. She would never hurt anyone."

"I'm sure you're right, and the truth will come out," Lillian told him. "But for now, this is what we need to do. I won't argue about it."

We spent the rest of the trip in silence. I couldn't believe this was happening. How had I let myself get into this situation? I should never have trusted these Mystics.

Instead of pulling up to the front door, Nate followed the driveway to the rear of the property and stopped near the shed, where just yesterday we had unearthed Olive's scooter and set off on a grand adventure. That seemed like ages ago. I remembered my bet that someone would end up in jail before midnight.

He owed me five dollars.

"I'll go inside with you," he said as we crossed the lawn.

"You can join Talia later," his mother corrected. "After you and I have had a chance to talk." When he opened his mouth to object, she cut him off with a lifted finger. "The best way for you to help Talia is to be completely honest with me so we can figure out why this is happening."

"She's right," I assured him. I didn't believe my own words, but I wanted him to feel safer than I did. There was no reason for both of us to be terrified. "You can do more for me on the outside. That's where I need you the most."

"Then I should have asked Olive to come with us," he said. "I don't want you to be alone."

Olive had stayed in the car, too weak for the short walk from the shed to the rear property line. I couldn't blame her. My own feet had begun to stumble from exhaustion. All I wanted to do was lie down and rest. I felt drained, from deep within my core, as though my soul had sprung a leak.

We reached the cottage, deceptively inviting with its matching flower boxes affixed to the walls. The three of us stepped onto a wide wooden stoop in front of the door. While Lillian fiddled with her key—an ordinary, non-magical key to operate an equally ordinary, non-magical dead bolt—I peeked through the windows on either side of the door to inspect my new living quarters.

The interior reminded me of my dorm room at the academy: small but functional, tidy but institutional, providing every basic need except the warmth of a home. The furniture consisted of a twin bed draped in white linens, a side table with one drawer, and a single wooden chair that looked like it had once belonged to a dinette set. On the other side of the room, a door stood ajar, allowing me to see a porcelain sink and a toilet.

That was it. No art, no books, no tablets or screens.

"Say your goodbyes here," Lillian told me, unbolting the door and pushing it open.

The air from the other side of the threshold washed over me, and at once, I noticed it smelled of lemon soap and laundry detergent, and something else, something familiar but also foreign, a scent that evoked a lonely sort of feeling. It was the staleness of a long-vacant room. The smell wasn't necessarily *bad*, but it didn't belong on Lumara. It belonged in the regular world, cut off from magic. And as a pang of grief shot through me, I realized how much I would miss the island's enchantments.

I didn't want to go inside the cottage.

Nate took my face between his hands and forced me to meet his gaze—his warm, dark eyes overflowing with so much passion it bordered on anger. "Listen to me," he said. "I will fix this. I swear."

I believed him. Or at least I believed that he meant it. Whether or not he could fix anything was questionable. I unbuckled the lie detector bracelet he had given me and handed it back to him. "You might as well take this, since it won't work in there. Maybe you can use it to figure out what's going on."

He nodded and fastened it around his wrist.

Neither of us spoke. The moment was starting to feel like a goodbye, and I didn't want that. So I stood on tiptoe and gave him a brief kiss. "Will you bring me some food later?"

"Of course."

"But real food," I said. "Not one of your protein shakes." Before he could respond, I walked into the cottage and closed the door behind me, trying to keep him from seeing how badly I was shaking.

I heard the dead bolt engage, and just like that, I was alone.

Footsteps retreated down the front porch steps and then faded to a soft patter on the grass. I was so distracted by following the sounds that it took a moment for me to notice the throbbing at my temples. It began as pressure, similar to my flashback episodes, but quickly intensified to a pain so sharp that waves of nausea forced me to the bathroom.

Trying not to vomit, I gripped the porcelain edges of the sink and inhaled deeply through my nose, then exhaled long and slow. Sweat beaded along my upper lip—a bad sign—so I tried again, pulling in another lungful of air. But as I did so, I happened to glance at my reflection in the mirror, and all thoughts of breathing vanished.

Glimmering, multicolored strands of what I could only assume was magic were woven tightly around me. As I watched, the shimmering cocoon of energy unraveled from the crown of my head, downward, as though a thread were being pulled.

Someone had put a spell on me, and the cottage wards were trying to undo it.

Where the enchantment unwound, my pain seemed to follow. Now at my ears, it pierced my skull and worked its way toward my jaw. I watched, panting and whimpering, forcing my eyes to stay open as my body, or the magic that had invaded my body, fought for dominance with the cottage wards. Both forces were strong; I could feel it. The push and pull of each side was almost equal, telling me that whoever had cast this spell was on the same level as the Grand Lumara.

A true master, I thought. *An insidious true master.*

When the battle reached my throat, I couldn't hold on to the sink anymore. I dropped to my knees and hugged the toilet just in time for the first round of heaves to start. I lost count of how many more rounds came next, but my stomach continued to turn somersaults even when it was empty. Finally, after what seemed like an hour, the waves subsided, and I slumped against the bathroom wall, exhausted but no longer in pain. I glanced at my hands and checked for signs of magic, seeing only my wiggling fingers.

It seemed the cottage wards had broken the spell on me.

Weakly, I pulled myself to the sink and washed out my mouth before standing up to study my reflection in the mirror. At first glance, I looked more or less the same. My eyes were bloodshot, my skin red from exertion. Nothing out of the ordinary, considering I had just purged myself half to death. Then my gaze settled on my mother's locket, and I knew something I hadn't known before.

There was a secret compartment inside it.

I opened the pendant, removed my mother's lock of hair, and pressed the inner oval wall. A hinge gave way, and the wall sprang open to reveal a collection of tiny bone fragments—the relics of my mother's ancestors—glued in place with my own dried blood in order to bind their power to me.

My world shifted on its axis.

I remembered the truth.

I remembered all of it—the full picture without any missing pieces, what the island had been trying to reveal to me all along.

CHAPTER
ELEVEN

"I think I'm in shock," I said to Kat's image on my cell phone screen. My Blaze Connect didn't work inside the cottage, but the wards hadn't blocked the Wi-Fi signal coming from the main house. "I feel like such an idiot. I can't believe I've been walking around for a year telling everyone how much I hate Mystics."

"Yeah." She cringed. "Now you know why your dad freaked out when you went to Mystic Con. He was sure one of those Aura hacks was going to try to heal you and mess up his spell work. You could've ruined everything. And then you started bashing your own kind . . . Not gonna lie, it was hard to watch."

I groaned, remembering that awful day at the convention, how clueless I had been when the "Legendary Madame Hector" had very accurately told me there was nothing wrong with my heart. What Hector hadn't known—what magic had made me forget—was that my father had woven a false memory charm over me. All of my recollections of hospital visits and medical tests were fake. I'd never had heart disease. My life energy was being drained by a curse—a hereditary curse that had killed my mother before passing on to me. And someone on Lumara had cast it.

I didn't hate all Mystics. I *was* one.

But the Mystics on Lumara could go straight to hell.

"What are you thinking?" Kat asked.

"It's like waking up from a dream," I said. "But a really vivid dream, and being all foggy, and trying to sort out what's real and what's not."

"Bet that's weird."

I made a face, disgusted with myself for how badly I had wanted to fit in here. "I can't believe I tried to get *them* to accept *me*."

"I know," she said. "I wanted to puke when we were coming up with wedding-present ideas. But the worst part was having to listen to you spew for a whole year about your undying love for *Nathaaaaaaaaaaaaaniel*." She pretended to gag herself. "I swear I died a little each time you said his name. Thank god that's over."

Pain bloomed in my chest. I knew she was right. I knew I was supposed to hate Nathaniel. He was from Lumara. He was the son of the freaking Grand Lumara. He embodied everything I was supposed to hate.

But.

Nathaniel hadn't done anything wrong. I knew that now. He was different from the others. But I couldn't say that out loud. Kat would never understand. I barely understood it myself. Somehow, I was still in love with him.

How was I going to look him in the eyes and tell him I had

cursed Lucy's puzzle? Or that I had planned it in advance. Or that the real reason I had transferred to Saint Wesleyan Academy was to befriend him; to make him think I shared his hobbies and interests; to be his dream girl, and mostly . . .

To make him fall in love with me.

To use him as my ticket to the island.

The truth would break his heart.

"Oh no," Kat said. "Please tell me you didn't catch feelings for him. Not *real* feelings."

I glanced down. "It's not my fault he turned out to be a good person."

"Oh, come on, Talia. Are you kidding me? He's, like, the prince of Lumara!"

"You think I don't know that? This wasn't supposed to happen. I mean, when I woke up from the spell, shouldn't my feelings have disappeared, too?"

"You'd think." Kat went pensive. "Unless they're so strong they transcended the spell."

I hung my head in my hands. "This is a nightmare. I love him, Kat."

"Well, you better get over him. Like, now," she said. "Because there's no right way to tell your boyfriend, *I'm sorry my dad enchanted me with a fake backstory that would make you fall in love with me and bring me home to your secret island, where I could find out which one of you murderous bastards cursed me and my mom.*"

She was right. He would never trust me again.

"*And,*" she went on, "*so I could curse a bunch of you assholes in return and force you to trade counter-hexes with me, because you're all evil and incapable of doing the right thing."*

"But they're not all evil," I said. "The bride was super sweet to me. I feel kind of bad for ruining her wedding. And Nate's sister, Olive, stuck up for me when everyone thought I was guilty."

"You *are* guilty."

"That's not the point."

"Ew, gross, stop." Kat flashed a palm. "These people are garbage. Even the ones who didn't kill your mom have been protecting her killer for years."

"But they all seem so . . . normal."

"Of course they do. Who's going to admit they knew about a curse on an innocent family?"

"That's true," I agreed. "That would make them complicit."

"So what if you ruined their wedding?" Kat made a fake crying motion. "Boo-hoo. I don't give a shit. The bride can have a hundred weddings after she wakes up. But you only had one mom, and you'll never get her back."

I set my jaw. Kat was right. Plus, it didn't matter who knew and who didn't. The culture of secrecy on the island had contributed to my mother's death. None of us had heard of Lumara until years after my mom had gotten sick, when my dad finally put together a group of Blood Mystics powerful enough to pool their strength and trace the curse through the island's wards. By then it was too late. With a little cooperation, maybe we could have saved my mom, but the Lumarans had made that impossible.

But the biggest question no one could answer—the question

that haunted me—was why? Why would anyone want to curse my mother . . . or me? We hadn't done anything wrong.

"Screw these people," I said.

"There's my girl! Now you sound like the real Talia!"

"The real Talia?" I repeated. "As opposed to what?"

"You know what I mean. The old you."

I tapped my head. "It's been me in here the whole time."

"Not really. You didn't know the truth. You didn't know who you were." She shrugged. "But now you do, right?"

Did I?

Maybe my dad's false memory charm had worked a little too well, because my real life and my fake life were still tangled up inside my head like two types of spaghetti noodles boiled in the same pot.

Logically, I knew I had never restored a car, but I could still picture the carbon-fouled spark plugs discarded on the garage floor. I could still smell the gear oil and feel the weight of a three-eighths drive ratchet wrench in my hand. And my aunt—all of my warm, fuzzy memories of her were fake. In truth, she was a fierce spell-caster with a reputation for making people disappear. She low-key terrified me. But despite that, I could still visualize her baking bread and singing in the kitchen.

It was a total mind freak.

"Hey, I just realized something," I told Kat. "That's why you didn't remember your mom tripping over a pumpkin. It never happened."

Kat giggle-snorted. "Can you imagine my mom picking pumpkins? Like some basic suburban loser?"

Yes, I could. That was the problem. And if I was being honest, I liked some of the elements of my made-up life better than my real one.

"It sucked keeping all those details straight," Kat said. "Not to victim-blame, but it's your own fault for being such a bad liar."

"Um, actually, you're welcome, because I saved us. Nate's bracelet, remember?" We hadn't known about that two years ago. "He would've busted me if I knew I was lying."

She flapped a hand. "Whatever. We're done pretending. That's what matters. Now you can make your demands, get your cure, and come home."

From somewhere out of sight, my father said, "The sooner the better."

Kat glanced over her shoulder and waved. She had messaged my dad to join our video call, but I hadn't expected him to come to her house. He entered the frame and peered at me as if checking for damage. I noticed how much more hair he had lost. Only a few gray locks remained, clinging stubbornly to his scalp. A clear sign of stress that he couldn't hide from me.

"Are you okay, Button?"

"I'm fine. Just shaken up."

"And the puzzle?" he asked. "Did it work like it was supposed to?"

"Like a charm," I told him. "You nailed it." In addition to the memory spell, my father had created the hex for my puzzle. He'd even helped me cast it during one of my sleepwalking episodes. If anyone deserved the title of *true master*, it was him—minus the insidious part, because there was nothing evil about a man wanting to save his daughter's life. "The Grand Lumara said your work is unlike anything she's ever seen."

He chuckled. "I'll bet she did. Let's hope it holds."

"Are you afraid it won't?"

"I'm afraid seven days is a long time to give someone as powerful as Lillian Wood to chip away at my magic."

"She shouldn't have to," I said. "All she has to do is give up the person who cursed Mom, and then she can save the wedding party *and* me. It's a win-win for her."

"I hope it works out that way . . ."

"But?" I prompted.

"But I'm not expecting it to."

"What?" My brows jumped in perfect time with Kat's. We stared at each other, equally confused, because there was no reason to think our plan would fail. I hadn't even talked to Lillian about my demands. Once I did, I was sure she'd see reason. "The whole point of cursing the puzzle was to force the killer to come forward," I told my dad. "You said it would work."

"I said it *might* work," he corrected. "And if we're lucky, it will. But your mom's killer has a lot to lose by coming forward. They might not confess."

"Not even to save fourteen of their own people?"

"Fear is a powerful thing."

"So what do you want me to do?"

"Make your demands, just like we rehearsed," he said. "But instead of sitting around and waiting for a response, I want you to keep digging. There has to be someone on that island who knew your mother, and my gut tells me it's one of the Woods."

"How am I supposed to do that when I'm trapped in here?" I asked.

"I can teach you how to pick a lock."

"And the security ward around the cottage?"

He made a face as if to say *gimme a break*. "It's child's play to undo a spell like that. Have I taught you nothing?"

"I don't remember the incantations."

"I'll remind you."

"But . . ." I shook my head, daunted by what he expected me to do. More than that, I didn't understand his lack of faith in our plan. If Lillian had the skills to trace the puzzle hex back to me, why would she have a problem tracing my hereditary curse back to the person who had cast it on my mom?

I studied my father's face and wished I could read his mind. My dad had never lied to me, but sometimes he tried to protect my feelings by downplaying bad news. I hoped this wasn't one of those times. "Is there something you're not telling me?"

"No, of course not, Button."

"Promise?" I said. "Because there's too much at stake for keeping secrets."

"I promise." He flashed an apologetic smile. "Sorry, I didn't mean to scare you. I just want to cover all our bases. It took a lot of work to get you on that island, and we won't get a second chance."

"All right," Kat said, as if to refocus the conversation. "So now that Talia's in the hornet's nest, what can we do to help?"

My dad sat down behind her. "Start by telling us what you know."

"Not much," I admitted. But when I thought about it, I'd

learned some valuable information during my short time on the island. Starting with the fact that Lumara wanted me there. "This is going to blow your mind. The island is trying to help me."

My dad blinked. "With what?"

"I don't know. Lillian said that remains to be seen."

"Could she be lying?"

I shook my head. "Nate's charm would've detected it."

"Well, that's . . . interesting," my dad said. "Keep me posted. What else?"

I told him about the people I had met, and I described the dynamic between the members of the Wood family, pointing out that Camilla had instantly pegged me as a threat.

"She might have the Sight," my dad said. "Watch out for her."

I went on to explain the magical nature of Olive's disease, and how her tumors grew back faster each time Lillian healed them.

"Do you like this Olive lady?" my dad asked.

"I guess so," I said. "As much as I *can* like anyone here."

"Invite her to bunk with you in jail."

I had just begun to ask why, when the answer hit me. "The wards negate magic."

"And symptoms caused by magic. That includes curses, so you should feel the difference, too."

I placed a hand on my chest. I had been too distracted to notice before, but he was right. I felt more energy than usual. Could the answer be so simple as staying inside the cottage until the wards negated my curse?

"The wards won't cure you," my dad said. "That was the first thing I tried with your mother. But they'll give you a lift, like a cup of coffee."

I slouched. I should've known it wouldn't be easy. "Better than nothing, I guess."

"Hey," Kat said, pointing at me. "Tell him about the ghost no one can see."

My dad arched a brow.

"I'm not a hundred percent sure he's a ghost," I said. "But I keep seeing this disappearing boy whenever I go near the water. He looks alive, but he's not solid. I can tell because he doesn't leave behind footprints or puddles where he walks."

"And he tried to lure her into the lagoon," Kat said.

At that, my father drew back.

"It's not as bad as it sounds," I promised. "I think he wants to communicate, but he can only do it underwater. He tried to talk to me at the wedding."

"You didn't tell me that," Kat said.

"I didn't have a chance." I leaned in closer to my phone. "Here's the interesting part. He kept trying to tell me who he loves, but he never gave me a name."

"What does that have to do with you?" my dad asked.

"My guess is the person he loves is Mom," I said. That would make sense—the missing link between my mother and Lumara. "Did she ever date anyone from here?"

"No."

"Are you sure?"

"Yes, one hundred percent."

He sounded so certain that I didn't want to press him. But even though my parents had married young—seriously young, as in eighteen—my mom had dated plenty of other guys before then. She had told me so. My dad couldn't possibly know everything about her past. Deep down, I felt a connection with the disappearing boy. He was tangled up in my family's mess; I knew it.

"What does he look like?" my father asked. "Skeletal? Decayed?"

"No, he's beautiful," I said. "The kind of face that belongs on a billboard. Mile-long lashes, dark brown eyes. He's about Nate's age, maybe a year or two older. Tall, built like an athlete. Long hair, down to his shoulders."

Kat waggled her brows. "Is he single?"

"I'll be sure to ask him." I rolled my eyes. Then I remembered another detail. "Oh, and he's always wearing the same thing: red plaid swim trunks."

"That doesn't fit the description of a wraith." My dad made a *hmm* noise. "I don't know who or what this boy is, but I can tell you all ghosts are bad news. You should steer clear of him. It won't end well."

"But he could be a clue."

"Or he could lure you into the water and drown you, just for fun," my dad said. "Want to guess which outcome is more likely?"

"Are you sure you're not being a tiny bit dramatic?"

"Stick with the Woods," he told me. "Especially Lillian. That's where you'll find your answers. The island *talks* to her. She has to know more than she's letting on."

"Fine," I agreed. "I'll see what I can find out about Lillian."

"And under no circumstances are you to go into the water with Ghost Boy."

"Oh, come on."

"Say it," he told me. "Out loud."

I heaved a sigh and chanted, "Under no circumstances will I go looking for the disappearing boy or follow him into the water."

"Good," my dad said, giving a satisfied nod.

He seemed to believe me.

Maybe I wasn't such a bad liar after all.

CHAPTER
TWELVE

"Thank you for meeting me," I said to Nathaniel and his mother, who were perched on the edge of my jailhouse bed, peering at me expectantly while I sat facing them on the wooden dinette chair in the corner. The room felt overcrowded—almost suffocating—and I kept trying to scoot back, forgetting there was a wall behind me.

Forgetting there was nowhere to go.

I swallowed with a dry throat, wiping my clammy palms on my dress. I had rehearsed this moment a dozen times, but only with the Grand Lumara as my opponent, not my boyfriend. I wasn't prepared for the way Nate unraveled me . . . the sweet look on his face, the tenderness in his voice, the smell of his cologne that lingered on my collar from the kiss he'd given me at the door.

The last kiss he would probably ever give me.

I shouldn't care about that, but I did.

"I wanted to be here sooner," Nate said. "I'm sorry it took so long."

"Don't apologize," I told him. It came out harsher than I intended, but I didn't take it back. Instead, I turned my focus to Lillian. "What I'm about to tell you should stay between us."

"I can't promise you that," Lillian said with none of her son's warmth. "I won't keep your secrets if it puts my people in danger. My first duty is to—"

"The island," I finished. "Yeah, I know." A flash of anger ignited inside me. I didn't need reminding that nothing mattered more to Lillian than the island—not my mother, not me. That was why I'd had to come here and strong-arm her into doing the right thing. "Fine. You can keep my secrets or not. But if the truth comes out and someone gets hurt, that's on you."

"Hurt?" Nate asked, gazing at me in concern. "Talia, what's wrong?"

Just like that, my anger dissolved. I should have asked Nate to stay outside.

"Whatever it is, we'll figure it out," he said. "Together."

No, we wouldn't. And the gentleness in his eyes only made me feel worse, because there was a very real chance he would never look at me that way again. Then it struck me: This might be the last moment he truly loved me. Without thinking, I moved my gaze over his face, taking a mental snapshot, preserving the memory so it would last forever. But a sudden pain in my chest stopped me, as though my heart couldn't hold him any closer and still survive letting him go.

I glanced at his bracelet. "I wish that worked in here."

"I don't need it with you," he told me.

"Yes, you do."

He scrunched his brow, confused.

It was time to be brave. No more stalling.

"My real name is Talia Malanovitch," I said. "And I'm not the person you thought I was." I took a deep breath. "I'm not the person *I* thought I was."

"Oh," Lillian said at the end of my confession. She blinked, parting her lips in a stupor, and repeated, "Oh."

I turned to Nathaniel, but he didn't say anything. He had let me speak the whole time, uninterrupted, and he hadn't uttered a word since. At some point, he had stopped looking at me, and he hadn't looked up again. I could easily imagine what he was thinking, because just last week, I had let *him* speak, uninterrupted, and I remembered how hard I had fought against the truth, how I'd silently begged him to stop talking, to take it all back. Now he had to be asking himself the same questions that I had: Which moments between us were genuine? Which were fake? What did he really know about me?

"Talk to me, please," I said, reciting the same words he had used when I had gone silent for too long. "You're starting to scare me."

He snickered bitterly. "Well played."

"This isn't a game," I told him. "Not even a little bit."

He raked a hand through his hair.

"This is life or death," I went on. "I hope that makes a difference. I only wanted to live. Can you blame me for that?"

He stared at the floor in silence.

"My survival depended on coming to Lumara," I said. "I hate that I had to lie to you to make that happen, but I can promise I never lied about my feelings for you."

He shot me a burning look.

"I mean it," I insisted. "The way we met was dishonest. I can't deny that. But the whole time we were together, I didn't know the truth about who I was. I had no agenda. Everything that happened between us was real."

"Stop," he said, flashing a palm. "I don't want to hear it."

But I needed to say it. I knew he could relate. "That day at the academy, you made me swear I wouldn't walk out on you until I listened to everything you had to say. Don't you think I deserve the same courtesy?"

"No. What we did is *not* the same."

"I never said it was."

"You used me, Talia!" he yelled. He had never spoken my name in anger before, and hearing it stung like a slap. Even his mother flinched. "I didn't do that to you!"

"I know. You're right."

"What if I had touched your puzzle?" he asked. "You could've killed me!"

"No one is dead," I reminded him. "Everyone's going to wake up as soon as the person who cursed my family undoes it."

"Assuming that's not a lie, too."

I glared at him. That was a low blow. "I'm not the bad guy here. I didn't start this war. I'm a victim just like you are, and both of us had secrets."

"My secrets didn't hurt anyone! My secrets didn't put fourteen people in a coma! My secrets didn't fill my head with a bunch of fake memories that turned me into someone else!" Nate flung a hand in the air. "Do you even *like* cars?" He shook his head. "Never mind. I don't care. It doesn't matter, because what we have isn't real. It never was. I don't know the first thing about who you are!"

"I'm the same person I was yesterday."

"Yeah," he said. "A liar."

"I didn't know I was lying when I was lying!"

"But you knew when you planned the whole thing! Jesus, Talia, you played me in a con that lasted more than a year! What kind of person does that?"

"The kind that wants to live," I told him.

He tore off his bracelet and stuffed it in his pants pocket as he stood up from the bed. I expected him to make another cutting remark before he left, but instead, he walked out of the cottage without a backward glance, closing the door ever so gently behind him. I wished he had slammed it. Something about his carefully controlled exit made me want to explode.

Lillian cleared her throat, reminding me of her presence.

"Yeah, well, that didn't go the way I rehearsed it," I told her. "But now you know the truth."

She raised an eyebrow. "Do I?"

"Hey, feel free to take me outside the wards," I said, pointing at the door. "You can cast an honesty charm on me. I have no reason to lie to you now. We both want the same thing—for no one to die in the next seven days." *And for me to get the hell off this island.*

She nodded. "As secrets go, yours was a bombshell."

"It was a shock for me, too," I told her. Not that I was looking for sympathy, especially from the Grand Lumara, but my life as I had known it had completely changed in an instant. "The shock still hasn't worn off."

"As sorry as I am to hear about your identity crisis, I'm more concerned about the fourteen innocent people you cursed."

"Then find a counter-hex to save me, and let's trade."

"It's not that simple. I have no knowledge of anyone on my island cursing you or your mother."

"I wouldn't expect you to admit it if you did."

With an icy calm, she folded both hands atop her lap. "I don't."

"Then track the person down, like you did with me and my puzzle." I gestured at my body. "Just pull their magical signature out of me. There has to be tons of it floating around in here."

"Again, it's not that simple," she said. "The magical link between an object and its spell-caster is direct. But there's nothing direct about a lineage curse. The spell that's affecting you originated with someone else, so as strange as it might seem, you're not the one who's cursed. That person was your mother."

"So if I'm not cursed, then what am I? Cursed adjacent?"

"More or less. And with your mother gone, I have nothing to trace."

"But there's dark magic inside me," I said. "I've felt it."

"Without a doubt," Lillian agreed. "But the magic draining you is a side effect of the original spell. It won't carry the signature of the person who cast it."

I swore under my breath. I had expected this to be easier. "So you're telling me you don't know how to find the person who did this to my family?"

"Not in seven days," she said. "And something else you might not have considered: Just because your father traced the source of your mother's curse to Lumara, that doesn't mean the person who cast it is still here. We do get visitors."

My stomach sank. It had never occurred to me that my mom's killer might not be a Lumaran. "You keep records, right? We can cross-reference my dates with your visitor list."

"Yes, but you have to give me more time."

"I can't," I admitted. "I don't have the counter-spell."

Lillian blinked at me. "Your father didn't give it to you?"

"No."

"Then how are you supposed to trade with me?"

"He'll make the exchange when I'm cured."

She blew out a long breath. "I need to see him in person."

"Okaaaay," I said, wondering how my dad would react. "This was never part of his plan."

"Arrange a meeting, here on Lumara." She nodded at my cell phone, which sat on the table in front of me. "I increased our security, but I can bring him through the wards in my personal jet."

My dad would never step foot on a plane controlled by the Grand Lumara. But I nodded and sent him a text.

Lillian wants to meet. Can you come?

"The sooner the better," she added.

ASAP, I told my dad. *She can send a plane in the morning.*

To my surprise, he replied right away with the coordinates to his nearest airport, and asked to depart at 8:00 a.m. I exhaled, relieved. My father would be here soon. He would figure everything out, and more important, I wouldn't be alone.

"In the meantime," Lillian said, "what can you tell me about him?"

"What do you want to know?"

"The question I keep asking myself is why he didn't contact me directly."

"How?" I asked. "He tried for months, but he couldn't get a message through your wards, and your contact information isn't exactly public."

"What about Nathaniel? You could have given him the message."

I had actually thought about that years ago. It had been my first suggestion to my parents. But they had pointed out the possibility that Nathaniel might not cooperate. Or worse, that he might warn his mother and make it impossible to infiltrate the island. "That was a risk we didn't want to take."

She wrinkled her forehead. "But sending you here was a bigger risk. Isn't your father afraid of what might happen to you if we don't make a trade?"

"We talked about that," I said. I chose not to mention that my father had promised to rescue me if negotiations went completely sideways. "I know there's a chance I won't make it off the island alive if things go wrong. But without my counter-curse, I'll be dead soon anyway."

"How do you know?"

"Well, I mean, I don't know *exactly* how much time I have left, but my symptoms are identical to my mom's. When she was like me, getting winded by ordinary things, she didn't last very long after that. It's not hard to predict what comes next for me."

"Do you think your father will follow through with his threat?" she asked. "You know him better than anyone, I imagine. Does he intend to let fourteen of my people die if I can't break your curse in a week?"

I wanted to say no. My dad wasn't the villain in this story. He was trying to save me, and that made him my hero. But he was also human. And like all humans, his pain had limits. "He's not the kind of man who usually makes threats."

"But?" Lillian prompted.

"But this is war."

"Is it?"

"To him, it is. Losing my mom changed him. Trying for years to save her and then failing . . . that broke something inside him. And then the cycle began all over again with me. So yes, I think he would do anything to save my life."

"Even if it costs innocent people their lives?"

"You're a mother," I told her. "Wouldn't you kill to protect your children?"

"I would," she admitted. "If I was defending them from a direct attack. But that's not what your father is doing. He's not defending you. He's making a deliberate choice to sacrifice other people's children—fourteen of them—for you. Being a parent doesn't justify being a monster."

"My dad's not the monster here. That's the person who killed my mom."

"And I empathize with both of you."

"Do you?" I asked. I doubted that.

"Losing a loved one is an unspeakable agony that no one deserves." She leaned forward, propping her elbows on her knees. "And I understand wanting to fight for your life. But tell me, do you believe your life is more important than Lucy's? Or Leo's? Do you think your soul has more value than theirs?"

I ignored the tug of guilt at my stomach and reminded myself I had come to Lumara to do battle. "You're talking like they're already dead. They're not. Every single one of them can wake up as soon as whoever cursed my mom comes forward and breaks the spell. That's the person you should be demonizing, not me or my dad."

"And if no one comes forward?"

"Then we force them out of hiding!" I pointed at the darkened window. "I can help. I know there's a connection to my mother here. Let me look for it. I can't do any good while I'm locked in a shack."

"Absolutely not," she said. "Even if I trusted you—which I don't—letting you roam the island would be reckless. Fourteen of my people are hovering between life and death, and they all have family and friends who are terrified and confused and angry . . . and looking for someone to blame. That *someone* is you. I'm responsible for your safety. What do you think your father would do if you were hurt on my watch?"

I didn't have to think about it. He would make sure the fourteen sleepers never woke up. But that would happen anyway if we failed to track down my counter-curse by the end of the week . . . and Lillian's motivation didn't impress me.

"Fine," I told her, because it was pointless to argue.

My father would straighten out all of this in the morning. And just in case he didn't, I had learned how to pick a dead bolt and disable the security wards around the cottage. I could find my own answers.

CHAPTER
THIRTEEN

Nathaniel never brought me the food he had promised, but at least his father cared if I lived or died. Adrian stood at the door to what I had started to think of as *my* cottage, bearing a covered platter that smelled of grilled steak and buttered potatoes.

"I thought you might be hungry," he said.

My mouth watered as I took the tray from him. "Thanks, I am. I appreciate you thinking of me . . . under the circumstances."

He nodded and then lingered at the threshold for a moment, avoiding my eyes and grinning awkwardly as if he wanted to convey some sort of positive message before leaving but couldn't think of the right thing to say. Finally, he told me, "Lillian and I put up new wards around the estate. No one's getting near you tonight."

"So no pitchforks and torches?" I asked.

"Not yet."

I remembered my father's suggestion to invite Olive to the

cottage. "Would you ask Olive to stop by? Maybe she can bring my suitcase or a change of clothes?"

"I'll make sure of it," he said.

I thanked Adrian again and shut the door behind him. He seemed nice, but that didn't mean I trusted him. His kindness could be an act, and even if it wasn't, feeding a prisoner was a pretty low bar for human decency.

The next morning, I awoke with the sun and discovered I wasn't alone. Olive sat on the wooden dinette chair in the corner, examining what appeared to be a loose strand of hair.

Not the visit I had expected.

"You really should sleep with your hair in a braid, you know," she said, turning the strand to face the light from the window. "And keep it in a ponytail during the day. People can do all kinds of nasty things to you with a binding agent."

She stood up and handed the strand to me, and I took it, though I didn't know what to do with it afterward. Another side effect of my yearlong fake life: I'd forgotten everything my parents had taught me about keeping my DNA out of other people's hands. "My mom used to freak out when she found my fingernail clippings in the trash," I recalled. "She would tell me to flush them."

"Or even better, burn them," Olive said.

That reminded me of the old charcoal grill my parents had kept in the backyard for exactly that purpose. They had even burned the contents of our vacuum canister each time we'd cleaned. "I always thought they were being paranoid."

"No, it's smart." Olive pointed at the window. "There's a crowd of very unhappy people on the other side of the perimeter ward, and if they can't get their hands on you, they'll gladly settle for an eyelash or a drop of blood."

"I'm already cursed." Or cursed adjacent. "What're they going to do? Kill me twice?"

"There are things worse than death," she told me, and the way she said it, with a soft break in her voice, plucked at my heart and made it impossible to argue with her.

"Got an extra ponytail holder?" I asked.

She pulled an elastic from her pocket and tossed it over. "I actually didn't come here to talk about binding agents. Your dad missed his flight."

I sat bolt upright. "What?"

"The plane waited for over an hour. He didn't show."

I grabbed my phone from the bedside table and found a missed message.

Sorry, Button. Change of plans. Call me.

"Just a second," I told Olive while dialing my father.

He picked up on the first ring. "Hey, honey. I'm sorry I wasn't there when you woke up. Are you all right? Are they treating you okay?"

"I'm fine," I said. "What happened?"

"I couldn't get on the plane," he said. "It didn't feel right, knowing Lillian is in control of it. I'll find my own way to the island."

"How? When?"

"Today," he said. "I already rented a boat. If I leave now, I should be there around lunchtime. But I want to meet Lillian in international waters. Tell her to pick a neutral spot, and you can text me the coordinates."

Olive spoke up from her seat in the corner. "That's not going to work."

"You can hear that?"

She shrugged. "He's a loud talker. Might as well put him on speakerphone."

I did as she suggested and made a basic introduction. "Dad, this is Nate's sister, Olive. She says there's a problem with your meeting spot."

"Let me guess," he told her. "The Grand Lumara won't meet me in a place where she's powerless."

"Can you blame her?" Olive asked. "Would you disarm yourself in the presence of a man who sends a child to do his dirty work?"

My dad went silent while my face flushed hot with embarrassment for him. Olive had it wrong. My father was no coward. He had sent me here to save my life, not to fight his battles.

"The meeting has to happen on neutral ground," Olive said. "You'll both have magic on Lumara. That's fair." She gave him a set of coordinates to Lumara's ocean border. "Drop anchor, and someone will pick you up and bring you to the harbor. Then you can be with your daughter. I imagine you're worried sick about her."

My dad didn't say anything at first. Then he told her, "Fine."

I took him off speakerphone. "Sorry about that," I whispered.

"Don't apologize, Button. We knew what kind of people we

were dealing with. I'll be with you soon, and then we can put this whole thing behind us."

I couldn't wait. "Love you, Dad."

"I love you, too, baby girl. More than life."

I ended the call and slid Olive a dirty look, which she ignored. "I want to go with the boat when they pick up my dad," I said.

"You can't."

"What about the docks?" I asked. "Can I meet him there?"

"Talia, did you miss the part about the angry mob outside the perimeter?"

I was about to suggest an invisibility spell, or hiding me in the trunk of Nate's car, when a loud noise erupted outside. I hurried to the window and glanced up at the sky, where several orbs were being launched high above the estate and bursting like fireworks. But instead of sparkling light, each one exploded into a different voice, loud enough to shake the windowpane.

"You can't hide forever!"

"Come out and face us!"

"Please wake up my sister! Please!"

"You're evil. Pure evil!"

"I hope you die!"

I covered my ears, but I could still hear the voices. They kept coming, dozens more of them, either screaming at me in rage or sobbing for my help. I didn't know which was worse.

Olive took my wrist and tugged me out the door. As soon as we were beyond the cottage wards, she murmured a spell that muted the voices.

I exhaled in relief and thanked her. Glancing up, I saw a new round of orbs launching, and I wished I could conjure one of my own to shout back at everyone, *You people started this! You're killing me, just like you killed my mom!*

Not that they would listen. Or care.

Lillian and her husband jogged onto the lawn, followed by Camilla and a few members of the household staff. I scanned the grounds for Nathaniel, but he didn't come outside. That stung worse than anything the mob had to say.

"I cast a sound barrier around the house," Olive told her mother. "But it's just a Band-Aid. The crowd can send visible messages, too." She pointed at me. "They're going to find a way to reach her unless you do something."

Camilla huffed. "The only person who needs to *do something* is Talia. I say let them reach her. Give her to the crowd. Maybe then she'll fix what she's done."

Adrian wrapped an arm around his sister-in-law. "Lucy will be okay. I know it. Have some faith in your Grand Lumara. Has she ever let you down before?"

Olive released a bitter breath. She didn't say anything, but I could tell she wanted to. Adrian shot her a look and a smile, a nonverbal *play nice*, while Lillian peered calmly at the hate mail bursting in the sky.

"Olive is right," Lillian said. "If my people are panicking, it means I haven't done enough to make them feel safe." She glanced at me. "It will help for them to see me in negotiations with Talia's father."

"He's on his way," I promised. "He'll be here this afternoon."

"Hmm," she said to me. Nothing more.

Two hours later, my phone rang.

"Button, you're not going to believe this," my father shouted over a heavy whine of machinery in the background. "I think the universe is trying to tell me something."

"What's wrong?" I asked.

"I blew an engine in the middle of nowhere, twenty miles offshore. Had to call a tow barge. They're taking me back to the marina now, but at this rate, I won't be able to rent another boat and make it to the island before dark."

My heart sank. "So I won't see you today?"

"I'm afraid not, hon. First thing tomorrow, though."

"What am I supposed to tell Lillian?"

"The truth."

"She won't believe me."

"Then remind Her Royal Highness that she's more than welcome to climb on board her private jet and meet me here," he said. "We can hash out everything tonight if she's willing to leave her magic behind."

"You know she won't do that."

"Then I guess she'll have to wait one more day."

"Or she could send a boat for you," I said. "She has a yacht called *Seas the Day*. It's really fast and—"

"Button, she could have a magic carpet with tassels that give foot rubs, and I wouldn't ride on it. I don't trust her."

I slouched in disappointment.

"Hey there," my dad said after a few beats of silence. "Who's my favorite person on the planet?"

"Me," I droned.

"That's right. Nothing is more important to me than you. *Nothing.* That's the whole reason we're doing this, Button—because I can't bear to lose you. Today was just a setback. I'll be there tomorrow, even if I have to swim through lava to find you."

"Well, don't do that. You'll disintegrate."

"Lava," he repeated. "I love you more than you can imagine."

Before I could say the same, he added, "Oh, and don't forget to keep digging. Have you found Lillian's grimoire?"

That shocked a laugh out of me. Lillian would never let me, or anyone else, get within a hundred yards of her personal spell book. She would protect it with the kind of enchantments I didn't even know existed.

"No," I said. "I haven't found the Holy Grail, either."

"Don't get smart with me."

"Of course I haven't found it. I need your help for that."

He exhaled hard into the phone as if I had frustrated him, and that pissed me off, because he had no idea what I was going through. No idea of the side effects of my fake life. He expected me to pick up magic where I had left it more than a year ago, and that wasn't fair.

"I'm doing the best I can," I told him.

"I know you are, hon," he said. "I'm sorry. It's been a hard day, and I didn't mean to take it out on you. Just go back to the attic and see what you can find. Any dirt is better than none. I'll see you in the morning."

CHAPTER
FOURTEEN

The call with my dad bothered me, and I couldn't put my finger on why.

I understood my father's concerns. I didn't trust Lillian, either. Lumarans had done us no favors, and we had plenty of reasons to be suspicious of their leader. But a nagging voice at the back of my head kept repeating the advice I used to give Kat when her boyfriends let her down: *If he wanted to, he would.*

Usually, motivation was that simple. People prioritized what they valued, so if a boy wanted to spend time with Kat, he would make it happen, not make excuses. And if my dad really wanted to be with me on Lumara, I doubted that anything could have stopped him.

Maybe I was being immature, but that was how I felt. And if my father wanted me to stay away from ghosts, then he shouldn't have left me unsupervised. The Woods' attic could wait. I had questions for my beautiful, disappearing boy. He was the missing link to my mother. I felt it.

Tonight, I would *prove* it.

I waited until Adrian brought me dinner. Then I drew the curtains and wolfed down my chicken Parmesan while I scoured the room for a set of bobby pins to use on the dead bolt. I couldn't find hairpins, but I discovered the next best thing in my bedside drawer—paper clips.

I could make that work.

I grabbed my phone and a baguette from my dinner tray and stuffed them in my back pockets. Peeking out the window, I scanned the lawn as I unbent both paper clips. When I finished, I inserted the wire ends into the lock the way my father had shown me. It took a few tries, but eventually I slid aside the dead bolt, opened the door, and left my prison cell.

Outside on the porch, jasmine blossoms perfumed the warm night air, thick with cicada calls and the lull of distant waves. There had been no more fireworks, no hate, no angry voices since Lillian had dispersed the crowd. A sense of peace washed over me, despite the curse retaking my body.

I crept across the lawn toward the shimmering static wall that stood in the way of my freedom. My father would scoff at the security ward. *Child's play*, he would call it. But I had forgotten as much magic as I had learned. I felt like a novice, starting from scratch, and also an impostor, pretending to be someone I wasn't.

Identity crisis, I reminded myself.

I needed to rediscover who I was.

I knelt on the grass in front of the static barrier. Making contact with the ground wouldn't increase my power, but standing up took more energy than I could spare. I sat back on my heels and inhaled slowly, then closed my eyes, cleared my mind, and recited the first of my father's incantations.

I could tell right away nothing had happened. There was no energy in the air. I pulled out my phone and read the incantation for the next enchantment, but that one didn't work, either. Not even a blip of magic passed through me.

I put my phone away. There was no point trying the third charm. My father didn't make mistakes. Any one of his spells could disable a simple security ward . . . in the hands of a competent Mystic.

That wasn't me.

I thought back to my earliest teachings, the basics I had learned from watching my mother cast. She had always stressed the importance of connection—of delving inward to find the current of power that flowed in our blood. She'd said the strength of our ancestors pulsed inside us, right below the surface, waiting for our call. She had even made up a rhyme to help me remember: *For power unchecked, you must connect.*

That had to be my problem. During the last year, I had lost my connection to my ancestors, even to my mother, and now I had to find it again. I felt a throb of shame to think of how much I had sacrificed to get here. Magic used to be a part of me—an extension of my body as real and natural as my limbs. I never imagined I could lose it.

I held my mother's locket tightly in my fist. I pictured her kneeling on the grass beside me, hugging me close to her, resting her head against mine. The mental image stirred a heavy sort of warmth inside my ribs, a painful sensation, as though my chest were a cage and all the love I felt for my mother was trapped there with nowhere else to go. I gave that love a destination. I turned it inward, found the part of my mother that still lived inside my veins. I latched on to it, and the bond that formed sent power surging across my skin.

I knew what to do now.

I recited the original incantation. This time, I had no doubt it would work. I didn't even need to open my eyes to watch the force field drop. I thanked my ancestors for giving me their strength, and then I stood up, strode forward, and made my way to the shed to retrieve Olive's scooter.

The road was quiet and empty, all the way down the winding hill. When I reached the sandy path leading to the lagoon, I pushed the scooter into the underbrush and continued on foot.

The moon was hiding behind a blanket of clouds, concealing the path ahead of me. I reached for my phone to light the way, but thought better of it. A flashlight would attract more attention than a neon sign. Before long, my eyes adjusted, and I picked my way across the sand to the lagoon.

The still water reflected the sky's meager glow, allowing me to see the rocks and boulders that stood at attention along the shoreline. I scanned the beach, looking for my beautiful disappearing boy and not finding him. That was all right. He would come to me. He always did. In the meantime, I peeled off my shorts and T-shirt, folded them neatly, and placed them on a boulder with my phone.

Then I stood in my underwear, nibbling on my leftover baguette while I waited at the water's edge.

Two bites later, the boy appeared, surfacing from the briny depths like a Greek god appearing among mortals. He stood before me, waist-deep in the water, his muscled torso gleaming in the moonlight, his chiseled face resolute, black eyes boring into mine with the unflinching confidence of a dozen men.

I, on the other hand, was stuffing bread crust in my bra.

"I'm coming," I told him, and waded out into the water. Something brushed my calf below the surface, and I stopped, suddenly aware of the creatures I couldn't see. I had watched enough shark movies to know better than to swim alone in the dark. I remembered a simple illumination spell, just enough to conjure a tiny ball of light below the water.

The boy had already turned away to swim farther out into the lagoon. I followed him until I could barely touch the bottom with my tiptoes.

"Stop," I called to him. "This is as far as I'm going."

He swirled around to face me and promptly dipped below the water.

Taking that as an invitation, I filled my lungs and joined him. Weightless below the surface, the boy's hair undulated around his face, which looked bolder and more angular in the glow from the tiny ball of light between us. The ethereal sight of him, combined with the distant, muted squeaks and clicks of ocean life, sent a chill skittering down my spine. I watched him intently, focusing on his lips so I wouldn't miss a single word when he spoke.

I . . . love . . . he began.

He stopped speaking.

I made a *keep going* motion.

I . . . love . . . he went on.

He stopped again.

I tipped up both palms to signal my confusion.

Who? I mouthed. *Who do you love?*

He glared at me in frustration and pointed at his mouth. Moving his lips in a slow, exaggerated way, as if talking to someone who didn't speak his language, he very clearly said, *I . . . LOVE . . .*

I shook my head. Maybe he *was* speaking a different language.

I . . . LOVE . . . he silently shouted at me, shaking his fists. *I . . . LOVE . . .*

I pointed upward, indicating for him to come to the surface so I could ask him a set of yes-or-no questions, which he could potentially answer with a nod or a shake of his head. But he didn't follow me. That would have been too easy.

I gulped a breath and went back under, surprised to find his face an inch from mine. The closeness startled me, and I jerked back, losing my footing on the sand. After that, everything happened in a rush. His body covered me, melded with me, filled me with a numbing cold that paralyzed my limbs. I couldn't move. My sight went black.

The next thing I knew, I was somewhere else entirely.

Chin-deep in a different ocean, with salt on my lips and laughter in my chest. It was daytime, and the sun reflected so brightly on the water that I had to shield my eyes. But the hand I raised to my face wasn't my own. It was the boy's hand: large and strong and solid.

Someone splashed me from behind, and I turned around to retaliate. In between dousings, I glimpsed a boy treading water with me. We were alone, far enough from shore that we couldn't touch the bottom, but well within the boundary of the red-and-white buoys that separated the beach from boat traffic. The glaring sun concealed my friend's face, but I could see his arms and shoulders in motion as he swam aggressively toward me. Anticipating his attack, I closed the distance between us and dunked him underwater. He resurfaced and did the same to me. I laughed, sending up a lungful of bubbles. But when I tried to come up for air, he shifted his grip to my shoulders and pushed me farther down. I accepted his challenge and wriggled in his grasp. I was stronger than he was, and I knew it. But no matter how hard I fought him, I couldn't get free.

Something wasn't right. It felt like there was a wall on top of me. Soon I stopped caring about winning or losing. I needed to breathe. I tapped his wrist twice, giving him a wrestler's surrender. That was our code: to honor the tap-out—always. I was so certain he would let me up that I opened my mouth in anticipation of drawing a breath. But I was wrong. He didn't let me go. He shouted something that sounded panicked, but I couldn't understand him.

Then something happened that I didn't know was possible. I lost control of my own lungs. My reflexes took over, and I inhaled water instead of air. For a fraction of a second, I felt betrayed by my body, but then an all-consuming agony hit me with the force of a freight train, pain beyond anything I had imagined. My lungs were on fire. My throat, my head, my nose—everything burned. I couldn't see, couldn't think beyond the pain. . . .

The flashback ended abruptly, and I slammed back into my own body, cold and submerged—and desperate for air. I felt a slithering sensation across my chest. Scales danced across my skin. Tiny teeth tore at my flesh. I opened my eyes to total darkness and found myself at the center of a feeding frenzy, a school of fish ravenously picking at the bread crust in my bra. I thrashed my limbs, too panicked to know which way was up. I needed to breathe. My lips parted, urging me to inhale. I remembered how the boy had lost control, and I fought my instincts while searching all around me for the surface of the water. But my light was gone; the boy was gone. He had shown me his death and then left me alone to repeat it.

Just when I'd swallowed my first mouthful of seawater, I felt pressure around my body, followed by a lifting sensation, as though an enormous, invisible fist had scooped me out of the lagoon. I drew a ragged breath and coughed so violently that I blocked out my surroundings. I didn't even notice when I had reached the shoreline. I came alert on my hands and knees, feeling the soft press of sand beneath me, still fighting to clear my lungs. I coughed again, over and over, until I gagged and heaved my dinner all over a pair of men's shoes that had just appeared in front of me.

I looked up at Nathaniel. Even in the dark, I knew his profile by heart.

"Sorry," I croaked, wiping my mouth.

He muttered an incantation that made my vomit disappear. In clean shoes, he widened his stance and folded his arms. "You're welcome."

"Yes, thank you," I told him, shifting onto my bottom to catch my breath. I expected to tremble or maybe burst into tears, but the only thing I felt was an immense gratitude for living. The emotion glowed inside me, casting a shadow over all the bad. Maybe shock would set in later, but for now, I scooped the rest of the baguette from my bra and flung the soggy bits into the water. "How did you know I needed help?"

"I didn't. My sister asked me to walk her to the cottage, and you weren't there." He flung his arms wide. "What the hell, Talia? I turn my back on you for one day, and you're already running off?"

"I was going to come back."

He blew out a sigh and offered me his hand. "Sure you were."

I took his palm and let him hoist me to standing. The contact felt good—warm and familiar—but the moment I was on my feet, he jerked his fingers from my grasp. Not knowing what to do with my hands, I touched the bare, wet skin below my navel and realized how little I was wearing. Nate had seen me in less, but I had never felt so exposed. He must have sensed my discomfort, because he whispered an enchantment that dried my skin and hair.

He handed me my clothes and turned around to give me privacy. "Hurry up."

"How did you find me?" I asked, shimmying into my shorts. "Did you track one of my hairs?"

"I could have," he said over his shoulder. "You leave enough of them lying around."

"I'm finished," I told him. "You can turn around now."

He faced me and held up his phone, displaying the Find My Friends map with a pin in my location.

"Oh," I said. "Technology for the win."

"But I didn't expect to find you drowning . . . in water you can stand up in. That was an interesting plot twist, so bonus points for having some surprises left up your sleeve." He shook his head. "I still can't believe you snuck out."

"I had a good reason."

He made a skeptical noise.

"I did," I said. "Trust me."

He snorted. "Trust you?"

"Sorry, poor choice of words."

"Whatever, tell me on the way to the cottage," he said. "Olive is in there pretending to visit you. We have to get you back before anyone knows you're missing."

"You didn't tell?" I asked. "You and Olive covered for me?"

"No, we covered for *me*," he clarified, jabbing an index finger in his chest. "I'm the idiot who brought you here. Everything you do is partly my fault, so I'd like to minimize the carnage, if you don't mind."

I bit my lip. "I didn't mean for you to take the blame."

"Yes, you did. You meant for all of this to happen."

"Please let me explain," I told him. I wanted so badly for him to understand me. "If I could go back in time, I would tell you the truth and I would trust you to help me, because I know you would have done the right thing. But I didn't know you then. I did what I thought I had to do to survive. You can't possibly hate me for that, can you?"

"Here's what you're missing, Talia. I don't have to hate you to want you out of my life. I don't hate sharks, and I still choose not to swim with them."

"You're comparing me to a shark?"

"Why not?" he said. "You're both willing to kill to survive. The point is I understand why you screwed me over. You wanted to live. Okay, fine, I get it. But that doesn't mean we can be friends. I don't need friends like you."

I knew he was angry, but that hurt.

"I'll help you clean up the mess you made," he went on. "Because I don't have a choice. You made sure of that. But if we actually make it out of here alive, and we go back to the academy, you're going to find an excuse to transfer. I don't care what you tell the headmaster or where you go next, as long as I don't see you again."

I felt an emptiness in my stomach that had nothing to do with hunger.

"It's not about hate," he said. "I just want to forget this ever happened, and I can't do that if you're around. Do you understand?"

I nodded.

"No hard feelings," he told me.

I couldn't agree with him on that point. The feelings he stirred inside me were full of sharp angles that stabbed every place they touched.

They were nothing if not hard.

CHAPTER
FIFTEEN

The scooter wouldn't fit in the trunk of Nate's car, so he enchanted it to follow along behind us. The conversation on our way back to the estate was torture. By the time I finished describing all of the sensations the disappearing boy had shared with me, my hands were so cold and clammy I had to sit on them. But as traumatic as the experience was, I would rather relive it than sit next to Nate in silence and replay his last words to me.

"Man, that's awful," Nate said with a grimace. "That poor guy. And having to feel him drown . . . that's seriously messed up."

It really was. I wanted to forget it—to ask my father for a spell to pluck the memory out of my head—but that would mean losing a piece of the puzzle. I needed all the answers I could find. Besides, to forget the boy's death seemed wrong somehow, like turning my back on him when he needed my help.

I glanced at Nate. "Is it weird that I feel guilty for wanting an anamnesis spell?"

"The whole thing is weird," he said. "Don't get me wrong; I feel bad for the guy. No one deserves to go out like that. But that was his death, not yours. You'll have to go through your own death someday. Why would you feel guilty for wanting to forget someone else's?"

I lifted a shoulder. "I guess because he shared it with me. That feels important, like I'm supposed to do something with what I learned."

"Sounds like you're overthinking," Nate said. "I don't know a lot about ghosts, except they're trapped where they don't belong, and that makes them miserable. And misery loves company. Maybe he just wanted to make you feel his pain."

I shook my head. "He doesn't act like a vengeful spirit."

"He's haunting you."

"Yeah, but not terrorizing me," I pointed out. "He wants to communicate. He keeps trying to tell me he loves someone."

Nate glanced away from the road and raised a brow at me. "Who?"

"I don't know. He won't say the name." I thought back to the look of frustration on the boy's face, as though we didn't speak the same language. "He tried a bunch of times to get through to me. When that didn't work, he possessed me, or whatever, and that's when he showed me how he died." The boy hadn't acted out of malice. He had learned that words weren't enough. "I think the way he died is part of what he wants to tell me."

"Maybe the person he loves doesn't know he's dead," Nate said.

I sensed that no one knew the boy had died. Or at least *how* he had died. Because if his body had been found, the news would have reported an accidental drowning. The story might not have traveled far, but a deliberate drowning—as in murder—would have made national headlines. I hadn't heard any stories about a game of dunking gone wrong.

"I think he wants his person to know the truth," I said, rubbing my hands together for warmth. "Maybe that's what I'm supposed to do—tell the girl . . . or the guy . . . or whoever that he was murdered so they can find out who did it and get justice."

"But why you?" Nate asked. He tilted his head and studied me as if seeing me for the first time. "Is that your specialty? Communing with the dead?"

That made me laugh. "You think I'm a necromancer?"

"How am I supposed to know what kind of magic you do?"

"Fair point," I said. Nate didn't know the Mystic side of me. *I* barely knew that side of me. "I do the ordinary kind. And not very well. I could barely conjure light under the water, and I lost it as soon as I freaked out."

"So there's no reason for this guy to choose you to convey his message?"

"Aside from his connection to my mother?" I asked. Because that was the obvious reason. "Do I need to remind you that I almost drowned in five feet of water? Would *you* choose me to avenge your death?"

"Yeah . . . probably not."

"Then you see my logic?"

"Something still doesn't make sense." Nate chewed his lower lip, peering thoughtfully at the steep road winding ahead of us.

"You said the guy drowned somewhere else, right? In the outside world?"

"Yes."

"Are you sure it wasn't Lumara?"

"I think so." The water in the boy's memory had looked like a normal ocean. The colors on Lumara existed on a different spectrum. "I saw buoys in the memory, the kind that mark boat channels. I've never seen those here."

"Okay," Nate said. "So if this guy drowned somewhere else, why are you seeing him in the water here? His spirit should be bound to the place where he died."

I opened my mouth to offer a theory, but nothing came. He was right. That part didn't make sense. "Too bad there's no rule book for the afterlife," I joked. But I quickly clarified: "I mean, there's not, right? Your mom doesn't have one of those, does she?"

"Afraid not."

"Still, she might know something." The question was whether I could tell Lillian about the boy without her twisting it into something to use against me. "Remember when I asked her about ghosts and curses? Her connection with the island taught her how spirits get trapped."

"And she said Lumara doesn't bind its dead," Nate reminded me. "Which brings us back to the question: Why is he here?"

All of a sudden, the answer came to me. "Love." The disappearing boy had been trying to tell me who he loved. "He's not bound to the island. He's bound to a person. If I can find out who it is, maybe we can release him."

"I hate to poke a hole in your theory . . ."

"But?"

"But spirits are bound by curses. You don't do that to someone you love."

I slouched in my seat. I didn't have an answer for that. "I need to figure out who this guy is. I have no idea if he actually lived here or if he was a visitor, but school seems like a good place to start. Do you have a library with old yearbooks? I think he was a wrestler. Maybe I'll find him in the team pictures."

"No school sports or yearbooks," Nate said. "Tiny island, remember? That's why I go to the academy."

"Oh, right."

"If this guy was from Lumara, he wouldn't . . ."

I waited for him to finish. "He wouldn't what?"

Nate didn't seem to hear me. His lips were frozen midsentence, as if something important had just occurred to him. I stayed quiet while the seconds ticked by. His body went as still as a grave. He may have even stopped breathing. I didn't want to break his focus, but whatever he was thinking about bothered him enough that he sped right past the road to his estate.

"You missed your turn," I said. "And don't forget the ward at the perimeter."

Nate swore under his breath and put the car in reverse.

"What were you thinking just now?" I asked.

He absently mumbled, "Nothing," while he used the rearview mirror to back up to the fork in the road. But as soon as he turned onto the correct lane, he added, "Maybe something. I don't know."

I watched his throat shift as he swallowed, his knuckles white from gripping the wheel. I had never seen him so shaken. "I can tell something's wrong. Talk to me."

"No," he said firmly. Out of habit, he cupped my knee, a gesture he had always used to let me know I wasn't the reason he was upset. When he noticed what he'd done, he pulled back his hand, and my heart sank. "I can't talk about it with you or anyone else until I check out some details first. It's hard to explain. If I bring this up and I'm wrong . . ." He shook his head. "Trust me, it would be bad for a lot of people."

"I do trust you," I assured him. "What can I do to help?"

"Go back to the cottage—and stay there. I mean it. Don't make trouble for me. That's what you can do to help."

He stopped on the driveway and nodded in the direction of the cottage, barely visible in the distance. Clearly, this was my signal to get out, but he didn't offer to escort me, or even ask if I had the energy for the long walk across the lawn.

It seemed he didn't care about me anymore.

"Oh, and listen," he added. "Don't tell anyone about the boy."

"I wasn't going to."

"Especially not Olive. Not until you hear from me."

"Okay," I agreed.

I stepped out of the car and watched him drive away until I couldn't see him anymore. I tried not to dwell on how unnatural it felt to leave without a kiss goodbye.

As I walked across the lawn, I noticed my feet moving at a brisk pace that was unusual for me. It was hard to believe the curse was still eating away at my body while I walked around Lumara, feeling fine. I should feel exhausted by now, especially after the wild night

I'd had. Not to complain, but my energy surges seemed to happen at random, and that bothered me. I wanted to find patterns, because patterns led to answers, and answers led to solutions. Patterns were safe and full of promise.

Unlike my life.

When I reached the cottage and climbed the stairs, I paused, holding on to the handrail while I waited for the effects of the anti-magical wards to subdue my curse. But standing on the porch, I felt no differently than I had on the lawn, or on the beach, or in Nathaniel's car. I glanced behind me, as though the answer might be written on the grass. When I had left the cottage, I had been so drained I could barely cast. At some point, that strength had returned to me. But why? It didn't add up.

"Nothing on this island does," I muttered to myself.

I had just begun to reach for the doorknob when I heard voices from inside the cottage, and I froze. If Olive wasn't alone, it meant I was busted.

I turned an ear toward the door and listened.

"You're the Grand Lumara," Olive snapped. "You have the power of a god! There's nothing you can't do!"

"All power has limits," Lillian replied in her usual cool tone.

"Stop it!" Olive yelled. "Stop pretending you don't know what I mean! You could have helped me years ago, and you chose not to!"

"Nothing would have changed."

"For *me* it would have," Olive cried. I heard the thumping of her hand against her chest. "You could have made my life bearable! You could have healed the one part of me that mattered the most."

"I'm tired of having this argument with you."

"And I'm tired of competing with an island for my mother's love!" Olive fired back. "You care more about Lumara than you care about your own family. You always have!"

Lillian's composure finally slipped, and she released a long groan. "Really, Olive. You're exhausting. I don't know how to talk to you."

"Well, there's the door," Olive said. "Feel free to use it."

I stiffened. I was on the other side of that door.

What should I do? Should I knock? Go inside? Sneak down the stairs and then clomp back up again, making a bunch of noise so Lillian wouldn't know I'd been eavesdropping?

Would that even work?

It didn't matter, because a voice from behind me said, "You're on the wrong side of that door, Talia Malanovitch."

I spun around. I didn't see anyone at first. Then I heard a single finger snap, and Camilla appeared, glowering at me from the bottom of the steps.

"I knew it," she spat. "I knew you didn't need protecting. Even before you cursed my daughter, I saw through your innocent act. You're as cold and ruthless as they come."

I couldn't think of anything to say that would change her mind. And to be fair, I *had* endangered her daughter's life. Maybe I was colder than I wanted to admit.

Lillian came outside, with Olive peering at us through the doorway.

"I caught her trying to sneak back in," Camilla said to her sister. "Were you going to tell me she escaped?"

"She was with Nathaniel."

"*After* he tracked her down," Camilla said. "Don't lie to me. I might not have the power of the Grand Lumara, but my instincts are never wrong. That's why I didn't touch her puzzle, and it's how I know her father has no intention of negotiating with us. It's also why I petitioned the Federation to hold a tribunal for attempted murder."

"*What?*" I said at the same time as Lillian.

"Under what authority?" Lillian demanded.

"Conflict of interest," Camilla said. "Talia was in a relationship with your son. You can't possibly be impartial. You should have removed yourself from the situation, and since you didn't do that, I did it for you. The adjudicator will be here tomorrow."

My stomach dropped to the floorboards. If the International Federation of Conjurers had deemed Lillian unfit to judge me, that meant she no longer had the power to send me home, even if we found out who cursed my mother and exchanged cures. Cures didn't matter anymore. The whole wedding party could wake up right now, and the tribunal wouldn't care. They would put me on trial for using forbidden magic.

And if they found me guilty . . .

"She'll be tried as an adult, you know," Olive said, staring daggers at her aunt. "Did that cross your mind before you jumped the chain of command and tattled to the IFC about our business? Do you know what it means if Talia is convicted?"

I knew what it meant. Capital punishment. The only people who used banishment as their severest penalty were Core Mystics, because they thought life without magic was worse than death. I disagreed, but the tribunal wouldn't ask for my opinion.

"Well, do you?" Olive pressed.

Camilla glared back. "Talk to me when *your* only child is in a coma."

Lillian held up both palms. "This isn't helpful. We can't change the past. Let's focus on what we can control."

"You need a lawyer," Olive said to me.

I gave her a hopeful look.

"Yes, I'll take your case," she told me. "It won't be pretty, though. The evidence against you is as damning as I've seen."

I raised my eyebrows and waited for the *but* . . .

"That's it," she said. "There's no bright side."

My pulse hitched, and instinctively, I looked to the main house for Nate. Every cell in my body cried out for him. I needed him to come to me and wrap me in his arms, to soothe my fear, to comfort me like no one else could. But Nate wasn't my drug anymore. He wasn't coming to rescue me.

That was my job now.

Olive touched my arm and brought my attention back to her. She gave me a soft smile, gazing at me with a tenderness that promised I wasn't alone.

"Come inside," she said. "We have work to do."

CHAPTER
SIXTEEN

To make the best use of our time, Olive arranged to have a folding bed and a variety of snacks delivered to the cottage, and we spent the night eating popcorn, drinking iced coffee, and going over the details of my case.

The world's most tragic slumber party.

But not as tragic as it would have been facing the tribunal without Olive to represent me. She had memorized more about Mystic laws and statutes than I even knew existed. The simple act of hearing my rights explained to me made the trial seem less like a monster in the closet and more like an enemy soldier on a sunlit battlefield. Olive had even found an old tribunal case similar enough to mine to use as a precedent for acquittal, or at least leniency. She warned it was a long shot, but it gave me a glimmer of hope I needed more than breath.

But the best part—the part that lifted a hundred pounds off my chest—was knowing my father was on his way . . . for *real* this time. After I told him about the tribunal, he'd gone full nuclear and called an emergency meeting of Blood elders. Even Kat had heard about it. She'd texted me at midnight: *Shit just got real! Your dad left five minutes ago, and he is NOT playing.*

As my legal guardian, my father had the right to attend my trial, so Lillian had been forced to grant him passage to Lumara on the same ship as the IFC adjudicator. That guaranteed my dad's safety. His last text had said to expect him at the docks midday. I didn't know how I would survive until then. I imagined him standing tall and bold at the helm of his ship, cutting though the waves, charging toward Lumara's harbor, ready to fight for me.

"Time to get up," Olive said, popping my fantasy bubble as she walked out of the bathroom, fully dressed in a pantsuit and flats, her hair pinned in a neat twist. She had already activated "lawyer mode," and the sun had barely risen high enough to cast a pink glow on the curtains. "We have a big day."

"Whatever I'm paying you, it's not enough," I told her.

She didn't respond, instead focusing on tidying and folding her bed.

It wasn't like Olive to ignore me. She didn't even smile, though she should have. She had offered her services pro bono. The money comment was a joke. "Get it? Because I'm not paying you anything at all?"

"Mm-hmm."

"Are you mad at me?" I asked.

"Of course not." She karate-chopped her pillow and placed it atop her folded bed. She still wouldn't look at me. "I'm just not much of a morning person."

I tried to believe that, but I was no good at lying, not even to myself. I thought back to the night before, replaying our conversations to see if I could pinpoint anything I had said to make her upset. I could think of only one reason for her coldness. I had told her the whole truth about what my father and I had done—all of it. Olive hadn't seemed angry at the time, but maybe she'd had a chance to think it over, and now she'd lost respect for me.

My heart twisted. I liked Olive. She had stood by me when my own boyfriend had cut and run. I didn't want her to hate me like everyone else did.

"I'm sorry," I told her, and then repeated the apology I'd given to Nate. "If I could go back in time, knowing then what I know now, I would—"

"Please stop," Olive interrupted. Her eyes were closed, accentuating the pained expression on her face as she pinched the bridge of her nose. "I want you to listen to me, Talia. *Really* listen, and believe what I'm about to say, because I don't have time to keep telling you this. Are you ready?"

I nodded.

"I am not mad at you. I am not judging you. I understand exactly why you did the things that you did, and I don't think you're a bad person."

"You don't?" I asked. "Why not?"

"Because I know what it's like to suffer," she said. "And to be so consumed by pain and sickness that you would do anything to make it stop." She drew a calming breath. "It's my job to win for you. Your life is in my hands, and that's a lot of pressure. Sometimes I'll have to fight dirty. Sometimes I'll be moody. It is not personal. Do you understand?"

Again I nodded.

"Take a shower and put on some light makeup," she told me. "And I do mean *light*. I shouldn't be able to tell you're wearing makeup at all. Style your hair in a plain, low ponytail. By the time you're finished with that, I'll have an extremely boring, unfashionable outfit delivered to you. Appearances shouldn't matter to an adjudicator of the law, but they do. I want you to—"

"Pretend I'm a good girl," I interrupted.

"You *are* good," Olive stressed. "There's no need to pretend. What we're trying to do is make you relatable. Judges are human; they have the same biases as the rest of us. Flashy clothes give off a reckless vibe. And designer labels are the worst. Nothing says 'spoiled, entitled, and above the law' like in-season Gucci."

As if I could afford that.

"The evidence against you is bad enough," she said, gathering her notes and tucking them into her satchel. "Let's not give the adjudicator a reason to pick you apart. That goes for your behavior, too. Don't try to be funny, or witty, or cute. Be the most cardboard version of yourself. Speak only if you're asked a direct question, and don't elaborate when you answer. Details are ammunition. Give them too much, and they'll kill you with it."

Another nod.

"And one more thing," she went on. "Before you leave the cottage, you'll be fitted with a disarming cuff. It's like an ankle monitor, but in addition to tracking you, it blocks you from casting. That means you'll be subject to other people's magic, but you won't be able to use your own. It will suck. You will be powerless. Don't complain about it."

I nodded for the hundredth time and assured her that I understood everything, mostly because I wanted her to leave. I was still grateful to Olive, but the dynamic between us had shifted, and neither of us seemed comfortable anymore. When she gathered her things and left for the main house, I was finally able to exhale. I had just started toward the bathroom when a knock sounded from the window.

I pulled aside the curtain and found Nathaniel making a shushing gesture. He pointed behind him at Olive, who was striding slowly across the lawn, and then motioned for me to wait. I wondered how long he had been hiding out there. And why. He had to know by now that Olive was my lawyer. I had already told her my secrets.

The instant Olive entered the main house, Nate unlocked the cottage and slipped inside.

"Why all the sneaking around?" I asked.

He released a weary breath and leaned against the wall. I could tell from his wrinkled shorts and T-shirt that he had slept in his clothes, and not more than an hour or two, judging by his heavy eyelids. All of that should have worried me, but instead, I felt a whisper of relief. Whatever had kept him away from me for so long had clearly been important.

"I have to show you something." He pulled out his phone and unlocked it before handing it to me. "Tell me if any of these guys look familiar."

I held the phone between us and glanced at the image. Nate had taken a picture of a picture. It looked like a team photo, with dozens of shirtless teenage boys arranged in three rows, the tallest in the back and the shortest in the front. Instead of bleachers, they stood on a grassy field that overlooked the ocean. A pegboard sign held by one of the boys read *Intra-Mystic Senior Varsity Wrestling Team.*

I drew a hopeful breath.

"Your ghost," Nate said, indicating the picture. "Do you see him?"

I started with the tallest wrestlers in the back row, enlarging the image and scanning their faces from left to right. It didn't take long for me to find my disappearing boy. Even with his hair pulled back in a ponytail and the wide, toothy grin, there was no mistaking his features.

"That's him," I said, tapping the screen. I enlarged the image so only his face showed. "That's the boy I've been seeing."

Nathaniel didn't share my excitement. He dipped his chin and slowly pocketed his phone. The color in his face drained, as though he had already known the answer but had hoped I would prove him wrong. He swallowed hard and asked me, "Remember when I told you the last person who left Lumara didn't come back?"

"Yes," I said. "And that's why people want you to move back home."

"He's the one I was talking about. This guy, his name is—was— Jude. He went missing from a summer wrestling camp eighteen years ago. No one ever knew what happened to him. But now I guess we do." Nate dropped his gaze and added, "He was my brother."

My mouth dropped open. "I didn't know you had a brother."

Nate sat on the edge of my bed. "We don't talk about him. Ever. We don't even have pictures of him in the house." His shoulders rounded, and he ducked his head as if ashamed. "Jude was so much older than me. I was a baby when he went missing. I don't remember him at all, so, in a way . . . it's kind of like I never even . . ."

"Like you never had a brother?" I offered.

Nate peeked at me. "Sometimes I forget he existed. Is that awful?"

I sat down beside him and briefly placed a hand on his shoulder. "Of course not. It's hard to grieve for someone you didn't know. You didn't have much time with Jude, not like Olive did." I paused to do the math and realized how close in age Jude and Olive had been. Maybe even the same age. "Wait. Were they . . ."

"Twins," Nate said. "Fraternal. Runs in the family."

I remembered Lillian telling me that. "Just like your mom and Camilla."

"Oh, but way, *way* closer. Like this." Nate crossed his fingers. "Jude and Olive had a freaky bond. People still tell stories about it. I wasn't old enough to remember, but I heard Olive knew something was wrong with Jude before the camp noticed he was missing. She went screaming to our parents about Jude needing help and how she felt like he was gone. She got so worked up she couldn't breathe, and they had to sedate her. After no one could find him, she stopped eating. Magic couldn't even help her. She kept getting worse, and eventually my parents had to hospitalize her. I don't know if that's what caused her tumors, but that's around the time she got sick."

Sympathy bloomed in my chest. I had always envied the twin bond, the love and safety and sense of belonging that came with being one half of a whole. But it hadn't occurred to me how shattered and incomplete one twin might feel without the other. Poor Olive. Now I knew what she had meant when she'd said her mother couldn't heal the only part of her that mattered. Grief was stronger than magic.

"That's why we don't talk about Jude," Nate said. "It's why there are no family pictures of him in the house, or any pictures, really. My parents packed it all away so Olive wouldn't be triggered." He glanced at me. "That's why I didn't want you telling her about the ghost. You didn't, did you?"

"No," I said. I could only imagine how traumatizing it would be for Olive to learn that Jude had been trapped and suffering for all these years. "She's going to . . ." I trailed off as a realization tingled in the back of my mind. "Olive," I repeated, paying attention to how my lips formed her name. "Olive," I whispered again, and then I finally understood what I'd been missing. "Oh, god, it's Olive. That's what Jude has been trying to tell me. He wasn't saying *I love*. He was calling for his sister."

The look on Nate's face mirrored my shock.

"Think about it," I said. "Olive never goes to the lagoon. That's why he can't reach her. He's bound to the water." It made total sense now. "Jude wants me to bring Olive to him."

"No." Nate couldn't shake his head fast enough. "You can't, Talia. When I tell you Jude is Olive's biggest trigger, I mean a trigger to an atom bomb that'll blow up our family. I don't even want my mother finding out, and she's strong enough to hear it."

"They have a right to know. Jude should be free."

"Absolutely," Nate agreed. "*After* your trial. *After* the cures are traded. Right now, we need Olive focused on you, and my mom focused on the people you cursed. Jude's not going anywhere. He can wait another week."

I chewed the inside of my cheek. I didn't want to wait. "Can you at least text me that picture? I want to send it to my cousin so she can find—"

"No way," Nate said. "Your family's a bunch of liars."

"Oh, come on. Not all of them. Someone has to dig into the wrestling camp: who was there, where the boys came from, who hung out together, where they are today . . ."

"They've already been investigated," Nate said. "First by the camp, then by the IFC, and then by a private investigator my parents hired. There's nothing left to find."

"Then explain why Jude keeps appearing to me and not to you. You're his brother. You've been to the lagoon plenty of times, and you've never seen him."

"That does seem weird," Nate admitted.

"He and I are connected," I said. "Maybe the PI report will tell us why."

Nate rubbed his temples and then nodded. "Fine. I'll try to find it."

Around lunchtime, I joined the convoy to pick up my father and the adjudicator from the harbor. Lillian, Adrian, and Olive drove together, and Nate and I followed in the Impala. Camilla had insisted on tagging along with us in the backseat, to make sure I didn't "accidentally get lost" and miss my pre-trial hearing.

As if I would risk my future by trying to run away.

Besides, Camilla was seriously overestimating my skill level if she thought I could outsmart the shimmering static cuff around my ankle. I couldn't cast a spell to move a feather, let alone escape the island.

At the dock parking lot, I stepped out of the car, preferring to wait outside. The sun was a warm contrast to Camilla's frost, and soon my father would be there, like a second sun. My heart fluttered with excitement to see him, but nervousness, too. Now that the IFC was involved, anything could happen. I wondered if they would file charges against my dad.

I tried not to think about that.

I had just shielded my eyes to gaze out at the harbor when something pushed me hard from behind, and I stumbled forward onto the pavement, landing on all fours. I glanced over my shoulder to find no one there, but at the other side of the parking lot, a man faced me, his stance wide as he prepared to conjure another attack.

I cringed and braced myself for a blow, but it didn't come. A young girl had run in front of the man and cast a shield between us. Nathaniel and the others rushed out to help me. Through the noise of car doors and shuffling shoes, I heard the girl shout, "Daddy, no!"

Lillian subdued the man in an instant, and then one of her entourage quietly whisked him away. I brushed off my skirt and limped over to the girl, who was now in tears. I noticed she was slightly older than I'd thought, about twelve or thirteen, with eyes so bloodshot I couldn't tell what color they were. She must have been crying for days.

"Thank you," I told her. I pointed at my ankle cuff. "I can't defend myself with this on. You saved me."

She nodded and wiped her cheeks. "Please wake up my sister

now," she said, her voice rough from tears. "Please. She's my best friend. I need her to come home."

My heart ached and sent a lump into my throat. I recognized the girl's voice from the fireworks, when she had begged me to save her sister. I had taken away this girl's closest friend, and instead of getting revenge, she had stood against her father to protect me. I couldn't say I would have done the same. In fact, I *knew* I wouldn't have.

"Who is your sister?" I asked.

"Mandy," the girl said. "The maid of honor."

"I remember her."

"Will you wake her up, then?"

I swallowed, but the lump wouldn't go down. "I want to. I'm trying really hard. I promise I'll do my best."

Someone came to return the girl to her family, and I walked numbly to the docks to meet the adjudicator's ship. I couldn't stop picturing the girl's face . . . or imagining how she would feel if her sister never came home. None of this was fair to her.

None of it was fair at all. What had we been thinking?

I held back and waited while Lillian boarded the ship and did what all politicians do: the hand shaking and the fake smiles of greeting other politicians. When she led the way down the boarding ramp, I stood on tiptoe and looked for my father in the line of people behind her. I didn't see him, so I scanned the decks, assuming he wanted space from the others. But I didn't find him there, either.

Olive veered toward me on the way back to her car. She touched my shoulder and said, "I'm sorry, Talia. He didn't come."

My stomach clenched. "What do you mean?"

"I mean he never boarded the ship."

"That's not possible."

"The captain told me himself," she said. "Your father's not there."

I pulled out my phone and dialed my dad. The call went straight to voicemail without ringing. I tried sending a text, but the message came back *not delivered*. My pulse rushed. I knew my dad was too careful to let his phone die, especially when I needed him.

Something was wrong.

"What if he's hurt?" I asked Olive. Then a terrible possibility occurred to me. "What if your mom had him killed?"

"Talia, listen to me." Olive gave me a gentle squeeze. "Take a breath. My mother has nothing to gain and everything to lose if your father goes missing. He's the only person who knows the counter-hex for Lucy and the others."

I nodded. She was right. But I could think of someone else who would benefit from my father's disappearance: the person who had cursed my mother. I had to find him.

I texted Kat, *Have you heard from my dad?*

Not since he left, she replied. *Why?*

He didn't make it here.

What??? Are you sure?

The ship just docked. He's not on it.

Okay, she said. *I'll talk to my mom and find out what's going on.*

I didn't tell her I was scared, or how alone I felt. But she must have known, because she added, *Stay strong. You got this!*

"Stay strong," I repeated. Easier said . . .

CHAPTER
SEVENTEEN

At the pre-trial hearing, it wasn't hard to be the most cardboard version of myself. I didn't have to pretend to sound bland when I answered the adjudicator's questions. I didn't have to remind myself to say as little as possible. Acting detached came naturally, because my insides were numb. My spirit was numb. There was nothing in me to tame.

"Excuse me." A throat cleared. "Miss Malanovitch?"

I blinked at the sound of my name. "Sorry?"

The adjudicator studied me from his seat at the head of the dining room table, where he had set up his temporary workstation. He had requested the use of the dining room instead of the Woods' home office, because like most formal dining areas, the space was quiet and clean and only used on special occasions, like holidays and anniversary parties . . . and attempted-murder trials.

The man had a name, but I had already forgotten it. Olive and I called him sir. He reminded me of an actor, someone soft-spoken and cultured, like Morgan Freeman, but with an edge that made my palms sweat. I was glad I didn't have to sit next to him. Olive had positioned herself between us, directly to his left. The empty chair to his right belonged to my father.

I tried not to look at it.

The adjudicator folded his hands atop the table. "You explained to me that it was your idea to infiltrate Lumara by way of the Wood family, particularly Nathaniel Wood. Did you also devise the plan to transport a cursed object onto the island?"

Olive flashed a palm at me. "Don't answer that."

The adjudicator gave her a withering look.

"My client was sixteen years old at the time this plan was conceived," she told him. "She was a minor—and she still is, for the record. Her parents were the adults. Whether or not the curse was Talia's idea, it was her parents' responsibility to act in accordance with the law. Her father is culpable for bringing the plan to fruition. He should be on trial, not Talia."

"Wait a minute," I said, because I didn't like where this was going. "The one who should be on trial is the person who cursed my mom. Why aren't we filing charges against them?"

"Give me a name and I will," the judge said.

"You'll have to help me find them first," I told him. "No one around here is looking for them. No one cares about the curse that's killing me. They would rather blame my dad, and he didn't do anyth—"

Olive lifted a finger and whipped her gaze around to me. "Stop. Talking."

I bit my lip and folded my hands on my lap.

"As I was saying," Olive continued. "The dark magic used on the puzzle originated with my client's father, Gregory Malanovitch. He provided the hex and then guided his daughter through the process of casting it while she was asleep. My client was merely his instrument, a sword in his hand."

I clenched my jaw to stay quiet. She made my dad sound so sinister.

"Based on what evidence?" The adjudicator indicated the empty seat at the table. "The 'hand' in question is not on trial today, nor is he present to defend himself."

"And that's rather telling, don't you think?" Olive asked. "How convenient that Mr. Malanovitch passed up three opportunities to be with his daughter. It's almost as though he knew the truth would implicate him as the mastermind behind this crime."

The adjudicator frowned and asked me, "Talia, did your father provide you with the spell for the puzzle you cursed, and did he assist you in casting it?"

I didn't want to answer him. I could see what Olive was trying to do, and I refused to let her throw my father under the bus. So what if he had broken more laws than I had? We were a team. I wanted my lawyer to fight the *system*, not my family.

"Talia?" the adjudicator prompted.

I tugged at my ear and glanced away. "I don't remember."

"Yes, you do." He held up his right hand, displaying a chunky golden ring embossed with a symbol I didn't recognize. "I can tell. Don't lie to me, Talia. It won't work."

I should have known he would have an enchanted lie detector.

"Answer the question," he ordered.

"Fine, I don't want to tell you," I said, and that was the truth.

Olive sighed and brought both hands together, as if praying for the strength not to kill me. She plastered on a grin and turned to face the adjudicator. "Sir, if I may, I'd like to request a declaration of incompetence."

"On what grounds?" the judge asked.

"Forced indoctrination," she said. "I believe my client was emotionally abused and manipulated during her childhood, and the resulting trauma has impaired her judgment."

I sat bolt upright. Was she calling me brainwashed?

"And you believe your client is unable to act in her own best interests?"

"I do," Olive said.

"No," I told her. "That's not—"

Olive flicked a wrist in my direction and instantly muted my voice.

I gasped in shock. *You silenced me?* I tried to say. No sound passed my lips. Rage heated my face until I could barely see straight. I felt violated. Betrayed. The same loss of control I had suffered when Hector's guard had taken over my body. *Take it back!* I mouth-yelled.

She wouldn't acknowledge me.

"Miss Wood," the adjudicator chided, wagging his finger at Olive. "You know better than to silence your client before I've issued a ruling on her competence."

"Please, sir," she told him. "My client is a danger to herself. She's sabotaging her well-being by continuing to defend her father.

She doesn't realize he's an extremely powerful spell-caster who doesn't need protecting. He should be in this room defending his child, not the other way around. Please let me speak on her behalf."

I pounded my fist on the table to get their attention. I mouthed, very clearly, *I AM NOT A DANGER TO MYSELF.*

Olive tried to block the judge from seeing me.

"Your client seems perfectly lucid to me," he said.

"She doesn't know what's best for her."

The adjudicator shook his head. "Miss Wood, a substantial burden of proof is required for me to restrict your client's free agency. You have failed to meet that condition." He waved a hand at me, restoring my voice, and declared, "Request denied."

Olive raked a hand through her hair, messing up her perfect twist.

I used my first words to tell her, "You're fired!"

She didn't argue with me, just hung her head in frustration.

"Do you mean that?" the adjudicator asked me.

"Hell yes, I do."

"Do you have another attorney in mind?"

"I don't want one."

The adjudicator leveled a serious gaze at me. "Talia, if you act as your own lawyer, you have a fool for a client."

I folded my arms. I would rather be a fool than a helpless bystander in my own life. No one would ever take away my voice again.

"Well," he said, and paused thoughtfully for a moment. "I'm going to delay your preliminary hearing until noon tomorrow. I hope that will give you enough time to make a more rational choice. You may not want an attorney, but you need one."

He adjourned the meeting, and Olive left the room without a word or a backward glance.

That was fine. I had nothing to say to her.

At the cottage, my afternoon continued to spiral.

I learned that no one had heard from my father since the night before. And thanks to his paranoia about binding agents, he had left behind no DNA for anyone to use to trace his location. We couldn't even trace his phone. The battery was dead.

As much as it terrified me, I had to consider the possibility that my father was hurt . . . or worse . . . and that I might not find him before the deadline he had given Lillian. Which was a problem, because I couldn't wake up the fourteen sleepers. I didn't know the counter-hex.

I was screwed.

And I had fired the only person interested in helping me.

Two knocks sounded from the door. The dead bolt slid aside, and Olive poked her head into the cottage. She had smoothed her hair into another perfect twist and even applied fresh lipstick.

"Ready to talk?" she asked.

I nodded.

The wooden chair in the corner had been removed to make space for Olive's folding bed, so she had no choice but to sit opposite from me at the foot of my mattress. She sat primly, her fingers inter-laced, and cleared her throat before speaking.

"I apologize for silencing you," she said. "That was wrong on multiple levels, especially now that you're defenseless against magic. I shouldn't have done that to you."

"You're right, you shouldn't have," I agreed. "And why didn't you talk to me about what you were going to say about my dad?"

"Would you have let me?" she asked.

"No, but that still doesn't make it right."

"There's another reason I didn't tell you," she said. "I was wor-ried that you would warn him and he would run. But he's smarter than I gave him credit for. He already knew he couldn't come here. His testimony would incriminate him. He's only safe as long as he stays gone and you keep his secrets."

"It's not like that," I said, even as a dark feeling took root in my chest. My father loved me—I had no doubt about that. But as powerful as he was, nothing should have stopped him from coming here to be with me. "I think he's in trouble."

Olive folded her hands and went quiet for a while. "Do you know why I became a lawyer?"

"You're fascinated by the law."

"That's not the whole story," she said, and stared down at her hands. "I lost someone special. The most important person in my life. I knew he was in trouble, and I couldn't do anything to help him. I had to sit in my house, hundreds of miles away, and feel his fear and his pain, and listen to him call out for me, and there was nothing I could do."

I chewed my lip. "Jude."

"Yes," Olive said, looking at me with tear-filled eyes, but also smiling, as though starved for the sound of his name. "He was the other half of my soul."

"I'm sorry you lost him."

"You know the worst part?"

I shook my head.

"The helplessness," she said. "All this magic, all this connection between us, and I couldn't even find his body. That's the real reason I went into the law. I needed to be able to do something, and I thought I would feel better if I could get justice for other people." She poked the bedspread in front of me. "People like you. But life doesn't work that way. I still wake up every morning feeling as helpless as I did the day I lost him."

I began to see the point she was making, the reason she had fought so dirty at my pre-trial hearing. "You thought saving me would be like saving Jude."

"More or less," she said. "I'll be honest. I still don't want to fail you, and I still believe you have a blind spot for your father. But you're not Jude, and it's not healthy—or fair—for me to transfer my feelings for him onto you. So if you hire me again, I promise to respect your wishes."

I grinned at her. "Same hourly rate as before?"

"I'll make you a deal," she said. "Half off my pro bono rate."

I extended a hand to shake. "You've got yourself a client."

"Good," she told me. "Because we still have a lot of work to do."

CHAPTER
EIGHTEEN

With my father missing, Olive and I agreed to make our top priority finding a counter-hex to wake up the fourteen sleepers. Kat hated the idea. She worried that no one would cure me if I removed the threat too soon. But I couldn't afford to wait. The judge would only show me leniency if the wedding party recovered, and regardless of whether or not my mom's killer came forward, I didn't want fourteen people to die because of me.

So for the rest of the afternoon, I brainstormed with Olive to unravel my father's spell, while that night, I scheduled a working dinner with Nathaniel to unravel my connection to Jude.

"Thanks for coming," I told Nate, and indicated the opposite end of my bed for him to sit down. He balanced my dinner tray on one arm and glanced at the corner, where the chair no longer stood. "Or you can sit on the floor," I added. "Your call, but I don't bite."

He placed the tray in between us and sat facing me on the bed. "I wouldn't say that." He tucked his curls behind one ear, revealing the quarter-size sweet spot I had discovered on the side of his neck. He used to go all kinds of crazy when I grazed it with my teeth.

I blushed. "Fair point. I don't bite *hard*."

He lifted the platter cover and filled the air with the rich scents of marinara and garlic. "Lasagna with mozzarella-stuffed bread sticks and an extra helping of shrimp fettuccini."

"Carb loading?"

"I figure we can use it."

He wasn't wrong. My head spun with all the work in front of us.

"Hey, um, listen." Nate picked up a bread stick and used it to push sauce around the plate. "Olive told me what's going on with you."

"What did she say?"

"That your dad bailed on you, and you're trying to undo his spell on Lucy."

Something stopped me from correcting him about my father. Maybe the doubt blooming in my chest. I distracted myself with a bite of fettuccini and nodded. "I never wanted anyone to get hurt."

"I believe you."

That took me by surprise. I glanced at him and asked, "You do?"

He pulled his bracelet out of his pocket. "I had this with me at the lagoon. It never vibrated. I don't know why it took me so long to figure out you were telling the truth. I was angry, I guess." He tossed it onto my side of the bed. "Anyway, you can have it."

"It won't work in here."

"Save it for later," he said. "I don't want it back."

"Ever?"

He shrugged. "Wasn't as useful as I thought."

I disagreed with him on that point, but I understood what he meant. The bracelet had failed him—but to be fair, he had expected too much from it. There was no such thing as safety in love or in life. Magic couldn't change that. If anything, magic caused more problems than it solved. But I thanked him for the bracelet and buckled it around my wrist. I would wear it because it reminded me of him. That was enough.

"So . . ." He poked at the lasagna. "What school do you think you'll transfer to?"

I laughed without humor. I hadn't thought that far ahead. "I'm kind of focused on basic survival. But, hey." I raised my water bottle in a toast. "I respect your optimism."

He clinked my bottle with his. "I'm next in line for valedictorian."

"That'll look good on your college apps."

"Feels wrong, though, taking the title away from you."

Class rank didn't seem to matter anymore. Even if I survived my curse and the adjudicator let me go—two big *ifs*—the original plan had been to train with my family and learn magic-for-hire. College might not be an option for me.

"Either way, neither of us deserves it," I said. "It's a school for regulars, and we both lied to get in."

He frowned. "I guess."

It hurt too much to talk about moving on without each other. So I changed the subject to Jude's summer camp. "Any luck digging up that report from the private investigator?"

"Yeah, I scanned it into my phone."

I held out a hand. "Can I see?"

When he passed me his phone, I quickly accessed his camera roll and texted myself the picture he had taken of Jude's wrestling team. I deleted the photo from our text thread before sending myself the investigation report. I hated tricking Nate, but desperate times . . .

"Thanks," I said, passing back the phone. "I'll read it tonight."

"Maybe you'll find something I missed."

"Nothing stood out?" I asked. Mostly I wanted to know if my mother's maiden name had come up. Despite what my father had said, I was convinced she had dated Jude. Their ages matched, and so did the timing. "Any mention of a Leah Clarke?"

"Not that I saw." His phone chirped, and he glanced at the screen. "It's Olive. She wants me to meet her at the house. I'll poke around the attic again tonight, see if there's anything I missed."

"Okay, thanks."

As soon as he left, I texted the team photo to Kat.

Do me a favor, I typed. *Ask your mom if any of these guys dated my mom.*

Kat responded right away. *Okay, on it.*

While I waited, I read the investigation report, starting with the team roster. I didn't recognize any of the names. The wrestlers were a mixture of Aura, Blood, and Core Mystics from all over the country—twenty-three boys in all, and only five Cores. I thought back to what Jude had shown me. Something had blocked him from surfacing, like an invisible wall.

Seemed like magic.

That eliminated the other Cores. So assuming the boy who had drowned Jude was a member of the wrestling team, the killer had to be one of the eighteen Auras or Bloods in the photo.

My phone buzzed with a text from Kat.

You dork! Yes, your mom was dating one of those guys.

Which one? I asked, not getting the joke.

OMG are you serious?

Yes! Which one?

Bottom row, third from the left, she said. *You don't recognize your own dad?*

I swiped up to the picture so fast I nearly dropped my phone. Enlarging the image, I found the third boy from the left. He didn't look anything like my father. I could almost see the resemblance in the face, but the boy had a head full of thick, dark, curly hair. My dad had gone gray at eighteen—and then totally bald. More important, there was no one on the team named Gregory Malanovitch.

Not gonna lie tho, Kat added. *I didn't know it was him either.*

I still wasn't convinced. My father had said he'd never heard of Lumara or the Wood family until a few years ago. If he had attended the wrestling camp, he would have known Jude Wood.

I cross-referenced the team roster and found the boy's name: Michael Machnowsky.

"Michael Machnowsky?" I whispered aloud.

A wild possibility came to me.

My father didn't talk much about his childhood, except to say he'd been raised in foster care. He knew nothing about his parents or his family tree, which was a big deal for Blood Mystics, because ancestral relics enhanced our power. What if he had a sibling—or multiple siblings—and the foster system hadn't been able to place them in the same home? That sort of thing happened all the time.

Maybe my theory wasn't so wild after all.

Hey, I texted Kat. *I need you to drop everything and snoop on someone.*

Sweet! Who am I stalking?

Michael Machnowsky, I told her. *That's the boy in the picture. IDK if he's my dad or not. Tell me whatever you can about him. His family, too. Dive deep, okay?*

You got it . . . Full Mariana Trench on the guy.

As fast as you can, I added. *This might be a game-changer.*

Not a minute later, a knock sounded from the door. Nate had returned.

"I talked to Olive," he said. "She asked me to get something from you."

"What's that?" I asked.

He cringed. "A drop of blood."

My eyes flew wide. Olive might as well have asked for my bank account and all of my passwords. Nothing held more value in the Mystic world than blood. It was the strongest of all binding agents. "Does she want the deed to my dad's house, too? How about my diary?"

"I know," Nate said. "It's a big ask."

"What does she want it for?"

"To test a theory about the puzzle curse."

"She wants my blood . . . for an experiment?"

"Just one drop, and she'll destroy it after." He held up a hand in oath. "I'll make sure of it. I swear."

I rolled my eyes and held out a finger for him to prick. "I can't believe I'm doing this."

"Neither can I, to be honest." He jabbed me and captured a single red droplet on a glass slide. "I wouldn't give anyone a drop of mine."

"Well, I must really trust you or something."

He locked eyes with me, his warm, dark gaze softening. "Yeah, you must."

My insides fluttered at the buttery tone of his voice, the unmistakable spark behind his eyes. I had almost given up hope that he would look at me this way again. I wanted more, to reach up and touch his face, but I was afraid to ruin the moment.

Instead, I told him, "That's my life in your hands."

He nodded. "I'll take care of it."

After he left, my phone started buzzing with texts from an unknown number.

It's Kat. This is my burner. She added a bunch of angry-face emojis. *Your dad or M!ch@el M@chn0w$ky or whoever TF he is owes me a new phone!*

What happened? I asked.

He cast a spell alert on his name. Strong-ass magic too! I'm guessing he gets notified when someone talks about him, and probably the identity of who's talking. As soon as I mentioned him to my chat group, my phone blew up. Literally! He killed it!!!

Damn, I'm sorry, I told her. I wondered why mine hadn't blown up, too. The cottage wards must have blocked his magic. *He reeeeeally doesn't want to be found.*

Well, that's too damn bad! she said. *Because it's ON!!! I'm gonna search so far up his ass that every time he has a thought, it'll refresh my browser!*

I couldn't help laughing. But my smile fell as a different text appeared at the top of my screen. Even from an unknown number, there was no doubt who had sent it.

Hey, Button. Call me. We have a lot to talk about.

CHAPTER
NINETEEN

I called Nathaniel to the cottage and asked him to take a leap of faith for me.

"A small leap, more like a bunny hop," I said. "I need your help sneaking out."

He cocked his head to the side.

"Listen before you say no," I told him, and then I confided that my father had texted me. I didn't mention Michael Machnowsky or the drama with Kat's investigation, only that the situation felt strange and I wanted to use my Blaze Connect to talk to my dad face-to-face. "The Blaze won't work in here—neither will your bracelet—and I can't get past the security wards because I'm cuffed."

Nate frowned at my static ankle monitor. His continued silence made me squirm.

"Whatever rules you set are fine," I said. "Put a tether spell on me if you want. I have no intention of running away, and even if I did, you have my blood, so I wouldn't get far." I peered up at him and made one last appeal that I knew he would understand. "I don't know what to believe anymore. I need to find out if my dad is telling the truth. Will you help me do that?"

"Fine," Nate said. "But I'm going with you."

He disabled the security wards and drove me to Jumping Rock Waterfall, a more remote location than the lagoon, with plenty of jungle greenery for concealment. After turning off the main road, he parked the car and cut the ignition.

"You go ahead," he told me, nodding toward the path that led to the falls.

"You're letting me go by myself?"

"You want the truth," he said. "Your dad's not going to tell you anything if I'm there."

"You're probably right. Thanks for the leap."

"Just hurry. It's not safe for you out here."

As quickly as I could, I followed the path until it ended at the falls. A thick layer of mist clung to the air, dampening everything it touched and absorbing the moonlight. The effect reminded me of standing inside a cloud. Most of the light came from the occasional dancing firefly, and then farther up the path, the waterfall glimmered with luminescent particles pouring out of the cleft-rock spring and emptying into the pool below.

A shiver tickled my spine despite the muggy warmth. If there was a more ethereal place on the island, I hadn't seen it.

I dialed my father, and his image appeared in front of me, so real and lifelike that my arms twitched to hug him. In an instant, my heart forgot that he had left me alone to wonder if he was dead or alive. He was here—more or less—and that was all that mattered.

"Button," he whispered as his face melted into a smile. "It's so good to see you. God, I miss you so much."

I scanned him to make sure he was okay. He looked fine, healthy and strong, with no visible injuries. I glanced all around him, trying to figure out where he was, but nothing existed in the background. I couldn't even pick up any noises. If I didn't know better, I would assume he was talking to me from inside a vacuum.

Or that he'd used magic to hide his location.

"Where are you?" I asked.

"Trust me, hon. It's safer for you if you don't know."

The buckle on my wrist vibrated. My heart sank. My father was hiding from me—from *me*, his own daughter. In an instant, all the hurt and anger from the past two days resurfaced, and I demanded, "Why aren't you here? Why didn't you at least call me? I thought you were in trouble!"

"There's a lot going on behind the scenes," he said, holding up both palms. "More than I can tell you. Honey, I'm so sorry I made you worry, but I promise—"

"Stop it," I interrupted. "Who's Michael Machnowsky?"

For a fraction of a second, my dad's eyes widened. The movement was so brief I almost missed it, but I hadn't, and his reaction left no doubt he recognized the name.

"I don't know," he said. Another vibration. "Why?"

"I found an old team roster in Nate's attic," I told him, unable to stop my voice from shaking with anger. "Michael Machnowsky has your face, and he went to a summer wrestling camp a long time ago with a boy from Lumara."

My dad swallowed hard enough to shift his Adam's apple.

"I thought Michael might be your brother," I said, heat rising in my cheeks. "Because he couldn't possibly be you, right? You said you had never heard of Lumara until after Mom got sick. You said you had never heard of the Wood family, and that wouldn't be possible if you had gone to the same summer camp where Jude Wood went missing."

My dad looked away and rubbed the back of his neck.

"Red plaid swim trunks," I went on, my pulse thumping. "That's what Jude was wearing the last time anyone saw him alive. That's what he's still wearing to this day. And I told you that, remember? I told you about the ghost in the red plaid swim trunks, and you ordered me to stay away from him."

"It's not what you think, Talia."

"Here's what I think: I think you wanted to keep me away from Jude so I wouldn't find out what happened to him."

"No, I was afraid he would hurt you."

"Why would he hurt me, Dad?"

"That's what vengeful spirits do."

My bracelet vibrated. "Or maybe you were afraid he would hurt me to get back at *you*."

"Do you have any idea how crazy you sound?" he asked, having the nerve to act offended. "If this is how you're going to be, I'm hanging up."

"If this is how *you're* going to be," I flung back, "I'm telling the adjudicator who really cursed Lucy's puzzle!"

He looked at me like I had stabbed him.

"Don't lie to me and expect me to keep your secrets," I said. "Tell me the truth!"

"What is it you want me to say?" he asked, flinging a hand in the air. "That I changed my name? All right, fine. I changed my name. I used to be Michael Machnowsky, and now I'm not. Are you satisfied?"

Satisfied was the last word I would use to describe myself. In the span of two days, I had gone from a Morris to a Malanovitch to a Machnowsky. I had learned I couldn't count on my father. That he would ditch me and lie whenever it suited him. I had lost trust in nearly everything I thought was real.

"So I'm not a Malanovitch?" I asked.

"No, you're a Machnowsky." He held out his wristwatch and popped off the crystal. I couldn't see what was inside, but I imagined it contained his ancestral relics. "From a long line of Bloods dating back to the Middle Ages."

"Do I have family? Grandparents? Aunts and uncles and cousins?"

"All of the above." He added in a sarcastic tone, "Mazel tov."

"Did Mom know?"

His face fell, the way it always did when I mentioned my mother. "No."

"You lied to her, too."

"I had to."

"Nobody *has* to lie."

"It was for her protection."

The bracelet vibrated. "Her protection? Or yours?"

"All right, mine," he admitted. "Yes, I was at that camp. I was the last one to see Jude Wood alive, and that made me the main suspect. You know how powerful the Woods are. You know what kind of influence they can buy. They ruin lives as easily as breathing. I didn't want their shadow following me around, so I changed my name so I could start over."

My wrist vibrated, the sensation dulled by my throbbing pulse. I wanted to cry. To scream. To tear off the bracelet and stop asking questions with horrible answers. More than anything, I wanted to be Talia Morris again: homecoming queen, valedictorian, cherished girlfriend of the most popular boy in school. But Talia Morris didn't exist anymore.

She never really had.

So I took a deep breath and kept pushing. "What did you do to Jude Wood?"

"Nothing," my father insisted.

Another vibration. "I went back to the lagoon the other night. Jude was there. I followed him into the water. Do you know what he showed me?"

My father mouthed the word *no*, shaking his head. He didn't want to hear it.

Too bad.

"He showed me how he died," I went on. "But he didn't just show me. He put me there. I lived it inside his mind. I felt every sensation that he felt—all the fear, all the panic, all the pain, the moment his spirit left his body. I drowned right along with him."

"Talia, please stop."

"It was awful. It hurt worse than anything I could imagine."

Tears welled in my father's eyes. "Button, stop."

"He was so scared, Dad. Why didn't you let him up? Why

didn't you let him breathe? He thought you were his friend. He thought it was a game."

"It *was* a game!" my dad cried in a broken voice. "I swear to God, Talia, I didn't mean to hurt him! It was an accident!"

My bracelet didn't vibrate. He was finally telling me the truth.

"I was an idiot and I used a spell," he said. "Jude was stronger than me—kept pushing me around and dunking me every chance he got. I wanted to get him back, so I cast a one-way glass on the water. It was supposed to keep him under for a couple of seconds, just long enough to make him take me seriously." He licked his lips, exhaling a shaky breath. "But the reverse incantation didn't work. I said the words wrong. Then everything happened so fast. By the time I reversed the spell, it was too late."

My lungs ached with the memory of that moment.

"After that, I panicked." My dad scrubbed a hand over his face. "I didn't think anyone would believe it was an accident. Even if they did, it wouldn't matter. The Federation would've made an example out of me. You know they would have. Think about the can of worms it would open if anyone thought they could get away with murder by claiming the magic went wrong.

"So I hid the body. I sank it to the bottom of the ocean and cast a concealment charm over it. A whole team of scuba divers could swim right on top of him, and they wouldn't notice." He raked a hand over his bald head. "It was the lowest point of my existence. That one day, that one choice, ruined his life and mine. And others' too."

I assumed he meant Jude's family. "They have no idea what happened to him. They never had closure or a body to bury."

My dad nodded. He avoided my gaze, saying nothing. The moments ticked by in silence, each second growing exponentially thicker and heavier, until I began to question what he wasn't telling me.

"You mean other lives, besides the Woods'?" I asked. "Whose?" And then it hit me. He was taking about my mom and me. Our lives had been ruined that day—that was when the curse had begun. "That's what started it all. It had nothing to do with Mom. *You're* the one who's cursed, aren't you? You're losing the people you love."

He hung his head.

"But how?" I asked. Hexes were only transmitted through cursed objects or binding agents. If no one knew my father had killed Jude, how could they possibly have hexed him? "Is it possible Jude cursed you? Maybe that's why his spirit can't move on."

"Anything's possible, I guess, but I doubt it."

"Who, then?"

"I don't know. I didn't know about any of this until now."

Another vibration. "I don't believe you."

"I didn't know *at first*," he clarified. "Not until it was too late to do anything about it. Your mother was the greatest love of my life. I would have given anything to trade places with her. But I couldn't. There was no way to save her."

As I heard his words, the last thing I expected was for my bracelet to vibrate again. When it did, all of the air leaked out of my lungs. What had he lied about? Had some other woman been the love of his life? Or had he known how to save my mother?

"You could have saved her?" I asked.

"No, Button. I promise."

Another vibration. I gaped at him in disbelief. None of this made sense. He had loved my mother—I knew it. Losing her had wrecked him. "You could have done something, and you chose not to?"

He splayed both hands. "What could I have done?"

"I don't know. You tell me!" An idea came to mind. "Maybe you could have gone to Lillian and asked for help. But then you would've had to admit you killed her son."

"Why would I go to the woman who probably cursed me?"

"To beg for Mom's life! To do whatever it took!"

"It wouldn't have mattered," he said. "Look at where you are now. We've got fourteen of her people on the hook, and she still won't fix you."

I shook my head. I didn't believe that. "Lillian's not my biggest fan, but I know she doesn't want me dead. If she hasn't broken my—*your*—curse yet, it's because she doesn't know how to undo it."

"Then you have to find the person who does."

I exhaled a bitter laugh, finally understanding the real reason my father had sent me here. He wanted me to find out who had cursed him because he was too afraid to do it himself. He really was a coward.

"Come help me," I dared him.

"You know I can't."

"Because the IFC will put you on trial, right along with me. That's what you're afraid of. That's what's kept you away."

He looked me dead in the eyes and said, "You're damn right I'm afraid. They'll execute me. Is that what you want?"

The grave reality of his words shook me. No, I didn't want

that. Maybe my dad was a liar—maybe he hadn't tried hard enough to save my mom—but he was the only parent I had left, and I loved him.

"You have to give me the counter-hex for the sleepers," I said.

"Not until you're cured."

"At least wake up a few of them. It will look like an act of good faith."

"Not. Until. You're. Cured."

I drew a breath to argue, but his image disappeared.

He had hung up on me. Abandoned me again.

CHAPTER TWENTY

The next day, the adjudicator didn't lecture me about my tantrum. He didn't even say he was glad I had come to my senses and rehired my attorney. Instead, he began the pre-trial hearing by stating our names for the record.

"Let it be known that the following individuals are present: Talia Malanovitch, accused; Olive Wood, representation for the accused; and Franklin J. Harland, presiding."

Franklin J. Harland. That was his name. I almost wished I hadn't heard it, because thinking of him as Franklin made him seem less like a harbinger of doom and more like a real person, the kind of man who enjoyed a nice cup of Earl Grey in the afternoons and bird watching from his kitchen window and reading presidential memoirs in bed.

The kind of man who wouldn't sentence me to death, which was a dangerous thing to assume about him.

"Miss Wood," he said to Olive, "does your client wish to share more information concerning the origin of the dark magic that was used to curse her puzzle, and whether she received assistance casting it?"

Olive cleared her throat. "I'd like to request a dismissal of my client's case. Attempted murder implies an intent to kill. My client meant no lasting harm." She pointed at his lie detector ring. "You know her testimony was true. At best, this is a case of illicit spell work."

The judge scoffed, grinning as if he admired Olive for taking a shot. "I might agree with you if the fourteen victims weren't hovering an inch from death."

I leaned forward in my chair. "We're working on that."

"Working on it?" he asked, his eyebrows jumping. "That doesn't inspire confidence. It almost sounds as though you don't know how to cure them."

Olive elbowed me to shut up.

"Miss Malanovitch," the judge said, "I've seen enough magic to tell the difference between masterful spell work and the sloppy conjuring of a novice. So when I encounter a hex so intricate that not even the Grand Lumara can reverse it, logic dictates it was not devised by a seventeen-year-old girl."

I couldn't say anything to dispute this, so I stayed silent.

"But ultimately, I have to base my ruling on evidence and testimony. If you refuse to admit that someone else supplied you with the dark magic, then you tie my hands. But if you implicate the other person, I can use my resources to apprehend them and transport them to Lumara—where they'll be forced to correct the damage they've caused."

"And then executed," I said. He'd forgotten that part.

The adjudicator shared a long, silent look with Olive. An entire conversation seemed to pass between them. It wasn't hard to imagine what they were thinking—that I was an idiot for protecting my father. And maybe I was. My dad didn't seem to care about protecting me. But if there was a chance I could fix this without him, I had to take it. I still had a little time.

The judge blew out a long breath. "Talia, do you know what will happen if your victims die?"

I didn't like hearing them called *my* victims. "I'll be convicted of murder."

"And do you know the penalty?"

"Death."

"I'll have no discretion in your sentencing," he told me. "The statutes I'm bound to uphold are very clear. Sentences are proportional to the crime. In your case, fourteen victims will equal fourteen executions."

I blinked at him, instantly going cold. I thought death was death. How could anyone kill me fourteen times? I turned to Olive, expecting her to refute him, but she didn't even raise an objection. What about cruel and unusual punishment? Didn't the Federation care about that?

"Have you ever heard of *Entrada v. Freedman*?" the judge asked me.

I didn't trust my voice, so I shook my head.

"I was summoned to a commune of Blood Mystics, where a man had died without leaving a will for his ancestral relics. Understandably, both of his sons wanted the relics. The brothers loved each other, but they were grieving, and emotions were high. What started as a rational discussion quickly escalated into an argument, and eventually, a fistfight. The younger brother used magic to cast an impact spell. He didn't intend for the spell to strike the left side of his brother's chin with precisely the right amount of force to twist and break the man's neck, but that's what happened."

The adjudicator fidgeted with his ring, a nervous gesture that told me he didn't want to keep going, but he did. "Joseph was the younger brother. By the time I arrived, he had already punished himself more than I ever could. There wasn't an ounce of malice inside that man. But the law was clear, and so was the penalty. I had to convict him." The judge locked eyes with me. "Just like I'll have to convict you."

I chewed the inside of my cheek and looked away.

"Do you know what that looks like?"

"No, sir," I murmured.

"Then let me show you."

He snapped his fingers, and, without warning, my senses vanished, as though a giant pair of scissors had snipped the tether between my body and mind. An instant later, I regained awareness in a different place, inside a different body.

My chest ached, so heavy with grief that I bowed over and propped both elbows on the table to relieve the burden from my spine. Through my swollen eyelids, I could see that the hands in front of me were callused and strong, with tiny flecks of white on my fingernails. I recalled that I had painted the ceiling in my bathroom. Half of the ceiling, actually. I had been working on the project when my brother had come to visit, and I hadn't finished the job.

Now I never would.

Not that it mattered. I had lost everything that mattered.

But still, I didn't like picturing the one small section of beige, untouched by the tidy swaths of stark white paint I had rolled on. My brother had made fun of me for doing the work by hand. He would have used a spell. But I enjoyed painting, found it cathartic. My favorite part of the process was applying the last stroke, the completion of coverage, creating a transformation that was simpler than magic and twice as satisfying, because of the very work that magic would have deprived me of.

I hated leaving a project interrupted.

But maybe that was appropriate for me. Symbolic of my life, and my brother's.

I rubbed my dry, burning eyes and wished I had tears left to wet them.

I wished a lot of things.

"Mr. Entrada," the adjudicator said from the other end of the table, "do you have any final words to share before I pronounce my judgment?"

I took a deep breath and then let it go. Glancing around the room, I didn't see anyone who would benefit from hearing more of my words. Not the lawyers, not the judge, and certainly not that asshole Freedman, the compound governor who'd filed the charge against me. I was sorry for what I had done. I had loved my brother with my whole heart. Anyone who knew me already understood that.

"You," I said, pointing at Freedman. "Do me a favor, will you? Go to my house and finish painting the bathroom ceiling. The supplies are all there. It shouldn't take long."

He nodded.

"That's all I need," I told the judge. "I'm ready."

"Very well." The adjudicator placed a metal box on the table, plain and dull and roughly the size of a cookie tin. He opened the lid, and I felt a slight

pull coming from inside, similar to the way an ocean current tugs at the shore. Leaning forward, I could make out a swirling black cloud at the center of the box. It was a vortex, a portal to another place. In my case, to an executioner's realm.

My pulse hitched with fear.

"Joseph Phillip Entrada," the judge announced, "you have been charged with the willful use of injurious magic resulting in death. I find you guilty as charged, and I sentence you to share the fate of your victim. May your spirits reunite in peace."

The pull intensified from inside the box. Reflexively, I gripped the table's edge and hooked my ankles around my chair legs. I didn't want to fight my sentence—I wanted to close my eyes and give myself up with dignity—but my instincts took over, and I couldn't help it. I held on tight, grunting and straining until my fingers grew slick, and I lost my hold.

The chair disappeared from beneath me, and then I was falling.

I screamed, surrounded by darkness. I flailed my arms to right myself, but I couldn't tell which way was up. There was no wind to blow back my hair, no sensation of movement against my skin, only stomach-tugging gravity and the absence of light.

Then came the pain, great jolts of it, electrifying my nerves. Blows landed on my chest and belly, sucking the air from my lungs. Another one struck the side of my jaw, and my face turned sharply . . . too sharply to the right. I heard a sickening crack. The sound was almost worse than the agony that split my spinal cord. I kept waiting for awareness to end, for death to take me, but instead, I lingered, continuing to fall, paralyzed and unable to move my lungs. I strained to breathe, my face swelling.

I wanted my life to end.

When would it end?

I returned to myself with a gasp, gripping the dining room table with both hands. I panted and massaged the ghost pains along the back of my neck. The horrible sound of snapping vertebrae echoed in my ears, giving me shivers. I swallowed against waves of nausea and fired a glare at the judge. My cheeks flushed hot with anger and hurt.

"Take it back!" I snapped. "You had no right to do that to me! I'm alive—damn it—for however long that lasts, and I'm sick of people forcing their deaths on me! I shouldn't know how it feels to drown! Or to break my neck! I shouldn't know any of that!"

"To drown?" the adjudicator repeated.

Olive wrinkled her forehead. "What did you show her?"

"Entrada v. Freedman," he said. "There was no drowning."

"Whatever, just take it back!" I jabbed a finger at him. "I don't want that memory inside my head!"

He snapped his fingers again, and the events from the memory began to fade away, gradually fraying at the edges, like a dream that vanished upon waking. Soon the only image I could recall was the box and the swirling vortex inside it, and the sinking feeling that came with knowing its purpose. My heartbeat slowed as reality returned to me. Whatever Joseph Entrada had experienced was nothing more than a distant nightmare.

"Are you sure there's no one else to implicate?" the judge asked.

"I can handle this on my own," I told him. "The way I live is more important than the way I die."

His gaze softened into sadness, and for the first time, he looked more like a Franklin than an adjudicator. "Oh, Miss Malanovitch. You wouldn't feel that way if you remembered what I had shown you."

Outside on the deck, Olive barely made a sound.

She had suggested we have a "working lunch," but so far, she hadn't touched her sandwich, or the wine she had insisted she would need.

"I have to tell you something," she finally said. "Two things, actually. And neither of them is good."

"Uh-oh." I set down my turkey on rye. "What's wrong?"

"Remember the blood sample I asked for?"

I nodded. The droplet had already been destroyed, so I'd put it out of my mind.

"I had an idea why we hadn't been able to break the puzzle hex. I really wanted to be wrong, but your sample proved me right." She picked up her wineglass and fidgeted with the stem. "The reason we can't break the spell is because it's linked to you."

"What?" I asked. "How?"

"Your father designed the hex so that anyone affected by it shares your fate. In other words, if you're cured, the sleepers are cured. But if you're not . . ."

My mouth went dry. All fourteen of them would die? No wonder my father had refused to give me the counter-hex. He hadn't made one. Which meant he had never intended on negotiating with Lillian. "Then we have to focus on curing me."

Olive stared into her wineglass. She cleared her throat and murmured, "We can't. There isn't a cure for you."

I started to ask how she could possibly know that, but the answer came to me with the force of an arrow to the chest. There was one person who had more motive than anyone else to avenge Jude's death. I held my breath, afraid to speak. I didn't want to say the words out loud and make them real.

Olive's chin wobbled. She peeked at me with tears in her eyes and said, "I did this to you, Talia. I'm the one who cursed your father."

CHAPTER
TWENTY-ONE

It made sense. Looking back, I should have seen it sooner. All of the signs were there. No one had loved Jude more than Olive. Their connection had shown her the moment of his death, giving her details about the drowning that no one else would have known. But my heart pushed back against the truth.

Olive was my favorite woman on Lumara.

Olive was my mother's killer . . . and soon to be mine.

I couldn't hold both thoughts inside my mind at the same time. They kept pushing each other out, making my brain spin.

All I could ask was "How?"

She dabbed her eyes with a cloth napkin. "I had a binding agent."

"How?" I repeated. My father didn't leave traces of himself behind, and supposedly, no one, not even Olive, had known the identity of Jude's killer.

"Jude used to call me from camp," she said, and then cleared the thickness from her throat. "He told me about a boy he had met, and how obsessed the boy was with his hair. So Jude stole his comb as a prank. He thought it would be funny to hide it outside their cabin, under the front porch overhang." She went silent for a long moment, staring at the horizon as if replaying a memory. "When Jude was drowning and he reached out to me, I saw an image of a comb, and I knew what it meant. He wanted me to know who was holding him under."

"There was hair in the comb," I realized.

"One strand," she said. "Right where Jude left it."

"But you could have given it to the police or the IFC. You could have gotten justice for your brother. You could have had my dad executed, and his death would have been as sick and twisted as whatever the judge showed me today."

"I didn't want justice," she admitted. "I wanted revenge."

"So you decided to kill everyone he loved?" I demanded. "What's wrong with you? What were you thinking?"

"I *wasn't*," she said. "I was young, and devastated, and out of my mind with grief. I didn't think about anyone else. I didn't care about the consequences. I did what felt right, and by the time I realized I had made a mistake, it was too late." She leveled her gaze at me. "Kind of like the girl who infiltrated a private island and cursed fourteen people."

"I didn't want to hurt anyone. *You* did. There's a difference."

"I won't argue with that," she said. "I don't want to argue at all. We don't have time." She reached for my hand but thought better of it. "Talia, I'm not the same person I was at seventeen. I hate what I did to you and your mother. I wish I could take it back, but I can't.

215

All I can do is help you now, and we have to stay focused, because there's a bigger problem."

I rolled my eyes to the sky. Of course there was.

"The curse I used is called Lucifer's Bane," she said. "It's not designed to kill everyone you love. It's designed to lie dormant until you experience the strongest love of your life, and then it takes that love away, and it doesn't stop until you lose the person who matters more to you than anyone else in the world. That's the only way to break the curse, when your most important person is gone."

My lips parted. The person my father loved most in the world was me. "The only way to break the curse is for me to die?" I breathed. And the only way to save the fourteen sleepers was to save *me*. It was an impossible contradiction.

"So you see why we don't have time to argue," Olive said.

Her icy control infuriated me. It wasn't fair, how quickly she had dried her tears after blowing up my life. I wanted her to hurt, to panic, to feel the same cold fear that I did. So I took the low road and I hit back. "While we're sharing secrets, I should tell you Jude has been trapped in the lagoon this whole time. Ever since his death."

Olive pulled back. Somehow, she went even paler. "What?"

"He's been appearing to me since I got here. He even showed me how he died."

Her lips tightened. "You're lying."

"Here's proof that I'm not." I held out my wrist, offering to let her wear my bracelet. "He calls your name, over and over. He wants you to know what you did to him."

"No. Lumara doesn't bind her dead."

"The island doesn't, but apparently, you do." I had wondered why Jude was tied to the lagoon instead of the ocean waters where he drowned. Now I knew. "You're holding him here."

"You're wrong. I've been to shore a hundred times since he died. I would have seen him."

"I don't think so," I said, finally understanding my link to Jude. "I'm dying from the same curse that trapped him here. We're connected. That's why I can see him and you can't."

"No, you must have imagined it. I didn't bind him here. I would never . . ."

"Maybe your magic backfired," I guessed. "You had to know a spell called Lucifer's Bane would come with a cost."

"The price I paid was my life," she said, splaying a hand over her chest. "The curse has been draining me from the beginning. That's why I'm sick."

"Sick, but not dead," I pointed out.

She shook her head over and over, murmuring *no* while her cheeks turned to wax. When her breath started to come in shallow pants, I felt a pinprick of guilt for the way I had thrown the truth about Jude in her face. She deserved to find out, but not like that.

"I have to . . ." She licked her lips, her hands trembling. "I have to go."

She pushed up from the table and stumbled inside the house, and I sat on the deck for a long time, feeling like my head was floating above my body.

The day didn't seem real. I had learned the answers to so many of my questions, but the truth confused me more than ever. I didn't know what to do anymore.

In a daze, I gathered my lunch dishes and took them back to the kitchen, then wandered into the foyer, not sure where I was going. I followed my footsteps to the basement staircase, where I paused at the top of the landing and considered what had brought me there.

Lucy.

I hadn't visited her, partly because she and the others were quarantined, but mostly because I felt too guilty to show my face anywhere near her. I stretched out a hand to test for a force field. Nothing stopped me, so I walked down the stairs as far as I could, until I reached a wall made of magical static at the bottom.

On the other side of the wall, fourteen bodies hovered above the floor in slumber, all of them dressed in their formal tuxedoes and gowns, their limbs relaxed and floating by their sides as if they were suspended in water.

Lillian stood with her back to me, her palms extended as she murmured an incantation. Camilla stood beside her, gazing down at Lucy and stroking her cheek. I stayed quiet until Lillian finished chanting. Her spell must not have worked, because she hissed in frustration and strode off into the basement, out of sight.

I cleared my throat to announce myself.

Camilla turned and glanced at me with an empty expression, not a hint of her usual contempt. The spark inside her seemed to have died. I recognized that hopelessness, because I felt it in my own chest.

"I dreamed about you last night," she told me. "I was wrong before. I didn't see below your surface, but I do now. My inner eye showed me your path. I know what's ahead of you."

"I wondered if you had the Sight."

"I do." She tucked a stray lock of her daughter's hair back into place.

"What do you see?" I asked.

"Love and loyalty, honor and sacrifice," she said. "You have a good heart. But there's darkness and pain coming . . . and unimaginable loss."

My lips parted. I wished I hadn't asked.

"But know this," she told me in the voice of someone pointing out the bright side. "Death brings new beginnings. Your loss will break the chains of torment for another."

She had to mean Jude—that my death would break the curse and release him. It warmed me to know that his suffering would end, that he would move on to the next great adventure because of me.

But still . . .

I thought of the graduation speech I would never give, the enchantments I would never learn, the hidden wonders of the world I would never discover. I pictured what my first apartment might look like, how I might decorate it if I had the chance. I imagined Kat and Nathaniel growing older and finding their way in life without me, gradually forgetting the color of my eyes and the shape of my face.

My vision blurred. I shook my head to clear it.

"There's one more thing you should know," Camilla added.

I nodded for her to continue. She might as well. It couldn't get much worse.

"Say goodbye while you can," she told me in a tone that raised the hairs on the back of my neck. "I promise you'll regret it if you don't."

CHAPTER
TWENTY-TWO

Say goodbye.

The words echoed in my head as I stumbled up the basement stairs.

Say goodbye.

Pressure multiplied inside my chest. The missing piece clicked into place, and finally, I could see my new reality. My time had run out. There were no more tricks, no more answers left to find. I had tried to change my fate, and I had failed. Now I had reached the end, all I could do was . . .

Say goodbye.

But how?

The phone in my pocket felt like a lead weight. I couldn't imagine picking it up, let alone dialing my family and hearing their voices for the last time. Just thinking about it made my throat constrict.

I couldn't do it.

I peered through a blurry lens of tears at the staircase to the second floor. To hell with goodbyes and responsibilities and bucket lists. If my days were numbered, I wanted to fill every moment I had left with joy and love and adventure.

I wanted Nathaniel.

With shaky knees, I made my way to the second floor and down the long hallway to his bedroom. I knocked twice and let myself in, not waiting for an invitation. I felt my composure crumbling like a sandcastle in the wind, and I needed him more than my next breath.

He glanced at me from his bed, leaning back with one muscled arm curled behind his head and the other supporting a photo album on his lap. "What's wrong?" he asked, sitting up and shoving aside the album. "Why are you crying?"

I closed the distance between us and wrapped myself so tightly around him that he couldn't push me away. Not that he tried. He stiffened for a moment, but he must have known how desperate I was, because he hugged me back. I straddled his lap and anchored my face in the crook of his neck. With his strong arms around me, I finally felt safe enough to let go.

I didn't just cry. I drained heartbreak all over his shirt. And he let me, saying nothing, holding me until I purged all of my pent-up darkness and my tears ran dry. Even then, he waited until my chest stopped hiccuping before he pulled back and asked me, "Are you ready to talk?"

For a moment, I wondered how much I should tell him, but then I realized all of my problems—every single one of them—had started with a secret or a lie. I was done hiding. I had to trust him with the truth, even if it hurt.

So I told him everything, every detail, leaving nothing unsaid.

I felt ten pounds lighter when I had finished. With a clear head, I could finally think straight again, and I knew what I wanted.

"Spend the day with me," I said. "I don't care what we do—we can go to the beach or stay inside—as long as we're together. I just want one perfect day with you."

Never in a million years would I have expected him to say no . . . or to lose his temper and sit up with so much force that he almost knocked me off the bed.

"Are you kidding?" he demanded.

I caught my balance and righted myself, searching his face for a clue of what I had done wrong.

"Let me get this straight," he said, flashing a palm. "Your dad killed my brother and hid the body. Then my sister got revenge by cursing your dad. Then your dad got revenge on my sister's revenge by cursing the wedding party. And now the best-case scenario is everyone dies?"

I hoped not, but it was looking that way.

"No, that's bullshit." He hitched his upper lip and added, "And Olive knew? You're telling me this whole time, she let us think she had magical cancer, when really she cursed a whole-ass family and didn't say a word to anyone?"

He glared down at the photo album, open to a page showing Olive and Jude as teenagers. In one image, the twins had joined hands, leaping together from the top of Jumping Rock Waterfall, their bodies frozen in midair, happy screams etched onto their faces. It was probably the last moment of real joy either of them ever experienced, the last shiny link in a chain of events that would cause misery for two families. Too bad Camilla hadn't seen *that* coming.

"I bet your mom knew or at least suspected," I said. "That would explain why she didn't try very hard to find out who cursed my family. Think how bad it would look for the Grand Lumara's own daughter to get caught using dark magic."

His eyebrows knitted together. "You're probably right. What the hell?"

"It's a lot." I stroked his arm. "I'm sorry."

"And you," he said, fixing his laser gaze on me. "You're done fighting? You're just going to trade your shot for one perfect day?"

"I don't know what else to do," I said, though, after everything, it was kind of gratifying to know he still cared.

"And you expect me to be okay with that?" he asked. "Do you even know me at all? Do you really think I'm going to say, 'Oh yeah, sure, Talia, instead of going down swinging, let's manufacture some fake happy memories for me to replay on a loop after you die.'" He threw one hand in the air. "Have you thought about what your perfect day would cost me?"

"What it would cost *you*?" I asked, my face heating. Did he have any idea how selfish he sounded? "I'm the one who's dying! I'm the one with everything to lose. So *excuuuuse* me for wanting a little happiness before I kick it!"

He thrust an index finger at me. "That's not you talking. That's not my Talia. My Talia goes after what she wants and doesn't stop until she gets it. My Talia doesn't settle for a crumb of happiness when she can have the whole cake. Or was that just part of the lie?"

"Oh, stop it! I never lied to you on purpose, so you can quit playing the victim." I poked my own chest. "*I'm* the victim here. I can't have the cake. It's impossible."

"How do you know?"

"Because . . ." *Olive said so.* I couldn't say it. It sounded pathetic, even to me.

"Exactly," Nate said. "Nobody knows when they're gonna die, and if they say they do, they're lying or fooling themselves."

"What about your aunt Camilla?" I asked. "What about the darkness and pain and unimaginable loss she saw in my future?"

He rolled his eyes. "When I was a kid, she told me my ice cream was haunted."

"You're making that up."

"She's the most negative human being on the island, and that's the truth," he said. "All lives are made up of pain—and happiness and boredom and everything in between. My aunt doesn't see joy in anyone's future because she doesn't think to look for it."

"So what am I supposed to do?" I tipped up my palms. "You tell me, since you have all the answers."

"Here's what we do, wise-ass," he said. "We put your dad in a room with Olive and my mom, and we force them to figure it out."

"I've been trying to get my dad here all week."

"Have you?" Nate asked. "Because it doesn't look like it."

I realized he was right. I had called and texted and complained, but I hadn't used any leverage against my father. "I could threaten to tell the Federation the truth."

"He's probably already prepared for that," Nate said. "And if not, threatening him will force him deeper underground, and we'll never find him in time."

"Then how do we convince him?"

Nate went thoughtful for a while. "You said Olive used a

binding agent to curse your dad. I wonder if she used the whole thing for the spell, or if she still has part of it."

I nodded in understanding. If Olive could give us a tiny piece of my father's hair, we would have the means to track him, maybe even compel him to come to Lumara. In theory, anyway. Compulsion was next-level magic. "Got any advanced spell books lying around? I haven't seen any."

Heat flashed in Nathaniel's eyes as he stood up from the bed. "You know what? We're done playing nice."

"I cursed fourteen people," I pointed out.

"Then *I'm* done playing nice. And you weren't looking in the right place." He held out a hand to me. "Not unless you found the invisible door to my mom's sanctuary."

I took his hand, intrigued.

"There's a portal at the back of her closet," he said, pulling me to my feet. "I've never snooped through my mom's things before. But hey, it seems like lying and sneaking around is a Wood family tradition. I have a lot of catching up to do."

"Are you sure about this?" I asked. "I don't want to corrupt you."

He answered with a wicked grin and led me into the hall.

"Whoa," I breathed, widening my eyes to take in more of the Grand Lumara's private chamber. "Home-office goals."

The portal had conveyed us to an underground cavern beyond the estate. I could tell by the thunderous roar of water coming from the other side of the stony walls that a river flowed nearby. But despite that, the air was dry and cool, without a hint of moisture to damage the leather-bound books that hovered in tidy rows behind a desk made exclusively of braided tree roots. The floor was carpeted with a thick, lush moss that prompted me to kick off my sandals and sink my bare toes into the ground.

I groaned. "It feels even better than it looks."

In the corner, vines had woven together to form a chaise lounge, topped by a pillow of fragrant blossoms, a light blanket draped over the back. Beside the lounge stood a shimmering geode table, the perfect place to set a mug of tea during an afternoon of reading. And the best part was the flickering glow emanating from a thousand bioluminescent crystals overhead, like stars captured in a bottle.

"I'm never leaving," I told Nathaniel. "I live here now."

He released a breathy chuckle. "See? The perfect day without even trying."

"We're off to a good start." I ran my finger along the leather book spines, noticing that none of the volumes had titles. It seemed Lillian didn't simply have a grimoire. She had an entire library. "What are we looking for?"

"I'll know when I see it," Nate said. "Or when I don't."

He crouched in front of the desk and skimmed his hands underneath the roots as if checking for a hidden compartment. The furniture didn't have any cabinets or drawers, not that I would expect anything so ordinary inside a magical lair. If I were a grand priestess, I would hide my treasures in another dimension or lock them in an invisible vault that responded to the sound of my voice.

"Aha!" Nate called, his arm disappearing into a deep, enchanted storage area within the desk. "She's so trusting. She didn't even lock it."

"Um, yay?" I tipped up my palms. "Joke's on her, thinking we're good people?"

"Well, what have we here?" he asked, having pulled out a small black book that resembled a journal. He leafed through it before tucking it in his waistband and reaching back into the desk. He felt around for another few minutes but didn't find anything else. "That's it." He stood up, brushing off his hands. "There's nothing else in there, just the notebook."

"It must be important. What's in it?"

"Sketches and notes," he said. "Observations about the island, that sort of thing."

It was interesting to me that she'd hidden it. Whatever Lillian had discovered about the island, she didn't want the public to know.

"We'll read it later," he said. "Right now we have to wrap it up and get going." He studied the volumes of books along the wall. "We won't be able to take these out of the room. It'll trigger an alarm. But if I find the right spell, I can take a picture of it and read it on my phone."

"Are you sure your mom has a coercion spell? That's dark magic, isn't it?"

"Depends on the intent," he said, pointing a finger down the rows of indistinguishable texts. He gave up trying to find the book on his own and chanted a locator spell. In response, a volume from the top row flew into his waiting hand and promptly opened to page two hundred and thirty. "Bingo."

"Show-off," I teased.

He snapped a picture with his phone and then returned the volume to its place. "There's one more thing I want to find before we leave."

"What's that?"

"A linking spell, so you can draw energy from me if you need to."

"What?" I cocked my head. "You would do that for me?"

"We're in this together," he said, shrugging. "We have a better chance of getting what we want if we share our strengths."

Something in his words triggered a connection for me. It had to do with my random energy boosts on Lumara. I hadn't been able to understand them before, but now I saw that each one had happened the same day Lillian had healed Olive. Looking back, I had also felt stronger when Olive had spent more time inside the cottage. That couldn't be a coincidence. The curse must have linked our energies.

"Hey, there's something you should know," I said to Nate, and explained my theory. "Are you sure this is safe? If I'm connected to Olive, she might draw from you, too."

"I'm not worried." He made a *come here* motion. "Quick, spit in my hand."

"Excuse me?"

"You heard me. Spit in my hand."

"You can't use my hair?" I asked. "I have to spit on you?"

He hawked into his palm and then held it toward me. "If you want to share my energy, this is what you have to do."

I cringed but leaned over his outstretched hand and summoned some drool.

"That's it?" he asked, scrutinizing his cupped palm. "That's all you got?"

"I'm dehydrated. Sue me."

"I guess this will work." He slid a glance at me, one corner of his mouth curving up. "I could have used a hair."

"Oh my god." I slugged his shoulder. "I knew it! You're so gross."

Through barely contained laughter, he recited the incantation to connect my life energy to his. I didn't feel any differently afterward, and I wondered whether or not the spell had worked. But then a quick burst of flame consumed the moisture in his palm and vanished. That seemed like a good sign.

"You're welcome," he said, replacing the book on its invisible shelf. "Now you've got some fight left in you."

"Thanks," I told him. "For not letting me give up."

"No problem." He held up his mother's journal and backed toward the portal to the main house. "Now let's go see what's in here."

"We shouldn't read it at your place, not with your mom around." I followed him to the portal and grinned innocently. "Probably safer to take it to the beach and read it there. Maybe pack a few snacks, throw in our bathing suits, fill a thermos with some fruity drinks . . ."

"You're relentless."

"I'm efficient," I corrected. "Multitasking is a critical skill."

"All right. You win." He offered me his elbow, and I took it. "Looks like you're getting your perfect day, after all."

CHAPTER
TWENTY-THREE

"Look at this view." I lifted my thermos toward the shimmering azure lagoon as I reclined in my oversize lounge chair. We had the whole beach to ourselves, but as a precaution, Nate had cast a concealment charm over the area so that only Olive could see us, assuming she responded to our messages to meet us there. "I told you multitasking is the best."

"Mm-hmm," Nate said from the chair beside me, his eyes fixed on his phone screen. "I'll be sure to follow your account for more tips and life hacks."

Clearly, he wasn't in the mood to play, so I left him to his reading and returned my attention to the Grand Lumara's journal.

At first, Lillian's notes about the island seemed random. She had described a cluster of orchids taking root and flourishing in the crack of a north-facing cliff wall; a rare species of butterfly gathering to spawn inside a mountaintop cave; the discovery of a "lucky fishing spot" near the north shore, where a tidal pool formed each night, teeming with the largest, healthiest fish any of the locals had ever seen. In the next entry, Lillian rated the changes in the strength and clarity of the island's "voice" as it spoke to her from different locations. It was then that I noticed a theme connecting the dots of each discovery.

"It's a power map," I said. Lillian had tracked Lumara's magic—the location of its figurative heart and the network of arteries that dispersed its essence through the island. "That must be why she hid the journal. She didn't want anyone getting greedy and bleeding the island dry."

"None of us would do that," Nate argued.

I slid him a disbelieving look. Had he learned nothing?

"All right, fine. People are unpredictable," he droned. "You never know what they're capable of." He jutted his chin at the journal. "Where is the magic strongest?"

"Up on the mountain, near the falls."

"Huh. I've cast up there."

"Did you notice a difference?"

"Not really."

"Maybe you need a spell to tap into the extra power."

"Maybe, but I don't think it would help much." He sighed, holding up the picture on his phone. "This spell is way over my head. I can barely decipher it, let alone cast it. If we want to pull this off, we have to go to my mom and tell her what's going on."

I bit my lip. I didn't trust Lillian.

"I know, I know," Nate said. "You think she's the enemy. But we have the same goals. Isn't that the definition of an ally?"

I couldn't agree with him on that point. Lillian and I only had one common goal: waking up the sleepers. Aside from that, we wanted different outcomes, specifically about who should suffer the consequences for the mess we had all helped create. She would point the finger at me and my dad, not at herself and Olive.

"Bottom line," Nate said. "She's the only one who can do the spell. So if we want your dad here, we have to go to her."

"I'll think about it," I told him, but he was right. We didn't have a choice.

I turned the page to the next journal entry and froze when I recognized my name scrawled in Lillian's handwriting.

Talia . . . Lumara wants to help her. With what? Grant Hammond type of situation? Purest love?

"Who's Grant Hammond?" I asked. And what did love have to do with it?

Nate wrinkled his forehead. "Not sure, but he sounds familiar. Why?"

Before I could answer him, my phone buzzed.

It was a text from Kat's burner. *I found him!!!*

My dad? I asked, sitting up.

Yes! He's good, but I'm better. Never mess with a girl who dates drummers. Cheating boyfriends will make you the Einstein of snooping.

Where is he?

Signal Hill, Pennsylvania, she said. *The Machnowskys have a compound there. It's fortified tho. That's the bad news.*

How fortified? Can you find out without him knowing?

She sent me an eye-roll emoji.

Sorry . . . didn't mean to doubt you, I said.

It's a good thing I love you.

Love you more, I told her. *LMK what you find out.*

I tucked my phone into my bag and noticed movement in my periphery. From a nearby path, Olive made her way toward us in slow steps, leaning on a cane for balance. She had changed out of her business suit into a bright red tankini and a long, matching sarong that billowed gently behind her on the breeze. A pair of dark sunglasses hid her eyes, but I could tell from her reddened nose that she had been crying. Sympathy plucked at my chest. I should have been more gentle when I'd told her the truth. To learn that Jude was trapped and suffering had to be more painful for Olive than losing him the first time.

"Your sister's here," I told Nathaniel.

He glanced up from his phone and grunted.

"Try to be nice," I said. When he slid me a glare, I repeated what he had told me in Lillian's office. "We're in this together, right? We have a better chance of getting what we want if we share our strengths. Besides, you can't punch down on someone that's already on the floor. She knows she bound Jude to the water. There's no punishment worse than that."

Nate glanced at his sister. He didn't greet her with a smile, but he at least acknowledged her presence by asking, "So, do you still have the hair?"

She nodded. "A bit of it. I cut it in half before I used it, just in case I messed up the spell and had to try again."

"Good," he said. "Now who's Grant Hammond?"

Olive blinked at the abrupt question. "Uh . . . an old Grand Lumara. Why?"

"How old?" Nate asked.

"I don't know," she said. "*Old* old. He's been dead a long time. I think he was two Grand Lumaras before Mom."

"What about his love life?" I asked. "Do you know anything about that?"

"Oh." Her face lit up with understanding. "You mean his wife, Alba Hammond." Olive used her cane to lower herself onto the sand. "She's a legend around here. They say she and Grant went hiking along a cliff face when they lost their footing and fell. In her last moment, Alba used magic to save his life."

"Huh," I said. That seemed noble, but not legendary. I had expected more.

"But Alba wasn't a Mystic," Olive added. "She was completely ordinary. Not an ounce of magic in her body. Supposedly, she had a big heart, and the island respected her for it. So when she called out for help, Lumara couldn't say no."

Nate quirked a skeptical brow. "I never heard that."

"You would have if you had gone to school here long enough."

"So the island gave her magic, but it couldn't save her life?" he argued.

"I guess that's not what she asked for," Olive said, shrugging. "I don't know. Why does it matter? It's just a story."

I shared a glance with Nathaniel. It had to be more than just a story, otherwise Lillian wouldn't have made a note of it in her journal. I could sort of see a parallel between myself and Alba. We were both outsiders. I knew Lumara wanted me here, enough to allow me through its wards. My guess was the island wanted to help me free Jude. Maybe Lumara would share its magic with me—assuming I could get rid of my ankle cuff.

I felt the familiar sensation of being watched, and I turned my gaze to the lagoon, where Jude had just surfaced. The sight of him didn't scare me anymore. I had come to expect him, almost like the tide. He stared at me with those impossibly dark eyes, his hair dripping torrents down his muscled chest, arms pumping as he strode toward the shore. He crossed the sand and knelt in front of me, sitting back on his heels.

Olive noticed the direction of my gaze and pulled off her sunglasses, glancing back and forth between me and the water. "Is he here?"

"Jude?" Nate asked.

I nodded. "Yes, he's here."

But he wasn't looking at his siblings. He watched me with soft eyes, as though he pitied me, which seemed backward. For the hundredth time, I wished he could talk to me or write a message on the sand. I wanted to communicate with him, but not enough to share another one of his memories.

Olive reached out to touch her twin brother. She managed to graze the edge of his shoulder, her fingernails passing though his image. Jude swiveled his head toward Olive and studied her, taking in her waxy skin and skeletal frame, tracing the lines and dark circles on her face, and eventually noticing the cane that rested by her side. His shoulders rounded. I didn't need magic to know what he was thinking. It hurt him to see his sister in pain.

"Please forgive me," Olive whispered to him. "I didn't mean for this to happen. I never would have cast the spell if I had known it would trap you here. I was stupid to think my life was the price. It's not a sacrifice to die when you have nothing to live for. I was a power source for the spell, nothing more. The real price I paid was hurting you."

So my instincts had been right. In order to take what mattered most from another, Lucifer's Bane had taken what mattered most to Olive, and Jude had been the trade-off. My heart hurt for them, despite what Olive had done to my family. She had shackled her brother underwater for eighteen years. All the agony she had wished on my father had multiplied and come back to her. No one deserved that.

"I'm so sorry," she told him, and then turned to me with tears in her eyes. "Can he hear me?"

"Yes," I said. "He's listening."

Olive pressed a hand over her heart. "I miss you every day. I even miss the things I used to complain about. Like finding your dirty socks in the bathroom. And how the bread was always stale because you forgot to close the bag. But most of all, I miss"—choking on a sob, she tried again—"the sound of your voice and your laugh. I would give anything . . ."

She broke down, covering her face with both hands, while Jude's expression crumpled. His throat visibly shifted, his eyebrows furrowed, and I swore I saw tears mingled with the ocean water on his cheeks. He turned and jogged back into the lagoon. He dove in headfirst, and moments later, he was gone.

"What is he saying?" Olive asked me. "Can you tell?"

I considered the best way to answer her. "You know that pain you feel in your chest right now? How it aches to know your brother is hurting?"

She nodded.

"He feels that way about you, too. He went back in the water because he couldn't stand to see you cry."

"You mean he doesn't hate me?"

Her question hurt my heart. "Of course not. Your brother loves you." I elbowed Nathaniel. "Both of them do."

"Doesn't mean I'm not angry," Nate said. "But I can be mad at you and love you at the same time. I'm getting good at multitasking."

Olive gave him a watery smile. "So, what can I do to help?"

The next thing I knew, a pair of eyes appeared on the pages in my lap, and I shrieked, shoving the journal away from me. It levitated in the air as the eyes blinked and studied us, one by one. Then Lillian's voice boomed, "To my study! All three of you. *NOW!*"

CHAPTER
TWENTY-FOUR

I had never been sent to the principal's office, but I imagined this was what it felt like. Standing with my co-conspirators in front of the Grand Lumara's desk, I clasped both hands behind my back and tried to avoid Lillian's searing gaze by looking at her forehead. But that only lasted until Olive confessed the truth about what had happened to Jude's spirit, and then Lillian did something unexpected.

She sobbed.

I stared at her, unable to look away. Her reaction shouldn't have surprised me—she was human, after all—but I had never seen her composure slip. And now, watching the Grand Lumara give herself up to her emotions, I was finally able to see her as a real person instead of my enemy.

"Did you know?" Nate asked her. "That Olive cursed Talia's dad?"

Lillian summoned a handkerchief and used it to blot her eyes. "Not for sure, but I always wondered. Olive came to me after Jude died. She wanted me to punish the boy responsible, and I refused to do it. I told her it would betray my calling to use the island's magic for harm. And besides, nothing would bring Jude back."

Beside me, Olive tensed. She didn't speak, but the flat line of her mouth told me she still resented her mother's decision, even after all these years. Maybe she believed Lillian had put Lumara above her family, or that if Lillian had punished my father the way Olive had asked, the disastrous consequences of Lucifer's Bane could have been avoided.

"Part of me suspected," Lillian said, avoiding her daughter's gaze, "that she took matters into her own hands. But I didn't ask. I didn't want to know."

"Plausible deniability," Olive murmured. "That's the legal term for burying your head in the sand so you can stay innocent."

"No." Lillian shook her head. "That wasn't it. I didn't want to believe that I failed you as a mother. Because what would it say about me if I made you feel so hopeless and alone that you threw away your future? I wanted to believe the best about both of us."

Olive's lips parted. She peered at her mother, seemingly at a loss for words.

After several awkward beats, Nate broke the silence. "So, now that you know what happened, will you use the compulsion spell to bring Talia's dad to the island?"

"For what purpose?" Lillian asked.

"So you can lay all your cards on the table," I said. "All three of you. You tell the truth about the spells you used—you share every line and every word—and then you put your heads together and figure out how to undo them."

"Lucifer's Bane is airtight," Olive said. "I've been trying to break it for years."

I pointed to Lillian. "But she hasn't. And my dad hasn't. They know more about magic than rest of us combined. Maybe they'll see something you missed."

Lillian thought for a moment. "Even with a binding agent, compulsion is an exhausting spell. And I can only use it with pure intentions, never to cause harm."

"This qualifies," Nate told her.

"And I have my dad's location," I said. "My cousin is analyzing his protective wards to see if we can disable them. I bet my aunt will help. All I have to do is tell her my dad abandoned me, and she'll strip the whole compound bare."

"I'm more concerned about his resistance," Lillian said. "The spell will create a powerful urge for him to come to me, but I predict he'll fight it. And the harder he resists, the more it will drain me."

My father would definitely fight it. He might even ask someone in his compound to restrain him, like Odysseus tying himself to the mast of his ship to resist the sirens' call. "Is there another way to get him here?" I asked.

"Short of hiring a team of mercenaries to kidnap him? I'm afraid not." She pulled in a deep breath and released it. "I think our best strategy is to cast the spell at full salvo."

"Full what?" I asked.

"A blitz," Nate told me. "A surprise attack with all your weapons. You hit the enemy hard and fast and overwhelm them before they can fight back. I've used it in gaming. It works, except when they have more weapons than you. Then you're screwed."

"Because you used all your ammo," I said. Or in our case, strength. I understood the concept, but a warning crept up the back of my mind. I had the vague sense that we were overlooking something. "Can you walk me through the steps?" I asked Lillian. "What will all of this look like for my dad?"

"When I cast the spell," she said, "he'll feel a need to come to me, like an all-consuming itch in a place he can't reach. I have no doubt he'll know he's been enchanted, but that won't stop the itch from driving him out of his mind until he can scratch it."

"How will he get here?" I asked.

"I'll arrange to have my plane waiting at the nearest airport. I can park a car outside the compound for him as well."

"Will he know that?"

"Yes, if I want him to."

Something still bothered me. My father was a brilliant man, but an even more stubborn one. If he knew he was enspelled, he would try to turn the tables on us. "What if he takes a boat instead of your plane? How will he pass through Lumara's wards? And what if he brings a bunch of people with him? Aren't you afraid of an invasion?"

Lillian tipped up a palm. "I can adjust the wards to admit him, and no one else. And remember, the island has a will of her own. Lumara knows how to defend herself."

All of that sounded logical. I wondered if the real reason for my doubts had to do with something deeper, like how my father would react when he learned I had teamed up with the Woods against him. He would see it as a betrayal. I knew it was the right thing to do—he had left me no choice—but I still hated the idea of disappointing him.

"I only hope I'm strong enough," Lillian added. "I wasn't exaggerating when I said compulsion is exhausting magic."

Nate asked his mom, "What if you tap into the extra power at the falls?"

"I was already planning to," she said.

"How about a linkage spell?" I asked. "Like what Nate did for me?"

Lillian snapped her gaze to Nate. "Excuse me?"

"It's just a vita navitas charm," he told her. "To give Talia a boost, so she can keep going."

Olive pointed back and forth between us. "You know that works both ways, right? You can draw energy from her, too. So if you get hurt or sick, you can wipe her out."

Nate cringed, peeking at me. "I'll be careful."

"Don't wait too long to undo it," Lillian told him. "No more than a couple of days. After that, the risk to Talia outweighs the benefit." She gestured at me. "Check in with your cousin and find out what she learned about the compound wards. We'll have to coordinate our plans if we want to keep the element of surprise."

I nodded.

"While you do that," she went on, "I'll make sure my plane and boat are both waiting at the nearest airport and harbor. I want to remove every barrier in your father's path. We only have one chance at this. Let's not waste it."

It took another few hours for Kat to diagnose the wards shielding the Machnowsky compound. By that time, evening was approaching, and because Kat and my aunt needed to travel closer to the compound in order to disable the wards, we agreed to wait until morning to put our plan in motion.

That night, I could barely sleep over the what-ifs playing in my head. Morning came too soon. When the sun rose, Lillian drove ahead of us to the falls to meditate and prepare for the exhausting day, while Adrian and Camilla stayed behind to monitor the roads and ensure no one interfered.

A few hours later, Nathaniel, Olive, and I left the estate. The three of us hardly said a word on our way to the falls. The mood had shifted since the day before. I imagined we all felt the same pressure, knowing this was our last shot, but I felt a different kind of weight in my chest, dark and cold and foreboding. I couldn't shake the feeling that something bad was about to happen, and I remembered what Camilla had told me about saying goodbye while I had the chance.

So I broke the silence.

"Hey, Olive," I said, turning around to face her in the backseat. "I want to thank you for being my lawyer. You never stopped fighting for me, even when no one else would, and I needed that more than you know."

She glanced at the cane on her lap. "It's my fault you needed a lawyer to begin with."

"Not really," I told her. "I made my own mistakes. I forgive you for yours, and I hope you can forgive yourself, too."

She smiled at me warmly. "Thank you, Talia. I appreciate you saying that."

I faced Nathaniel, but he warned, "Don't."

"Don't what?" I asked.

He raised an index finger at me. "You know what. The sappy words, the fake gratitude."

"It's not fake!"

"Whatever. It feels like giving up."

"I just want us to be friends again, like we were before. I want you to forgive me. Is that too much to ask?"

"Talk to me when all this is over," he said. "When everything is back to normal. Then we'll see."

I heaved a sigh, and we resumed riding in silence until we reached the turnoff to Jumping Rock, where we parked on the side of the road. We continued on foot from there, taking the dirt path that led to the falls. As I walked, I noticed I didn't have to stop and catch my breath, unlike Nathaniel, who lumbered ahead of me, panting like a mule hitched to a wagon. The energy-transfer spell had clearly worked.

We kept going until the path brought us to a wide stone ledge, and the land turned to sky. I crept toward the ledge and peered through the mist at the opposite cliff face, where the giant stone slab known as Jumping Rock jutted out above a spring-fed waterfall spewing from a cleft in the mountainside. The only way to reach the falls was to teeter along a narrow hiking trail etched into the mountain. Not something I wanted to navigate. I shielded my eyes and searched for Lillian, hoping she was on this side of the cliff and not the other.

It wasn't until I heard a rustling behind me that I found her. She sat cross-legged in the underbrush, so concealed by the jungle greenery wrapped around her body that I had walked right past her without noticing. Nate and Olive had known what to look for. Both of them stood quietly beside their mother until she spoke.

"The island is ready," she said, glancing at me. "Tell your people to attack the compound wards."

I texted Kat, already in position with my aunt. *It's go time.*

OK, she replied. *Wish me luck.*

She didn't need it, not with the power and the fury of my aunt alongside her.

It's done! she texted moments later.

"Now," I told Lillian. "His protection is down."

Lillian closed her eyes, tipped her head to the sky, and began chanting. Somewhere in Pennsylvania, Kat and my aunt should be taking cover to watch my father's movements from the road. Not ten minutes later, Kat texted me to say, *He's on his way!*

Are you sure? I asked.

Girl, I just watched him drive out of the compound like his ass was on fire!

"It worked," I told the others.

"Now for the hard part," Olive said. "Now we wait."

CHAPTER
TWENTY-FIVE

Lillian weakened as the hours passed. She continued to chant the compulsion spell, even after my father boarded her private plane. We knew that if the magic lapsed before he landed, he might find a way to turn the craft around. So the goal was to get him to the landing strip, where a security team would escort him to the estate.

But I doubted Lillian's strength would last that long. The plane was still miles away when she started to slur her words and break the enchantment. Restarting the spell seemed to drain her even more, until after the third lapse, she couldn't speak. With sweat slicking her forehead, she looked at us one last time before her eyes rolled back, and she collapsed into the hammock of vines that had woven around her.

Olive lowered herself with her cane and checked Lillian's pulse. "She's alive."

She and Nathaniel exchanged a relieved look.

"What about the plane?" I asked. "How close is it?"

Nathaniel closed his eyes and murmured an overview spell. "It landed. I can see it on the ground. Security opened the hatch, and now they're going up the steps."

"Then we should go meet my dad," I said. "Olive can stay with—"

"Wait," Nate interrupted, his eyes still shut and his brow furrowed. "There's no one in the plane."

"What?" I asked.

"They're searching it. The pilot is on board, but the cabin is empty."

"That's impossible," I said. "Your mom felt him getting on the plane. The pilot confirmed it." Then it hit me. My father had done exactly what I'd expected him to do. He had turned the tables. "He's here. He's hiding in plain sight. He probably used a cloaking charm and snuck off the plane before anyone noticed."

Olive swore under her breath.

"Can we track him?" Nate asked. "Is there any hair left?"

"No," Olive said. "I gave Mom everything I had, and she used it for the spell."

"So what now?" I asked. "I seriously doubt he's going to come to us. He doesn't even know we're here."

From somewhere distant, my father called out, "Oh, Button, you have so little faith in me."

I followed the sound of his voice across the ravine to Jumping Rock, where he came into view sitting cross-legged on the slab. He gave me a tiny wave, more of a sarcastic taunt than a greeting. I had no idea how he had gotten there so fast or low long he'd been watching us, but the cold, stiff set of his smile confirmed my fear that I had hurt him.

I cupped my mouth and shouted to him, "I'm sorry. I had to do it."

"I'm not angry," he called back, causing my bracelet to vibrate. "Well, maybe a little. But I admire you, Button. Not many people can say they pulled one over on me. It's good to see you finally rising to your potential."

That didn't feel like a compliment, but I told him, "I learned from the best."

He laughed and stretched out his hands. In response, a pathway of stones flew into formation to create a bridge between us, nothing elaborate, but flat and straight and easy to cross . . . as long as I didn't look down. "Come over here so we can talk."

"Wait," Olive said, blocking me with her cane before I had even thought about moving. She raised an invisible shield wall. "I don't trust him."

In truth, I didn't trust him, either. I knew my father would never hurt me, but I wouldn't put it past him to punish me somehow, and with the disarming cuff around my ankle, I had no way to defend myself.

"All right, I'll come to you," he said, climbing down onto the bridge he had built. He strode toward us in brisk steps and stopped about ten paces from Olive's shield wall, where he raised a shield of his own. He waved a hand, and a parchment appeared on the bridge. Tightly rolled and tied with a red ribbon, the scroll resembled a fairy-tale document. "This is what you wanted from me, isn't it? The reason you forced me to come here?"

"What is it?" I asked him.

"The counter-hex for your precious sleepers."

"I thought there wasn't one," I said. "You tied them to me."

"Yes, I did," he admitted. "But any decent spell crafter knows how to make a back door, a fail-safe, just in case his plans change." He jutted his chin at Nathaniel. "I'll make you a deal. I'll give you the counter-hex right now. You can look it over and verify that it's legitimate. But in exchange, I want your word that as soon as your people wake up, I can leave here with my daughter, and no one will stand in our way. Agreed?"

Nate looked to Olive for approval. She considered for a moment and then lowered the shield to let him pass. "Go ahead," she told him. "See if it's legit."

Nate crept forward, testing the bridge with one foot while peeking into the abyss. When the stones held his weight, he inched toward the scroll until he reached it and then carefully lowered at the knees to pick it up. He pulled off the ribbon, unrolled the sheet, and began reading under his breath.

"What do you think?" Olive asked.

Nate shrugged, still scanning the page. "I guess this could work. I won't know until we try it, though."

"Bring it to me," she said.

In the time it took for Nathaniel to roll up the parchment, his whole demeanor changed. A pained look crossed his face. His eyebrows pinched together, and he bent at the waist as if he'd been punched. He swayed once, dropping the scroll and reaching out for balance. The next thing I knew, his eyes rolled back in his head, and I watched in slow motion as he collapsed toward the edge of the bridge.

Panic squeezed my chest. I barely had a chance to gasp when my legs seemed to disappear from beneath me, and I fell faceup, cracking the back of my head and rattling my teeth with an audible *snap*. I opened my eyes and winced at the pain pulsating in my skull. Instinctively, I tried to touch the tender wound on my scalp, but I was too weak to move my arms. I couldn't even turn my face to the side to see if Nate was safe. All I could do was blink at the canopy of leaves high above me, whipped into a frenzy by dark storm clouds rolling in.

"You idiot!" I heard Olive shout. "She's linked to him! You're killing your own daughter!"

Nathaniel must have been drawing from my energy to keep himself alive. *Good*, I thought. That meant he *was* alive.

I heard the strained sound of Olive groaning, as though she were pushing a boulder up a hill. I focused all of my strength on the simple act of turning my head. I only managed an inch or two, but it was enough to catch Olive in my peripheral vision.

She had dropped to her knees, one hand outstretched and trembling with the effort of levitating Nate's limp body above the falls, the other maintaining the shield. With a pained cry, she pulled her arm inward, and Nate flew to her side, where he landed half on top of me. Olive didn't hesitate to pluck a hair from his head and mine. She joined them in her fist and spoke the incantation to unbind our life forces.

I felt the difference at once. I stretched my back and inhaled a long, ragged breath, feeling tingles buzzing through my veins as the sensation returned to my body. It took another moment before I could sit up, but the first thing I did was cradle Nathaniel's face in my hands. His skin was warm, and a faint pulse ticked at his throat, but I couldn't wake him.

"What did you do?" I asked my father while lightly slapping Nate's cheeks. He was completely unresponsive, comatose like . . . Lucy. "Oh no." I glanced at the discarded scroll and then at my father, searching his face for some sign that I was wrong, that he hadn't cursed Nathaniel with the same hex from the puzzle. "Tell me you didn't."

My dad tilted his head in casual acknowledgment.

"Why?" I breathed. Why would he do that?

Olive used her cane to stand up and face my father, her chest heaving with exhaustion and fury. "I didn't think you could sink any lower!" she shouted. "But cursing my brother and nearly killing your own daughter in the process? You're even more of a selfish bastard than I gave you credit for!"

"Why?" I asked again. My mind reeled with excuses for my father. Maybe he had felt threatened. Maybe he had acted out of fear. But that didn't make sense. The only person who could hurt him was the Grand Lumara, and she had passed out. "You were in control of the situation. Nate wasn't a danger to you."

"I'm sorry, Button. I had to do it."

My bracelet vibrated. He was lying—again.

"You asshole!" Olive yelled. "We brought you here to cooperate! To try and save your daughter's life!"

In one swift motion, my father clenched his fist and shattered Olive's shield wall. Before she had a chance to defend herself, he froze her with a paralysis spell. The whole thing happened in the span of a single heartbeat.

"I heard what you said before," he told her. "About the leftover strand of hair. I always wondered who cursed me. Now I finally know."

I gaped at Olive's stiff, motionless body. She moved her gaze briefly to me and then to my father as tears of rage welled in her eyes. Her anger glowed inside my own chest. I would never forget how violated I had felt when Hector's guard had used that same spell against me.

I whipped around and glared at my father. "Who *are* you?"

"Hey now," he said, holding up his palms and approaching me as though I were a wounded animal. "We're on the same side, remember?"

"Are we?" I asked, and pointed at my ankle cuff. "Then help me take this off. I know you can do it."

"I can, but I won't. You're mad at me, Button, and I've seen what you're capable of when you're angry."

"What *I'm* capable of?" I yelled. "You left me stranded here! Charged with fourteen attempted murders!" I pointed at Nathaniel lying on the ground, his limbs splayed, his eyes closed in slumber. It struck me that he would never wake up. The boy I loved would *never* wake up. "Fifteen! You tied him to my fate. He's as good as dead!"

My father lifted his chin. "I did it for you."

"Don't say that!" I tore off my bracelet, unable to stand the constant vibrations. "If you were doing any of this for me, you wouldn't hurt the people I love. You did this for *you*. And it's sick! You're sick!"

He proved me right when he glanced at Olive, narrowing his eyes in contempt. That was why he had kept her alive and paralyzed—to inflict maximum pain, to force her to watch as he took away the only brother she had left.

"You hate her," I said, "more than you love me."

"Grow up, Talia," he snapped. "Not everything is about you."

And he was right. None of this was about me. It never had been.

"You didn't send me to Lumara to save myself, did you?" I asked. I thought back to our first phone call after Lucy's wedding, when my father had doubted our plan would work before I'd even had a chance to make my demands to Lillian. "I think you already knew I couldn't be saved. You sent me here to help you get revenge."

"Oh, stop it. You know that's not true."

But did I? The fake memories, sending me to Nathaniel's academy, helping me infiltrate the island, arming me with a cursed object—an overly complicated plan if the only goal had been trying to save my life.

"You used me," I said. "You never intended to trade cures with anyone. That's why there's no counter-hex. You just wanted to kill as many Lumarans as possible, and the only way to do that without getting caught was to send me to do it for you. Olive was right. I was just a sword in your hand."

"Don't be ridiculous, Talia. You're my daughter. I love you."

I believed him, and I loved him, too. But I was wrong to think that I mattered more to him than anyone else in the world. There was one other person above me, someone he would always put first. "I had it wrong," I told him. "Olive's curse ends with you. The person you love most in the world is yourself."

CHAPTER

TWENTY-SIX

Hurt flashed in my father's eyes. "Take that back."

I almost did. The truth was agonizing, and I wanted more than anything to deny it. But with Nathaniel lying on the ground and Olive frozen by my side, I couldn't pretend my father had acted out of selfless love.

"No one comes before you," he said. "You're my whole world."

I shook my head and took a backward step. As much as I wanted it to be the case, I knew the curse wouldn't end with my death. It would end with his.

But what did that mean for me?

Nothing had changed. I could still feel the dark magic draining me with each labored breath. I thought back to what Olive had said about the curse: that it would punish my father with heartbreak until he lost the person who mattered most to him. So it seemed the only way for me to live—the only way to save Nathaniel and the fourteen others—was for my father to die.

And we were running out of time.

A shadow passed over my heart. As if to match my mood, dark clouds covered the sun, and the wind whipped my hair into my face. I glanced at Lillian, unconscious on the ground. She couldn't help me. No one could help me.

Thunder cracked in the distance, the air thick and heavy with the promise of rain. I sensed Olive watching me, and as soon as I locked eyes with her, I could tell she had put the truth together, too. She silently urged me to take action. But what could I do? Did she think I was capable of killing my own father?

Just looking at him stirred the little girl inside me. He was my first love, my safe place, my home. Even now, knowing what horrible things he had done, I ached for him to wrap me in his arms and shield me from the coming storm.

I shook my head at Olive. I couldn't do it.

"Don't look at her," my dad said, placing himself in between me and Olive. "She did this. All of this is her fault."

"Daddy, no," I told him, but he wasn't listening to me.

He spun on Olive, his face red and his voice wild as he shouted, "It was an accident! I didn't mean for Jude to die! We were just messing around! You had no right to take my wife away from me! No right to destroy my life!"

"But what about Nathaniel?" I asked, tugging on my father's shirt. "What about the fourteen others? You had no right to take them away from their families."

My father flinched as if I'd thrown water in his face. "You're defending her? The woman who killed your mother?"

"I'm not defending anyone. I'm trying to make you see that you and Olive both made mistakes that killed people. But the difference is Olive changed, and you didn't. You're still hurting people, but now you're doing it on purpose."

"Only to save you."

"Not to save me!" I pointed at Nathaniel. "Stop pretending that what you did today is any different from what Olive did to you all those years ago. You haven't learned! And you don't care about the people you hurt! That scares me!"

"*That's* what scares you?" he demanded. "Not the lunatics who put you on trial?" He thrust a finger at Olive. "Her family did that! They called the tribunal. They don't care about you, so why should I give a damn about them?"

"Because you love me."

"*What?*" He fisted both hands above his temples as if to pull the hair he didn't have. "Damn it, Talia, that's why I want to burn down this whole island! Because I love you! How can you not see that?"

I shook my head. "How can *you* not see you're hurting me? You basically killed the boy I love! You had to know that would break my heart, but you did it anyway because it made you feel good. That's not what love looks like. That's what hate looks like, and your obsession with Nate's family has nothing to do with me."

My father clenched his jaw and stared at me with a cold gaze that told me I hadn't reached him. Maybe I never would. "You care more about that boy than about your own mother," he said. "She would be ashamed if she were here right now."

"Yes, she would be," I told him. "But not of me."

For a long moment, he went unnaturally silent, amplifying the sound of the whistling wind and the rustle of leaves. Darkness shrouded the mountain and chilled the air. I hugged myself, feeling the weight of Olive's gaze on me. This time, I couldn't bear to look at her. I didn't know what to do. My head swam with guilt and confusion, my pulse ticking harder and faster as I stared down my father and waited for something to happen, for the pressure to break.

A flash of lightning, a crack of thunder. And then my father moved his lips and chanted a spell I couldn't hear—or defend myself from. All I could do was stand there while his magic surrounded me, bled into my skin, and severed the connection between my body and mind until I couldn't talk back to him anymore.

He had rendered me helpless.

The same charm he had used on Olive, the same charm Hector's guard had used to violate me on one of the worst days of my life. Part of me had seen this coming, but I still felt a throb of betrayal. My father had comforted me after that horrible day at Mystic Con. He knew the terror I had felt, the shame of being stripped of my free will and my dignity.

And now he was doing the same thing to me.

Deliberately? Had he planned it out in his mind, chosen the one spell that would cut me deeper than the rest?

Yes.

The answer rocked me to my soul.

My father was cruel, and he was dangerous . . . and he would probably never stop. I didn't know when he had turned into the kind of man who liked to hurt people, but the knowledge that he would hurt me, too, nearly broke me in half.

Tears flooded my vision. My heart ached, because the little girl inside me didn't care what kind of man my father had become. I still loved him—enough to protect him from his own darkness. Lillian couldn't help me, but maybe the island would. I closed my eyes and channeled all of my energy toward Lumara, visualizing its core within the mountain. I called out to it with a heart full of perfect love, and I asked for a single favor.

Rain struck my face in fat pellets, streaming down my cheeks and mingling with my tears. From the ground, a surge of warmth entered the soles of my feet and shot all the way up to my scalp. Raw power hummed along my skin, so intense that I worried my cells might split apart if I held it inside for too long.

Lightning rent the sky, and thunder shook the mountain. I looked down, fully in control of my body, and discovered the island had granted my wish.

My disarming cuff was now around my father's ankle.

"I'm sorry, Daddy," I murmured.

He blinked in shock as I spoke, and again when he noticed the cuff above his foot. He stumbled back a few paces toward the cliff ledge and gaped at the static ring, then furiously tried to dislodge it with his opposite heel. I could feel my guilt building, so I hurried to Olive and gripped her shoulders before I lost my resolve. With the last remnants of my power, I spoke the words to break the paralysis spell, and I freed her.

Olive exhaled in relief, arching her back and lifting her face to the rain. Leaves rustled behind us, followed by a soft groan as Lillian awoke and pushed herself to sitting. She massaged her temples and glanced up at her daughter just in time for Olive to whisper, "I love you, Mom."

Olive looked to me with a question in her eyes. I gave her a nod. After that, everything happened in a flash.

Olive tossed aside her cane and lumbered toward my father with her head down and her arms outstretched, building a momentum with her full weight behind it. Too late, he glanced up from his ankle cuff. Their bodies collided, and Olive wrapped herself around him, knocking them both off the ledge.

Lillian cried out while a scream lodged in my throat. Olive was supposed to use magic, not sacrifice herself. I scrambled to the ledge, but the two of them had disappeared.

"Olive," Lillian croaked, weakly dragging herself to my side.

Together, we stared down into the darkness. I could hear the rush of the waterfall, but I couldn't see all the way to the pool at the bottom. Maybe that was a blessing, sparing us the sight of their broken bodies. But still, I lowered onto to my hands and knees and held my breath while I kept searching. I had to know what had happened to them, or I would lose my mind.

I didn't notice the wind had stilled until a distant sound of snapping twigs caught my attention. I turned around and did an immediate double take. I almost didn't recognize Jude standing on the narrow hiking trail that led to the falls. Instead of red plaid swim trunks, he wore jean cutoffs and a wide smile that lit up his face and made him so beautiful it almost hurt to look at him.

"Lillian," I whispered. "It's Jude."

She traced the direction of my gaze and then gasped. She could see him, too.

His hair was dry and loose, gently blowing in the ocean breeze as he surveyed the view with a contentment that warmed my fractured heart. As if on cue, the clouds parted and bathed him in sunlight.

Jude was finally free. That was almost worth the pain.

Almost.

But then a girl's voice called out to him from the falls, and Lillian and I turned to find a young, bikini-clad Olive standing on top of Jumping Rock, smiling and waving at her brother with so much excitement it set her ponytail swinging.

Jude waved back at her and laughed, and then jogged along the narrow trail until he reached his sister. They stood next to each other on the stone slab above the falls. Neither of them seemed to notice me or Lillian, but that was all right. After all the years Olive and Jude had spent apart, they deserved to have this reunion to themselves.

This—this was worth it.

"Race you to the bottom?" Jude asked his sister.

She shook her head and held out a hand to him.

"Together?" he asked.

"Always," she told him.

He took her hand and gripped it tightly, and together they leaped into the mist.

Through my veil of tears, I watched them vanish. I stood up, and at once, I noticed the added strength in my limbs, the absence of the dark magic that had drained me for so long. A glance at Nathaniel showed his forehead wrinkling as he began to stir.

The curse was broken. The storm had cleared.

CHAPTER
TWENTY-SEVEN

Magic could do wonders for the dead. Not bring them back to life, of course. No spell had the power to do that. But the right charms could repair any amount of physical damage, even the trauma of a twenty-five-meter fall, and that was a gift to the living.

A gift to me.

I sat alone on the beach with my father, counting down the minutes until sunset, when Lumara would claim his body and commit him to the sea. I had wanted this: no ceremony, no burial, no announcements or wakes or receiving lines. Just the two of us, father and daughter, and his peaceful, quiet return to nature. I hoped my dad wouldn't mind that I hadn't taken him home and buried him next to my mother. But if he did, then oh well.

I made the decisions now.

Which terrified me.

My whole life stretched ahead of me, and I had no idea what any of it looked like. Were my legal troubles over? If so, would I leave here and go live with my aunt and Kat? She wanted that, but did I? Or did I want to finish my senior year at another boarding school? What about after high school? Did I want to apply to college or hone my magic through an apprenticeship? What about my father's family? How much did they know about me? Did I want to meet them?

My mind spun. There were too many decisions to make. I would think about them later. For now, I shook my head clear and focused on my father.

"I miss you," I whispered.

Miss you too, Button, I imagined him saying.

No one else called me Button. I would miss that, too.

I took his hand, surprised to find it cold. It was such a mind freak, how I kept forgetting he was dead. Maybe it was denial or grief or exhaustion. Or maybe Lillian had done too good a job restoring him. If I squinted, I could make believe he had fallen asleep in the shade, stretched out on the sand beneath a palm tree, hands folded atop his belly. There was only one thing out of place. I had taken his watch and tucked it in my pocket. Its crystal face had shattered, but the ancestral relics he'd hidden inside it had survived. Now a part of him would always be with me, just like my mother and her locket.

The sun slid closer to the horizon, lengthening the shadows and casting my father in a rosy glow. I straightened the orchid blossom on his lapel and admired how handsome he looked in the linen slacks and the white button-down shirt. Lillian had helped with that, too, all while grieving the loss of her daughter.

Guilt gnawed at my stomach. On the other side of the island, the community had gathered for Olive's funeral. I knew I should be there to honor Olive and support Nate and his family. But I couldn't do it. I couldn't face them, not after what my father and I had done. Everyone knew I was the reason Olive had sacrificed herself. I had received enough icy looks to tell me the people of Lumara would never forget.

Who could blame them? All I could do was hope they'd forgive me someday.

My chest turned heavy, tugging me into a slouch. I glanced at the setting sun, merely a kiss from the horizon, and then took one last moment to study my father's face. I memorized the cleft in his chin, the stubble along his jaw, the subtle arch of his brows. Pressure built behind my eyes when I noticed a narrow ribbon of tide snaking its way toward my father. The sea had come for him.

Soon it cocooned his body in clear, swirling water, and for a moment, he floated peacefully above the sand. I knew what would happen next, so I crossed both arms to stop myself from reaching out for him as the water carried him away. I didn't see him join the waves. My vision was so blurry that I blinked once, and he was gone.

"Goodbye, Dad," I choked out, and then it struck me that Camilla had been right after all. I hadn't told him goodbye, and I regretted it. I cleared my throat and added, "I wish we'd had more time."

A man's voice from nearby said, "Don't we all?"

Adrian Wood had joined me, standing there barefoot in his suit and tie. I was surprised to see him. He should be at his daughter's funeral, along with everyone else.

"Did the service end early?" I asked.

He shook his head and gazed out over the ocean with his hands tucked in his pockets.

"Then why did you leave?"

"Because my little girl is gone," he said. "Olive doesn't need me anymore." He gave me a quick glance, an unspoken *but maybe you do.* "I don't think Olive would have wanted you to be alone right now. She cared about you."

I nodded, my throat thick. I had cared about her, too.

"She came to me yesterday," he went on, "and told me something in confidence. She wanted me to know, just in case anything happened to her, that she made a deal with the judge on your behalf."

"What kind of deal? She didn't mention it to me."

"She didn't want to get your hopes up. But you should know that Olive took full responsibility for your mother's death. She gave her confession to the judge in exchange for a dismissal of your charges. The only stipulation was that the sleepers woke up, which they did. So now your record is clear."

I peered at him in shock. I had no idea Olive had done that for me.

"You're free to go," he said.

"I can't believe she confessed. My own father wouldn't do that for me."

"Ah, well . . ." Adrian rocked back on his heels. "I won't speak ill of the dead. I think the main takeaway is that they both loved you, in their own ways."

"Olive was special. I'm sorry you lost her."

"You've lost a lot, too," he said. "Is there anything I can do to help?"

I started to say no, but then I thought of something. "Actually, yes. Do you know an amnesia spell?"

"I do. Why?"

"I want you to remove a memory for me." I explained how Jude had appeared to me and shown me his drowning. "Now that his spirit is free, I don't need to know how he died."

"Oh goodness, of course you don't," Adrian agreed. "Close your eyes and remember what he showed you. I'll do the rest."

He placed his hands near my head, and I let myself return to that awful day one more time. As I recalled the sunlight glinting on the whitecaps and the weightless feel of the ocean beneath my limbs, the details of Jude's memory began to dissolve at the edges. Like rice paper on water, they faded and thinned until nothing remained aside from the vague sense that I had forgotten something.

"Is that better?" he asked.

I nodded, thinking how lucky Nate was to have Adrian for a dad. I'd been wrong to dismiss Adrian's kindness as a nice-guy act. He was simply a nice guy. The world needed more like him.

"You're stronger than you think," Adrian said. "You'll survive this. I promise."

His words made me smile. It felt good, familiar, like the promise of a sunrise after a cold and moonless night. "Thanks," I told him. "I know I will."

At the cottage, I packed my suitcase and took one last look around for anything I might have missed. My boat would leave the next morning and return me to the real world, where I would finally have to face all of the choices I had been avoiding.

Funny how I used to dream about this—being an adult and having the freedom to make my own decisions. Now I would give anything for a mom or a dad to tell me what to do. I had never realized how stressful freedom was. It messed with my head, the knowledge that from this day forward, the only person to blame for anything that went wrong in my life was me.

So far, I didn't recommend adulthood. Zero out of five stars.

A knock sounded from the door, and Nate let himself in, balancing a dinner tray on one arm. My stomach flip-flopped at the sight of him. I had been looking forward to this moment and dreading it at the same time, our last dinner together before I went back to the academy and filled out a form to withdraw. I hated that our paths were going in different directions. Keeping Nate in my life was the one choice I didn't have the freedom to make, and ironically, the only one I was certain about.

"Before I forget," Nate said. "I'm supposed to invite you to stay for Lucy's wedding do-over tomorrow night."

"Oh, that's really sweet of her to offer, but—"

"I already told her you couldn't make it."

"Thanks." It had been hard enough to look Lucy and Leo in the eyes and apologize to them. Attending their wedding might actually kill me. "So, what's on the menu tonight?" I asked, changing the subject as I settled at the head of my bed. I sniffed the air and guessed, "Steak and potatoes?"

"Close." Nate sat down at the opposite end of the bed and placed the tray between us. He lifted the platter lid to reveal two hamburgers with a side of seasoned curly fries. "Olive's favorite."

I smiled. "Solid choice."

"She had excellent taste," he agreed.

I held up a curly fry and toasted, "To Olive."

"To Olive," Nate echoed, tapping my fry with his. "The best sister—"

"And lawyer," I cut in.

"That anyone could ever ask for," Nate said, his voice thick.

"Until we meet again," I added, because I knew we would.

"I'll eat to that."

After those first curly fries, neither of us touched our dinner. My stomach was too full of butterflies to make room for food. And besides, I had the rest of my life to eat but only tonight to tell Nathaniel everything that was in my heart.

I started with an apology. "I'm sorry I wasn't at Olive's funeral. I should have been there for you. I was too afraid of what people would think, and that's backward, because the only opinion that really matters to me is yours. I hate that I let you down."

"It's okay," Nate said. "I'm sorry I wasn't at your dad's."

"My dad tried to kill you," I reminded him.

Nate lifted a shoulder. "So what? The funeral wasn't for him. It was for you—to say goodbye to the only parent you had left. A real friend wouldn't have let you go through that alone."

"I wasn't alone. Your dad was there."

"It should have been me."

"So," I said. "Does this mean we're friends now?"

"I'll forgive you if you forgive me."

I extended a hand to shake. "Friendship do-over?"

His lips curled into a breathtaking smile that reached all the way to his eyes. "Friendship do-over," he agreed, and pumped my hand up and down. Instead of releasing me, he held on to my fingers and went thoughtful for a while. "You know," he said. "A real friend wouldn't make you change schools. Not after everything you've been through."

I bit my lip. "I see your point. A real friend would want me to have stability. Even if it cost him the valedictorian's spot."

"I think he'd be fine with salutatorian," Nate said.

"But Mystics aren't allowed at the academy. That's the rule."

"Did you use magic to cheat?" he asked me.

"No."

"Me neither," he said. "I can't even use magic away from the island. That makes me as ordinary as everyone else."

"So what you're saying is the rule is pointless."

"And pointless rules deserve to be broken."

"All right, then it's decided," I said. There was just one problem. "We're not together anymore. What are we going to tell people about the breakup?"

I held my breath while I waited for him to answer. Silently, I willed him to say, *Let's not tell them anything. Let's go back to the way things were.* I loved Nathaniel. I wanted him with every atom in my body, and if he couldn't see that, then he wasn't paying attention.

He dropped his gaze and seemed to remember that he was holding my hand. When he let go of me, I had my answer. "Um, how about we keep it simple and say you caught me texting some other girl? People break up for that all the time."

I swallowed hard and hoped my voice didn't shake. "That'll make you the bad guy."

"That's okay. I can get away with it easier than you can."

I winced, because he was right. When a girl at school cheated, she was forever branded a slut. But when a boy cheated, he was simply being a guy. "Well, thanks for taking one for the team."

"What are friends for?" he asked.

I couldn't think of a reply.

After that, we avoided each other's gazes and fidgeted with our uneaten curly fries until Nate stood up and thumbed at the door. "I should go. Olive's wake is still—"

"Of course," I blurted. "Don't worry about me. I'll see you . . ." I glanced up at him with a question in my eyes. I didn't know when I would see him again. I left the invitation open, in case he wanted to walk me to the boat in the morning.

"At school, I guess," he said. "Right?"

"Right," I told him while my heart sank. "I'll see you at school."

CHAPTER
TWENTY-EIGHT

EIGHT MONTHS LATER

"Fellow graduates," I said into the microphone as I gazed at a sea of identical blue square caps and white dangling tassels. From the stage, I could see the entire senior class occupying the auditorium floor, and in the tiered rows behind them, all of the friends and family members who had traveled in for the ceremony. I spotted Lillian and Adrian Wood seated in the same row as Kat and my aunt. All of them smiled at me. Kat added an enthusiastic wave and shouted, "I love you, Talia!"

A few chuckles broke out.

"I love you more," I told her, and then I returned my attention to my classmates. "As your valedictorian, it's my job to deliver a speech that will inspire you to go out into the world and embark on a new adventure. And that's what I'm going to do. But the adventure I want to talk about has nothing to do with college degrees or internships or launching a career. Today, I want to talk to you about empty gloves and thrift-store tap shoes."

The audience laughed.

"I know, sounds random. But stick with me and it will all make sense."

I glanced at my note card, a quote from Lewis Carroll. "There's a line from *Alice's Adventures in Wonderland* that stands out to me: 'I know who I *was* when I got up this morning, but I think I must have changed several times since then.' I can relate, because not too long ago, I wasn't the person I thought I was.

"It's no secret that I had a tough year. During fall break, I lost not only my father, but one of my best friends, too." I glanced down at Nathaniel, seated in the front row, and gave him a soft smile, my way of saying *no hard feelings*. "I'm not going to lie; it was brutal at first. I felt like a glove without a hand. There was nothing holding me up inside. I was devastated and lonely, and I didn't know what to do with myself. So I hid out in my room and I studied around the clock." I pointed at my valedictorian sash. "That's why none of you stood a chance at beating me."

Soft chuckles filled the auditorium.

"I knew it wasn't healthy to stay cooped up forever. I wanted to go out, but all my hobbies were things I used to do with my dad or my boyfriend. Restoring old cars, going to football games, watching true-crime documentaries. None of it sounded fun to me anymore. And then I realized it never had. Those were their hobbies, not mine. I had only tagged along to make them happy.

"I started to see why I felt like an empty glove. I had been living for other people, and when they disappeared from my life, they took my passion and my purpose with them. In small doses, there's nothing wrong with doing things for other people. But when you abandon your interests for someone else, you risk becoming an empty glove. And it can happen easier than you think."

To make a point, I asked my fellow seniors, "How many of you played a sport because your parents signed you up for it as a kid? Or because your friends were on the team?" Dozens of hands went up. "How many of you only go to church when your grandma guilts you into it?" A few more hands. "How many of you joined a club or signed up for a class because your crush was in there?" Even more hands. "Now be honest about this one—how many of you picked a career based on money or clout?" More seniors than I could count raised their hands. "See what I mean? It's almost scary how hard it is to untangle your passions from the ones that belong to other people. But that's all right. The first step of the adventure is taking off the glove to see whose hand is underneath.

"For me, once I realized what didn't bring me joy, I had to figure out what did. It was overwhelming at first, but luckily, I had help. Every week, the athletic department taught me a new sport until I tried all twenty-three of them. I learned I'm not much of an athlete—sorry, coaches—but I love tennis. I don't care how horrible I am at it. I enjoy every minute I spend on the court, and I'm glad I figured that out now instead of twenty years from now . . . or worse, never.

"At that same time, I spent my weekends volunteering at animal shelters, food banks, and churches. I met people who are different from me, and I listened to their stories. I took an internet sewing class because I thought it would be fun to make my own clothes. I ended up not liking it—*at all*—but that's okay. I'm richer by one slightly misshapen poncho.

"Now for the best part. One day my roommate, Farah, took me to a consignment shop in the city, and I scored a pair of flawless vintage tap shoes in my size, autographed on the soles by some dancer I'd never heard of. When I showed them to Mrs. Gervasio, she practically had an aneurism and told me to auction the shoes." I shrugged. "I think Ginger Rogers would be proud that I put them on instead. Because that's when the magic happened. As soon as I heard that sound, the clicking of taps on a hardwood floor, I was hooked. From that moment on, I spent all my spare time in the studio practicing choreography I copied from a third-grade YouTube recital." I paused to grin at how silly I must have looked. "Thank you to everyone who saw me in the studio and had the grace not to point and laugh. There's something about tap dancing that turns my brain into a serotonin factory, and I never would have discovered that if I hadn't been actively looking for it.

"I'm not going to say I'm grateful for the pain I went through this year. That would be a lie. I lost two people I love, and I miss them every single day. But I can honor what I learned from my pain. I can celebrate the fact that I finally know who I am, and what fills me up inside. I know that I'm the hand beneath my glove. And years from now, when I take my final breath, it won't be someone else's life passing before my eyes. I want that for you, too.

"So here's my challenge: Go out into the world and find the sport that brings you joy. Listen to the music that makes you sing. Choose a career that doesn't feel like work. Play your games and dance your dance. Watch slapstick comedies and read books with happy endings, and whatever you do, don't call them guilty pleasures. If something puts a smile on your face, then own it, grab on to it with both hands. The world can be a dark place sometimes. Don't shame yourself for turning on the light.

"So . . . to all of my fellow graduates, there's only one thing left for me to say, and that's congratulations!" I pumped a fist in the air. "We did it!"

The crowd roared with applause as everyone stood up to cheer and whistle. I waved at my family at the back of the auditorium and blew them a kiss. Then I stood back from the podium so the headmaster could take my place. He led the graduating class in moving our tassels from right to left, and then with a shout, we tossed our caps into the air.

Afterward, the students and guests began filing outside to the picnic the academy had arranged for us. I lingered on the stage to shake my professors' hands and to give them my thanks. By the time I finished saying my goodbyes, the auditorium had emptied, except for one graduate who stayed behind.

Nathaniel beamed up at me from his seat in the front row, his dark curls loose, his cap tucked beneath one arm. "Congrats, Miss Valedictorian."

I climbed down from the stage to join him. "Same to you, Mr. Salutatorian."

"That was an amazing speech."

"Really?" I asked. "I didn't sound too nervous?"

"You were perfect," he told me, his rich brown eyes simmering in a way I hadn't seen from him in months. "Perfect," he repeated.

I rubbed a hand over the flutters that had broken out in my stomach. "I heard you got into Cornell. That's exciting."

He nodded. "How about you? Did you get your top choice?"

"I did, but I'm going to defer."

"Taking a gap year?"

"Mm-hmm. I want to check out some other options first." I glanced over both shoulders to make sure we were alone. "My aunt helped me set up an apprenticeship tour. I'll spend three months with four different spell masters, kind of like a sampler to see what kind of magic is out there. I start in September."

"Wow," Nate said. "You weren't kidding about the whole adventure-of-discovery thing. You really leveled up."

I stood straighter with pride. "Thanks, that's the goal."

"Now you've got me rethinking my summer plans."

"Which are?" I prompted.

"I *was* going to hang out at home. But how uninspired is that? I've explored every inch of Lumara. There's not much left for me to discover."

I seriously doubted that, but instead of telling him so, I blurted, "Then come hang out with me this summer." I was mostly joking. I didn't expect him to take me seriously. But when he tilted his head with interest, I took a shot and kept going. "I reached out to my dad's family in Pennsylvania. I'm going to meet them for the first time and stay for the summer, get to know my grandparents and a few cousins who live there. I rented a place in town. Nothing fancy, but there's a pool and an extra bedroom if you want to come along." I waggled an eyebrow. "Should be interesting, from what my aunt told me."

"Interesting how?" Nate asked.

"She said they're kooks, but more or less harmless."

"More or less harmless," Nate repeated. "You know, maybe I

should go with you. These people are strangers. Might be a good idea to have someone watching your back, just in case."

"You can't do magic there," I reminded him.

"I can't do magic *here*." He shrugged. "Never held me back before."

I peered at him for a moment. "Would you really go with me?"

"That depends." He slid me an impish glance. "Do you really miss me every single day?"

My cheeks heated. "You shouldn't have to ask. You know I can't lie."

"That was the old you. The new you can do all kinds of things you couldn't do before."

"But the new me isn't into cars," I pointed out. "Or any of the other things we used to have in common."

"I guess we'll have to discover some new ones." He tossed aside his cap and reached out a hand to me. "Didn't you say it's part of the adventure?"

My heart glowed as I smiled at him. For me, there was no question of what to do. I had said it in my speech: *If something puts a smile on your face, then own it, grab on to it with both hands.* So I followed my own advice, and I took his outstretched hand in both of mine.